un break
this heart

AMAZON BESTSELLING AUTHOR
BETTY SHREFFLER

UNBREAK THIS HEART
Published by Betty Shreffler
Copyright © 2018 by Betty Shreffler

This is a work of fiction. Names, characters, places, and incidents are either the product of the author's imagination or are used fictitiously, and any resemblance to actual persons, living or dead, business establishments, events, or locales is entirely coincidental.

Printed in the USA
ISBN: 978-0692164914

This story is close to my heart. I have personally suffered from sexual assault and the aftermath of depression and PTSD that comes with it. I wanted to write a story that reflects the struggles a woman goes through, but that she can also overcome those inner wounds and find the strength to live a fulfilling life as well as to be able to love and trust again. I hope you enjoy Alex's journey as much as I did writing it.

Thank you Lorilee for your expertise on all things MMA. You made my research much easier and enjoyable especially with your enthusiasm to answer every one of my questions no matter how late I was up writing.

Thank you Lorilee and Tashia for being my beta readers. Your love for Carter motivated me to keep writing this story during the hardest times.

To book nerds everywhere;
you are my tribe
you make my dream possible
and for that
I thank you.

The pain you feel today is the strength you'll have tomorrow.

PROLOGUE

I lay here teetering on the edge of my own sanity. My despair and fear have become a black hole from which I can't escape. I fear the dark. I fear sleep. I fear what comes to me every night. Over and over. When morning comes, I gasp for air, drenched in sweat, my fists clenching my sheets. I remind myself he's not here. He can never hurt me again. He's dead, and I'm alive.

CHAPTER ONE

—

ALEX

The loud, obnoxious buzzing of my cell phone on my nightstand reminds me it's time to wake. I only fell into an exhausted sleep three hours ago. Dragging my heavy legs off the bed, I stumble to stand and make my way into the kitchen. The cool tile floor feels refreshing against my warm feet. It's the first thing every morning that jolts my body awake and reminds me I can still feel something—*anything*.

With the direction my life has gone these last several weeks, it amazes me I haven't lost everything. My boss has taken pity on me and given me many passes, but it will only last so long. I need to get my shit together. I'm trying. I swear I am but surviving an attack in your own home isn't something you recover from quickly.

Moving to a new apartment in Villa Heights was a way to cope. Every time I walked into my old apartment, I was reminded of that night. Leaving behind all of my furniture and telling my landlord to sell it or use it was an easy choice for me. The apartment had become a desolate cave, filled with despair, anger, fear, and disgust. It was no longer my home. I would've burned it down to the ground and watched it incinerate if given the chance.

The Keurig machine grinds and hisses, and I'm snapped back to the present. Pulling the mug from the base, I hold it between my narrow fingers and bask in the warmth before bringing the hot liquid to my lips. As it warms my throat, it sheds the last of the lingering night.

My hand curls around the white curtain and pulls it away from the floor to ceiling window, letting the Florida sunlight illuminate the room and fill every crevice of my apartment. After another sip, I close my eyes and concentrate on the sensation warming my skin. I need these little moments—moments where I forget the pain, the desolation, the loneliness.

Ever since the attack, I haven't dated. I had a fiancé, but the coward took off when I needed him the most. I can't blame him though. I became a broken woman. I was no longer the spritely, kinky, fun Alex I used to be.

Now I'm the workaholic, structured, paranoid, can't bring myself to love Alex. If not for my best friend, Jane I may not be here at all. Her spunk and loyalty gave me a string to hold on to—something to grasp onto in my deepest, darkest moments.

Glancing at the gym certificate on the table, I smile. After mentioning I wanted to take a self-defense class, it was Jane who left me a sparkly card on my birthday with a gift certificate for eight weeks of kickboxing and self-defense classes, all expenses paid. You see why I love her?

My first class is at nine and I don't want to be late. After a quick shower, I carefully choose something comfortable. I'm not a gym enthusiast, but I do know I'm gonna need as much flexibility as my clothes will allow. Settling on a peach racerback tank and black, knee-length, athletic, yoga pants, I wrap my chocolate hair into a ponytail, grab my bag and keys, and head out the door.

As I pull up to the gym, I'm already feeling good about the place. It has large windows across the front of the building. With the sun shining, I can see inside clearly. There's a class now, a group of women hitting and kicking bags with all their might. I take a breath, committing to my endeavor. It's now or never.

Opening the door, I'm overwhelmed with nerves. The eyes that descend on me, the smell of sweat and metal, and the symphony of grunts do nothing to calm them. A pretty girl with short, wavy, dark hair gives me a toothy grin from behind the front desk.

"Welcome to Raise the Bar. What can I do for you?"

I hand her my certificate.

"Oh great! You'll be with Carter. He's the best. He's finishing up the eight a.m. kickboxing class. If you want to take a seat and fill out this sheet, he'll be over when he's finished."

"Thanks," I reply, taking the clipboard from her hand.

Moving to the small waiting area that blocks my view of the current kickboxing class, I listen to a guy with a smooth and authoritative baritone instruct the women to stretch and drink water before telling them they did a great job this morning. Filling in my name and information, I wait for the next class participants to arrive.

My nerves etch wrinkles across my forehead when no other women show up, but several depart from the class that just ended. Stepping up to the counter, I place the completed form on it.

"Excuse me."

The sweet girl turns to me. "What can I help you with?"

"The certificate says nine. Was it printed wrong? No one else seems to be showing up."

"No, it's printed correctly," the young woman smiles kindly. "It's a certificate for private classes."

"Private classes?"

"Yeah, here's Carter now."

She points behind me, and I turn to see a magnificent specimen of a man walking toward me while he lowers what appears to be a fresh shirt. Flapping wings go into a tizzy, giving my stomach an unfamiliar sensation. I stare, a bit mesmerized by the broad shoulders, muscular arms, and the peek I saw of his chiseled chest and the tribal tattoo laced across his torso. And those abs! I've never seen someone in the flesh with an actual eight-pack.

Before I embarrass myself, I peel my eyes off him, glance back at the girl, and smile. The warmth of my flushed cheeks adds to my embarrassment. She gives me a knowing grin.

A smooth baritone breaks me from my internal anxiety attack.

"Hey, you must be my nine o'clock. I'm Carter."

Turning to face him, I accept his extended hand and give it a firm shake.

"I'm Alex."

Deep blue eyes study my face for what seems like an eternity. Steadying my trembling knees, I give what's probably a crooked, awkward smile.

"Come on back. I'll show you around, then we can get started."

I follow like a loyal, scared puppy as he points and explains where things are and what equipment is what. He leads me into an area with padded floor mats, kickboxing bags, and equipment hanging from the low ceiling.

"Do you have a pair of good gloves?"

"No. I should've got some. I didn't think of it."

"It's all right. I have a pair you can borrow for today, but it will be better if you have your own pair to train with."

"Got it. I'll take care of that later today."

Carter smiles and that incessant flapping in my stomach startles me. His smile is too charming, too sexy. Avoiding his gaze, I find a place to drop my bag.

"When you're ready, we'll start with some stretches, then we'll move into some simple exercises of punches and kicks. I'll try not to work you too hard on your first day. I want you to come back," he chuckles, pinning me with that sexy smile.

"I kind of have to. My friend paid for these classes. I'm not going to let her waste her money, and honestly, I'm here to learn."

6

He moves to a stereo and hits a button. Upbeat music filters out through the speakers but not loud enough I can't hear him clearly.

"What would you like to learn, Alex? What are your goals?"

I cross my arms, unsure of what to do with them.

"I'd like to learn to defend myself."

Carter observes my body language with every one of my movements. He's studying me and that makes me uncomfortable. Biting my lip, I rub my suddenly chilled arms.

"Have a seat. We're gonna stretch, then I'm going to help you reach your goal."

Sitting down, I outstretch my legs. Sitting in front of me, he outstretches his. I copy him as he moves one direction, then the other. He stands, and I follow his movements, stretching limb after limb, loosening my tight muscles.

"Good. You ready to start?"

When I nod, he grabs me a pair of pink gloves. With his assistance, I get them on, then he slides on a pair of punching mitts. Standing in front of me, he raises them eye level.

"What I want you to do is put your front leg forward and get a confident, steady stance, then punch with your right, left, then duck."

Repeating the words in my head—*right, left, duck*—I start swinging. My glove makes impact, then I lower my body before his left mitt hits me in the face.

"Good, again, but I want you to keep your gloves close to your chin. Protect your face."

Everything repeats in my head—*right, left, duck—keep gloves to cheeks.* I put power into my punches and make contact. He swings, and I hurry to duck, just missing the mitt to my face.

"Good," he winks. "Again."

This repetition continues several more times before he tells me to switch my leg and punch the opposite direction. Once more, I have to tell my brain where I'm supposed to hit before being able to make contact. The words repeat, and soon, I'm anticipating his swings and falling into a rhythm.

"Good." He lowers the mitts as I catch my breath.

"You're a natural, Alex, and your form isn't far off either. Take a drink, then we'll start on kicks."

After drinking water and getting my breath regulated, I return to him on the mat. He motions for me to follow him to an elongated kicking bag, sticking up from its floor anchor.

"I want you to kick this bag. Here first." He toes the bottom. "Then here." His shoe points to the middle. "Then here." Lastly, his shoe faces the top. "But when you kick, I want you to put your weight on the front pad of your foot. Let your body swivel and you'll be able to put more power into your kicks."

He demonstrates, and I stumble back, startled by the sheer force and speed of his kicks.

"Got it?"

"Yeah," I reply meekly, "I think so."

Replicating his movements, I swivel too far and my ankle dips. Strong hands catch my fall and stabilize me. "I gotcha."

The touch of his hands to my waist ignites an odd combination of sensations. I haven't been touched affectionately by a man in over a year, and my response to the graze of his hands is equally startling as it is tantalizing. Immediately, I wiggle from his grasp.

"Thanks."

My shy embarrassment appears to amuse him. Staring at me, his eyes soften.

"It's all right. It's your first day. A strong core takes time and practice. We'll get you there. You ready to try again?"

Nodding, I approach the bag. With concentration, I attack, giving it everything I have.

"Switch," I hear behind me.

Lowering my leg, I rotate my stance and begin my kicks on the other side. He says switch two more times before our time on this bag is through.

"Great job, Alex. That was better. You have the drive to do well, and that will get you through all your training."

Silly as it is, I feel warm and fuzzy from his praise. "Thank you."

"You need a break or you ready for more?"

"A quick water break and I'll be ready."

The next thirty minutes, Carter puts me through more punch and kick practices, and I begin to think, *wax on, wax off.* He's teaching me proper form and how to keep my stance strong which makes my punches and kicks more powerful. By the end, I'm panting and wiping sweat from my brow. He tosses me a towel and nods for us to sit.

"You've done really well today, it being your first time. You had serious power in your kicks."

Little did he know who I was imagining when kicking those bags. I stumble through removing my first glove, and Carter smiles.

"Here, let me."

Strong hands that were demonstrating how to demolish a punching bag earlier are now providing a gentler touch as he pulls the wristband off my glove and eases my hand out of it. He takes my hand in his and I flinch at the unexpected touch. His observant gaze watches my response and tilts my hand back and forth for inspection.

"This is why your own set of gloves will work better. These are MMA gloves. You won't have these marks on your knuckles with your own hand wraps or kickboxing gloves."

Deep blue irises meet my gaze and lock me in his stare. Something passes between us like an unruly itch running across my skin. I quickly withdraw my hand and tear my gaze from his mesmerizing eyes.

"Any recommendations of where to buy gloves?" I ask as I remove my second glove and avoid getting locked in an awkward stare again.

It's been a very long time since I found a man attractive. I came to the conclusion love and men are a loss for me. I'm destined to live alone and be married to my work. These odd sensations coursing through me at the scent of his masculine soap and sweat, his beautiful blue eyes, and the innocent touch of his hands are unfamiliar territory for me.

"You can buy some at the shop here, on Amazon, or any MMA site. I'll walk you to the shop and help you pick out a pair if you'd like."

"That'd be great."

I'm ready to get away from him before I get any dizzier, but I genuinely need his help with picking out the right kind of gloves. He nods and a deal is struck. Taking the borrowed gloves off the floor, he wipes them out and tosses them in his duffle. Grabbing my own bag, I follow him to the store, packed full of workout gear.

He points to different gloves in different colors, and I catch myself staring at his short, milk chocolate hair, strong pronounced jaw, and the scruff lining it. His eyes though are what keep me from being able to look away. They're a deep, soft blue that give the impression of tenderness beneath the masculinity. Turning his head at the right moment, he catches me staring, and I quickly point to a pair of gloves.

"Those ones will work."

"Good choice." Pulling a green pair off the peg, he carries my gloves to the register, leaving me tagging behind and still unable to escape his distracting presence.

"Give her my discount," he tells the clerk.

The shaggy-haired fella nods and rings up the gloves.

"You didn't have to do that."

"I do it for all my clients," Carter smiles and traps me in the pool of deep blue.

"Of course. Thank you." Embarrassed, I hide my flushed cheeks by digging my wallet out of my bag. Carter watches me as I check out. His lingering is causing a twitch in my jaw and my weight to shift from one foot to the other.

"So, I'll see you Tuesday evening then?"

"Hmm? Oh, yes, Tuesday's session. Thanks for everything today. I'll see you then."

Carter taps the counter and makes his way back into the gym. I let out a breath and stare at the clerk, almost forgetting why I was there in the first place. He hands me my bag and I dart out of the gym. Before I make it to the car, I'm dialing Jane.

"Hey, babe! What's up? How was your first sess?"

"*Jane Marie Anthony.* Private lessons? That had to have cost you a fortune!"

"Eh, don't worry about it. It's a gift from Kyle and me. You mentioned it so many times, I thought it was time to make you do it."

"And the trainer? Have you *seen* him?"

"Oh, yes. Carter," Jane laughs. "He's great. He's friends with Kyle. Kyle suggested him, and when I met him, I thought he was perfect for you."

"What do you mean *perfect* for me?" I ask, leaning my weight against my car.

"Well, you know? He's hot and single, and you're hot and single. Figure it out, babe."

"Jane, you know I can't even fathom a relationship."

"Honey, you won't know until you try. You do think he's cute though, right?"

Shuffling my foot, I let out an exasperated breath. "Yes, he's gorgeous and his eyes... Jane, he has the most beautiful eyes I've ever seen."

A tap on my shoulder sends me spiraling and falling into Carter's arms. I move like lightning to get out of his grasp and gather my exploding emotions.

Oh my God, did he just hear that?

Carter stabilizes me, then waves my water bottle in the air, grinning ear to ear. "You forgot this."

I can hear Jane giggling through the phone.

My hand grabs the water bottle as my expression no doubt reveals how mortified I am. Carter doesn't say anything about the comments I'm sure he just heard.

"Would you like to have dinner with me tomorrow night?"

Heat rises to my cheeks. I know my face is a solid, rosy red at this point.

"I can't. I'm sorry." Turning away from him, I dive into my car and leave before I embarrass myself any further.

"You seriously bolted after he asked you to dinner?"

Jane brings her freshly filled wine glass to my table and sits across from me, her long, lengthy legs wrapping around each other. She takes a sip, and I fidget at the sight

13

of her bold, brown eyes scrutinizing me over the brim of her glass.

"Yes. I'm not ready. It's too soon." Raising my glass of wine to my lips, I pause. I hadn't expected to feel a tinge of regret at saying no to Carter. *Am I ready to date again? Have I laid my demons to rest enough to be able to give my heart and body to a man?*

"If you think any harder, you're going to form permanent wrinkles on that pretty face of yours."

I chuckle before letting the refreshing liquid soothe my edginess.

"He's the first man you've been attracted to. Why not give it a try?"

Jane's persistence is understandable. She knows me better than anyone even better than I know myself sometimes, but the thought of opening myself up emotionally and physically is terrifying. My apprehension and fear are a gap that lays between us, and she'll never be fully able to understand it.

"One step at a time. I'd like to conquer my first goal and make it through my classes. Trying to date my instructor would only make things more complicated."

"Sure, babe," Jane agrees, tapping her manicured nails on the table, "one step at a time."

I glance at her emotionless face. I know her too well not to recognize the intellectual wheels turning behind the expressionless mask.

She's not going to let this go.

CHAPTER TWO

—

ALEX

Entering the gym for my Tuesday evening session is more difficult than I expected. My hands tighten on the steering wheel as I take calming breaths. No doubt Carter will want to know why I said no and ran after hearing me gush about how good-looking he was. It's the potential questions that create a fist-tight ball in my gut and make me stumble over my words. You can't come out and explain you were a victim of rape and haven't been touched by a man since. It's not something anyone is ready to hear nor do they know how to respond. They stare at you with a mix of shock, pity, and an expression that says, *What the hell do I say to that*? The usual go-to is, *I'm sorry*. Yes, thank you, so am I.

Gathering as much gumption as I can muster, I grab my bag and head into the gym. The young dark-haired girl waves hello. Stepping to the counter, I smile.

"I'm sorry, I didn't catch your name last time."

Her smile widens. "I'm Rachele."

"Rachele, it's nice to meet you."

"You too, Miss DeMarco."

"Call me Alex."

"So, you aren't married?"

My head snaps in the direction of Carter's voice. Curiosity brimming in his eyes, he smiles as my cheeks grow warm. Rachele bows her head with a grin then busies herself with work.

Stumbling over my cement tongue, I manage to form words. "No, I'm not married."

"Boyfriend?"

"No."

"Girlfriend?"

His barrage of humorous and entertaining questions pulls my lips back into a smile.

"No girlfriend."

"Well then, what made you bolt like a scared kitten?"

I go for a simple and satisfactory explanation, one I'd come up with this morning while I debated coming back to the gym. "You're my trainer. I don't want to complicate things."

Carter nods, clearly defeated. He turns on his heels, and I follow, feeling like a total asshole. I tell myself it's better this way. The alternative options are unsettling.

As I pull out my gloves, Carter joins me and offers to help put them on. Blue eyes survey me, roaming over my face, causing an unfamiliar sensation to twist in my gut and trickle down to my core.

"You're very pretty, you know that?"

His subtle compliment jolts my attention back to him. I smile awkwardly as an unusual flutter of excitement does a loop-the-loop in my belly.

"Thank you."

"You sure you don't want to have dinner with me?"

"Carter..." My head drops and guilt punches its way into my gut.

"I can guarantee if you have a terrible time on our date, I'll still train you. I'd even get you a new trainer if you decided you never wanted to see my face again."

The humorous undertone brings the smile back to my lips.

"I'm gonna wear you down, Alex. You should save yourself the torture now," he quips.

"It's complicated. I'm not open to dating right now." My smile morphs into a frown. "Can you respect that?"

Carter's jaw tightens as he nods. Giving a blow to his ego felt as bad as it sounded.

"Sure, I can respect that." He motions toward the mats and I step forward. "For now."

Glancing over my shoulder, I take sight of his sexy smirk and bite my lip to keep from giggling at how cute he looks.

"What's the plan for today?" I ask, taking our conversation in a new direction.

"Same as the last session, but today, we'll also do some exercises to focus on strengthening your core."

Following Carter's lead, he guides me through a circuit exercise. Each activity is focused on building up the muscle strength in my abdomen and back. As soon as he says,

"Time" I drop the ropes and step off the yoga balance ball. Lifting my water bottle to my lips, I guzzle the water and stop myself from pouring it all over my face. Carter tosses me a towel.

"You continue to impress me. You don't balk at anything I have you do."

"No pain, no gain, right?"

Laughing, he takes a seat on the bench next to me. The scent of his cologne mixed with his masculinity is all too enticing.

"Yeah, it's true. You're gonna be really sore tomorrow. I have a massage therapist I can recommend."

"Yes!" The word *massage* has me tuning in intently. "I'll gladly take you up on that offer."

"I'll get you her number before you leave. So, what is it you do for a living?"

"I'm an operations specialist at Kevlar and Kline. They make the vests for law enforcement officers and military personnel."

"That's a cool job," Carter's eyes widen, "an important job."

"For a while there, I thought I was going to lose my job, but I'm finally getting my shit together." Carter studies my face, and I realize I divulged too much information. "I had a rough patch with some personal issues," I backtrack.

"I get the impression you're focusing on you right now, that's why you're not dating."

"Yeah," is all I say. It's not completely off from the truth.

"You ready to practice a few rounds with me?"

Nodding, I grab my gloves out of my bag. Raising my glove-covered fists, I prepare for his instruction.

"Double punches, left, right, duck, left, right."

As I repeat the words, I pound the gloves into his mitts. He lowers the mitts after the last round. "Let's correct your form."

He motions for me to follow him to a boxing bag. Demonstrating on the bag, he shows me how I should place my feet and move my body. I move in and replace him in front of the bag as he steps away. Replicating his movements, I punch the bag. I startle when his hands briefly take hold of my hips and adjust their placement. A warming sensation spreads through me and my cheeks flush.

"Good, Alex. Another twenty."

When he calls time, my arms drop like limp noodles. Carter runs his hand along my arm and gathers the glove in his hand. With his free hand, he removes the wrist wrap. To my surprise, I don't jump at the contact.

"You did great today. Like I said, you're gonna be sore tomorrow. I recommend a lot of water, an easy run or jog to loosen your tight muscles, and I'll get you Connie's number for the massage."

"You're a great instructor."

Carter's smile is sweet. "You're a good student."

His affectionate praise creates an unusual warmth in my chest.

"After we stretch, you're free to go."

Once I put my gloves away, I join Carter on the mats. He reaches his hands out for me to take. Hesitantly, I place mine in his palms. He pulls me forward, stretching my hamstring.

"Lay back."

Lying back on the mat, I look up at Carter with no doubt a deer in headlights expression as he moves forward and takes my leg in his hands. Pushing it forward, he stretches the muscle. It's a relief as much as it is painful.

He does the other leg, and I shift when I feel the length of him accidentally brush up against the backside of my thigh. My body's reaction shakes my reserve. Arousal ignites in my gut and travels south. Easing my leg down, he reaches out his hand for me to take. I'm frozen in his gaze as he smiles down at me.

"See you at our next session."

CHAPTER THREE

—

ALEX

After shimmying into my skinny jeans, I pull my green sweater over my chest. One look in the mirror has me tearing it off and throwing it to the floor. My phone buzzes on the bed, and Jane's face lights up the screen. I know she's anxious for me to arrive at her St. Patrick's Day party.

"Where are you? Don't be late. Just pick something out and go with it."

Moving to the closet, I rummage through my shirts. "Everything I own looks terrible on me."

"Go with the long-sleeve green shirt, the V-neck with slits in the arms."

"How is it you know what's in my closet better than I do?"

"I'm in that closest nearly as much as you are. Now hurry up. Don't keep me waiting. I made Jell-O shots!"

Finding the shirt, I pull it from the hanger and finish dressing before her calls become sequent, rapid-fire dials.

A quick look in the mirror, touch up of my lipstick, and I'm grabbing my purse, rushing out the door.

My nerves combust as I step up to Jane and Kyle's home. Music is thudding, and several cars are parked outside already. I barely get a couple knocks on the door and it's swinging open. I'm dragged inside by Jane's long arms. Squeals erupt from her as she shoves a green Jell-O shot into my hand.

"Get in here! You have catching up to do."

Taking my hand, she pulls me into the kitchen as I slurp down the Jell-O shot. As we enter the kitchen, I take note of the people standing at her kitchen island, taking shots and another handful at the makeshift beer pong table in her dining room. My eyes focus in on one person in particular—*Carter*.

My gaze sweeps to her, and she winks and shrugs. Carter waves at me, and I shyly wave back. He misses his next shot as his attention is on me and not the cups in front of him.

"I'm out," he says to a friend before eliminating the space between us.

"Alex."

"Hey, Carter."

"It's good to see you outside of training. You look beautiful."

"Thank you." His penetrating gaze makes me shift in my heels. "You look great too." In an effort to hide my awkward staring, I lean over and grab another Jell-O shot. His long-sleeved, black shirt with wheel tracks across the front is pulled up to his elbows and semi-tucked into a pair of worn jeans, sporting a silver buckle on the belt. A brown leather band covers his wrist, and his look is completed with brown boots. He looks even more delicious outside of the gym. His style is sexy, it's a mix of edgy, rocker, country boy. A style I didn't realize I found so appealing until now.

"Want a beer?" he nods to the fridge.

"Can't stand the stuff. I'm a liquor or wine gal."

"Jane, you got any wine?"

She looks over from the other side of the kitchen with an expression of amusement. "Ah duh! Yeah, I have wine."

"You mind getting Alex a glass?"

"You didn't have to do that." The chivalrous gesture tugs at my lips. "I could have drank what she had out."

"You're special, Alex. You deserve special."

Heat flushes my cheeks. He's really putting on the charm, and it's affecting me whether I want it to or not. The affectionate look in his eyes holds me hostage, and I begin gnawing on my lip.

"I'm glad you're here tonight."

"You are?"

Jane hands me a glass of wine, then bolts, leaving me behind like a comrade too far gone to save.

"Yeah, I was hoping you'd be here so I could get to know you better."

I take a strong gulp of wine as my nerves start to fire like pistons.

"Do I make you nervous?" Carter suddenly asks, his brows pinched inward.

It must have been the liquor and wine hitting me because my mouth opened and spilled out the words.

"All men make me nervous."

Carter's expression twists as his thoughts take shape. "What do you—"

His words are cut off as Jane shouts. "Blindfolded coin search time! Pair up with a partner."

"Would you like to be my partner?"

"Yes, she would." Jane's hands take hold of my shoulders. "Everyone has to play. Everyone needs a partner."

She sprints off in search of something, I assume the blindfolds.

"All right, then," I laugh. "I guess the answer is yes."

Carter leans against the island. "How do we play this game?"

"One of us is blindfolded and the other one directs the blindfolded person around the room in search of gold chocolate coins. The coins will have little messages on them with tasks for us. The first couple to find five gold coins and complete their tasks wins."

Jane returns and hands out the blindfolds. She places one in Carter's hand and smirks at me. She's too clever sometimes. She probably orchestrated this entire party around getting Carter and me together.

Carter holds out the black blindfold. "Do you trust me?"

Apprehensively, I nod and turn. The blindfold is gently placed over my eyes and tied. He places his hands on my shoulders and leans in close.

"You can trust me. I won't let you fall," he whispers.

The heat of his body so near and the touch of his hands on my shoulders turns my stomach into a tight knot. The blindfold, his heated breath, it's too much. Tears threaten to escape my eyes, and I tear the blindfold off.

"I can't do this." I rush out of the room, trying not to draw any excess attention to my panic attack.

"Shit," I hear Jane say behind me. "Kyle, tell everyone the rules. I'll be back."

My body trembles as he ties the blindfold over my eyes. The cuffs around my wrists keep me from being able to remove it. He's taken one of my senses from me, leaving me terrified and blind in the dark. His hand grazes along my inner thigh, and I try to squirm away from his grasp, but he presses his weight down on me, trapping my legs beneath him. He straddles me, pinning me under him, and I feel his finger swipe across my cheek and gather my tears.

My ears pick up the sound of his lips sucking his finger.

"Your fear tastes sweet. Keep them coming. It's so much better when you cry."

Jane enters her bedroom. I look up at her through my tears.

"I'm so sorry, Alex. I didn't think about it. I'm such an asshole."

"It's okay. It isn't your fault. I used to love that game. The son-of-a-bitch took that from me too! He's ruined my life! I can't have normal interactions with a man without freaking out because of him!"

25

"Alex, listen to me." Jane bends down in front of me and takes my hands in hers. "He hasn't ruined your life. Look how far you've come. You used to be scared to close your eyes. To do anything. Now, you've taken control of your independence, your success. *You* own your life."

A creak at the door has me whipping my attention toward it. Carter steps in, and my head goes foggy, and my cheeks flush with embarrassment. He's holding my glass of wine and wearing an expression of concern.

"Jane, could I speak with Alex, alone, if she's all right with that?"

Jane looks at me for approval, and I nod. She glances at Carter.

"Yeah, sure. Let me know if you need anything," she says to me before leaving the room.

Carter's soft, blue eyes fall on me, and he moves forward, carefully and slowly as if I'm a wild animal he's trying to pet. Finally reaching me, he sits down on the bed next to me and hands me the wine glass.

"Thank you." I take it and swallow several times, trying to soothe my frayed nerves. "I'm sorry I freaked out."

"You don't have to explain anything to me. I wanted to make sure you're all right."

"Something terrible happened to me and I still have unexpected panic attacks because of it."

"I understand. My mother had something bad happen to her too. Every once in a while, a certain trigger would leave her emotional for a few days."

I look at him, completely shocked by what he's sharing.

"It was before my brother and I were born. She only talked to me about it once."

The knot in my stomach loosens and my trembling hands steady.

Carter's hand gently slides into mine, and to my surprise, I appreciate the gesture and the warmth of his skin. Soft, blue eyes entrap me.

"I'd never ask you to share anything you don't want to, but I do want you to know you can."

I can't even form words. The sincerity in his voice and his thoughtfulness soothe the remaining aches and pains.

"Would you like to come back out with me? You can blindfold me instead," he grins playfully, and I can't help smiling.

"Yes, I would like to join you."

"Good." He pulls the blindfold from his back pocket and hands it to me.

I place it back in his hand. "I'd like to try it. I trust you."

With his pretty blues glistening, he raises the blindfold and gently places his hand on my hair and brushes it aside. Slowly, carefully, he places the blindfold over my eyes. His whispered breath warms my ear.

"It means a lot to me that you trust me."

His hand slides into mine again and my jittery nerves settle.

CHAPTER FOUR

—

ALEX

The first coin was the easiest. Carter spotted it on the window sill, behind the curtain, and gave me great instructions to locate it.

"You have an advantage. You instruct for a living. So, what's it say?" I outstretch my hand and he takes it from me.

"It says to take two Jell-O shots each."

Thinking he's going to walk away and leave me there blindfolded, I reach for the blindfold to remove it. His hand takes hold of mine and I instantly relax. "I'm not leaving you. Not for a second. You're coming with me."

Several steps put us back in the kitchen and he places my hand over the Jell-O shot. I gobble them up, then giggle as the liquor I've consumed since arriving takes effect. Carter takes my hand in his and kisses the top making me giggle again.

"You really are beautiful."

I jump when I feel his lips touch my cheek. The sweet gesture warms me and sends a tantalizing sensation over my skin.

"You ready to find the next one? I wanna win whatever prize Jane has in store for us."

With my grin of approval, he takes my hand in his, pulling me around the room. His hands gently take my shoulders like before, his breath warming my ear. I know he's located another one.

"On the TV stand—" His words are cut off as a crash bang meets my ears. I move into his arms and he holds me protectively. "It's all right. That girl, Anna, just tripped and fell. You good?" He rubs my arms and I realize I don't want to move out of his grasp. For the first time, in a very long time, I feel safe.

"Yeah, I'm good."

"On the TV stand, there's one next to Kyle's Xbox console. If you reach into the center of the TV stand, you'll touch the console. It will be to the right of it, about five inches in."

Walking forward, he lightly touches my shoulder and redirects me anytime I'm close to tripping over something. We reach the TV stand and I move my hand as he instructed. Feeling the wrapper of the chocolate coin, I pull it out and hand it to him. He doesn't read it aloud, and now I'm curious.

"What's it say?"

"For me to kiss you…on the lips."

I shift my footing. I want him to, but I'm not sure I'm ready for it, now, at this party with people watching. I hear movement and his hand takes mine.

"I'll save that one for later. Let's keep looking."

Within moments he finds another one and I pull it out.

"What's this one say?"

"To feed the chocolate to your partner." The sound of the wrapper crinkling reaches my ears. "Do you like chocolate?" he asks.

"Of course, I love chocolate."

"Good. I'm gonna place it to your lips."

Wondering how I look, I chuckle before I open my mouth. He places it on my tongue, and I lift the chocolate from his finger. His finger lingers on my lip, and I playfully swipe my tongue across it. Removing his finger, I'm left in silence, feeling odd about the encounter.

"I'm sorry."

"No, Alex. That was…there are people around us. I don't want them to notice how incredibly attracted I am to you."

"Oh." I realize what he's saying. He liked it, maybe too much. *Incredibly attracted.* My cheeks couldn't get any warmer as the words dribble around in my head.

His hand takes mine. "You ready to find the next one?"

"Yes."

It's taking more steps than before, and I know we've gone into the guest room. He lets go, and I'm left standing there, anxious about what to do next. Fidgeting uncomfortably, I freeze when warm hands cup my face and soft lips touch mine.

His kiss is affectionate, tender, and it lights up my whole body. When he ends the kiss, I let out a whimper. I don't want it to end. It's incredible, he tastes of lime, liquor, and delicious man. His hands take hold of my shoulders and caress me.

"There's one by the foot of the bedpost."

I'd nearly forgotten the game entirely. Reaching up, I place my hand on his chest.

"Please, kiss me again."

Instantly, his hand holds me at the nape of my neck and the other wraps around me as he pulls me in close. His lips meet mine and I fall into oblivion.

We pull back from the kiss with heavy breaths, Carter's fingers caressing my cheek.

"We're gonna lose this game if I don't stop kissing you." He kisses my cheek, moves away, returns quickly, placing the gold chocolate coin in my hand.

"What's it say?"

"To switch the blindfold."

I giggle and reach for it, but he stops my hand.

"One more before you take it off."

He kisses me and I lean into him. Holding me close, he offers me the same affectionate, passion-filled kiss as before. My knees go weak, but he holds me steady. The kiss ends and he takes my breath with him.

"I can't take how beautiful you are." Slowly, he removes the blindfold and I stare up at his warm, inviting eyes. His thumb swipes my lips. "I want to keep kissing you, but we should get back to the party."

"And it's your turn to wear the blindfold."

"Yes, it is." Turning his back to me, I place it snuggly over his eyes and tie the ends. "Where to, beautiful?"

The term of endearment brings a smile to my lips. I take his hand, moving around the room, looking for the last coin we need. *The closet. Jane would hide one in there.* Carter follows the sound of my voice as I look around inside.

"There." I point, then roll my eyes.

"You just pointed, didn't you?" Carter laughs.

"Yes."

"You're cute."

"It's sitting right next to one of her high heels. Raise your hand straight out in front of you. Lower. Good. Move forward a step. Yes. Right there. You got it."

Carter lifts the blindfold off and reads the message. "It's another shot each."

Pocketing the coin, he takes my hand, and we walk out to the kitchen where he places all five on the counter. He glances around at the others still searching.

"What did we win?"

Jane's smile couldn't get any wider as she looks at our intertwined hands. She reaches above the fridge and hands Carter two tickets. "Movie tickets."

Carter takes the tickets from her hand and turns to me. "What would you like to see?"

Grabbing another Jell-O shot, I swallow it as my nerves prickle my skin. A date, alone, with Carter who likes to kiss me. Not sure I'm ready for it, but I'm not going to turn him down in front of everyone.

"Action or comedy."

"Perfect."

The party continues with an Irish whiskey and beer tasting contest, then a Who's the Greenest outfit contest. After several more drinks, I lose my bashfulness and join Jane on the dance floor. We shake our asses to the beat of the music and I notice Carter watching my every move as he chats with Kyle.

CHAPTER FIVE

—

CARTER

"Dude, if you stare any harder, she's gonna think you're a creep."

Fuck. Kyle's right. I wonder if Alex even knows how stunning she is. I feel like a damn moth drawn to a flame every time I look at her. Tugging on my beer, I try to pry my eyes away, but the way she moves those curves has my semi growing in an uncomfortable upright direction. Her long, straight, milk chocolate hair curves around her face in layers, but it's those bold, green eyes that draw me in, the hidden sensuality under that shy and apprehensive exterior. It's an adorable and wicked combination. She's drank enough liquor her guard is down and she's letting me in. My shoulders are now heavy with an angel and devil whispering sweet nothings in my ears.

"What's her story?" I press Kyle. I have an idea, but assumptions aren't facts.

"Don't say anything. Jane will fucking kill me if she knows I told you."

"Not a word," I promise.

"She was attacked by a serial rapist. She was his last victim."

I nearly spit out my beer and quickly gulp it back down. "Are you shitting me right now?"

"No, dude. I'm for real. She doesn't trust men. She hasn't dated since her attack. She had a fiancé, but he ditched her 'cause she was too sensitive about being touched and he couldn't handle the emotional aftermath."

"What a prick? You know him?"

"I did. We were buddies, but after he left her like that our friendship ended quickly. She spent a lot of nights here. She'd wake up screaming from nightmares. Jane would sleep in the bed with her so she felt safe and everyone could get sleep."

"That's fucking nuts." I pull on my beer as tension tightens my chest. "What happened to him? You said she was his last victim."

"The cops had him as a suspect and put a tail on him. He'd already done what he wanted to her by the time they broke in. He fired at the cops and the cops took him down."

Tugging harder on my beer, I mentally try to absorb the sick fucking details I'm hearing. No wonder Alex is so skittish and uncomfortable being touched. The last man who touched her hurt her in the worst possible way.

"How long ago did this happen?"

"A little over a year ago. It was the one-year mark of her attack about three months ago. She backtracked and got depressed for almost a month, but she came out of it, determined not to let it affect her life."

35

"She's incredibly strong."

"She is, Carter. She survived this guy's twisted games and abuse for three hours. She fought to survive, and she's come a long way. You're one of the best guys I know. If you're truly into her, you need to know you have the potential to end up with a great woman, but I can't promise it will be easy to win her over. Her scars run deep."

Meeting Alex's gaze, I can see the curiosity taking shape. There are moments where I see a woman much like myself—observant, determined, independent. Yet so much is shadowed by the fear she harbors. I've never seen myself as much of the hero type, but for the first time in my life, I find myself wanting to rescue someone.

"What about family? She got any around?"

"A sister and father. She and her sister are estranged, and her father doesn't live in the country anymore. Took a job in the UK. Jane and I are her family."

"I'm glad she has the two of you."

With sweat glistening their skin, the girls take a break from dancing. Alex goes for water and I watch carefully. Now that I know what she's been through, I'm better prepared to move forward.

CHAPTER SIX

—

ALEX

"He's smitten, Alex. He's watching your every move."

Tipping the glass back, I take several swallows before setting it on the counter and claiming one of the stools at the island.

"I know. It's an odd sensation. It excites and freaks me out."

"Carter is one of the good ones, babe. Kyle says so."

"I believe him, but it's difficult. I'm trying. I promise."

"Are you gonna go to the movie with him?" She asks as she preps a whiskey shot and downs it.

"I don't know."

She pours another and slides it towards me. "You should go. It'll be fun. Pick a movie you really want to see."

Lifting the glass to my lips, I swallow the fiery liquid.

"You wanna dance some more? Anna is waving us over."

"No, I'm gonna get some air. If I'm going to make it home, I need to stop drinking."

"No one is going home," Jane laughs, "I hid everyone's keys."

My eyes widen and I grab her wrist. "You're joking, right?"

"Nope, it's a cab or my guest room for you."

Yes, of course, a cab. Releasing my grip, I rub her arm. "I'll call a cab soon."

She puckers her bottom lip. "It would be more fun if you slept over."

"Jane, you and Kyle are gonna hump like rabbits the moment you hit the sheets. I'd rather not be present for that. You get loud."

Jane giggles. "We do, don't we?"

"Very."

"Ok, well, be that way then. I do have a pair of earplugs in case you change your mind. I think Carter is crashing here tonight," she winks and leaves me to go dance.

Stepping off the stool, I make my way out to her back deck. It's small but equipped with the necessities—a shiny grill and an elegant set of matching table and chairs. I lean on the railing and suck in the breeze, letting it cool my warm, damp skin. I hear the sliding door behind me and Carter approaches. Putting his elbows on the railing next to me, he leans over it.

"Having a good time?"

"One of the best nights I've had in a long time."

"I hope you say that after dinner and a movie with me."

"Carter—"

"Don't say no. I understand you're not looking to date, but it doesn't mean we can't hang out."

I look away before I lose myself in the deep pool of blue. Carter pulls the tickets from his pocket and hands me one.

"We'll go as friends. You can even pay for your own dinner…maybe."

His grin is so delicious, my heart pitter-patters, and I struggle to say no to his charm. Taking the ticket from his hand, I smile.

"All right. We'll go, *as friends*."

"So, friend, what kind of food do you like to eat, or should we hit up a fast food drive-through on the way to the movie?" I laugh and his eyes light up. "You're stunning when you smile."

"Only when I smile?"

"Touché. What I really mean is, you're beautiful all the time, no matter what you're doing."

"Those are nicer words than you tell a friend."

"You women tell each other you look pretty all the time. I'm just stating the obvious."

"Well, you're not so bad yourself."

"You sayin' you think I'm pretty?" Carter grins, the corner of his eyes crinkling. His own humor cracks him up, making him even more attractive.

"Very pretty."

Laughing, he moves closer. Feeling the warmth radiating off him, I find myself wanting to be held in his arms.

"Anything wrong with two friends kissing? I can't stop thinking of earlier."

Chuckling, I turn to him, admiring the tenderness I see in his eyes. "You have seriously blurred lines of what friendship is."

"Can't blame me for trying. I enjoy kissing you."

Gently swiping his finger over my hand, his gaze lingers on me. I can see his interest and desire. My stomach knots, and this time, it's not out of fear. It's guilt. I enjoyed being kissed by him, but it's all happening much quicker than I'm prepared for.

I withdraw my hand from his touch. "I think I'm gonna call a cab. It's getting late and I'm pretty tired." Stepping away from the railing, I fumble with my steps. Carter grasps my arm and stabilizes me.

"I'm not comfortable with you taking a cab home alone. Why don't you crash in Jane's guest room? I was gonna stay there, but you can have it. I'll take the couch."

Part of me wants to tell him I'll be fine and take the cab back to my own bed, but the dizziness in my head is telling me to drink some water and lay down.

"Yeah, I think I'll stay. That last shot did me in."

Carter keeps contact with my elbow as I go back inside. I grab a bottle of water from Jane's fridge and head toward the guest room. Carter follows and my nerves bunch.

"What are you doing?"

"Making sure you don't fall or pass out."

"I'm good, I promise." I stop mid-way through the hallway, "Thank you for a really fun night."

Carter nods, seeming to understand I want my space.

40

"Goodnight, Alex."

Breath warm on my ear, he whispers, "You're gonna be my favorite. I can already tell."

"Please don't do this," I whimper between trembling lips.

"It's going to happen. Cry if you want to. It'll add to my pleasure."

He tests the ropes tied to my ankles, and I flinch at the touch of his hand on my bare skin.

"Why me? What did I do?"

A slap slams into my cheek, feeling as though a soccer ball was just kicked into my face. I taste blood on my lip before it spills into my mouth.

"Stop talking!"

A tear sings through the air as my underwear is ripped to shreds.

"No, NO! Stop!"

My eyes jolt open and panic rises as I feel a man's hands on my arms. I squirm and thrash at his body and face. *Please, no, please no!*

"Ssh, Alex. It's me, Carter. You're having a nightmare." His voice breaks through the vicious memories. Pulling me into his arms, he holds me as I weep into his bare chest, spreading tears everywhere. Hand caressing my hair, he gently rocks me.

"Ssh, you're safe with me, I'm not gonna hurt you."

Safe. I'm never safe. That monster took that security blanket from me and I've been fighting ever since to get it back.

Through the little bit of moonlight coming through the window, I realize I'm exposed. Snatching up the comforter, I pull it up over my bra covered breasts.

"I'm sorry I woke you."

The door swings open and Jane barrels in. "Alex. Are you okay?"

"Yeah, I'm so sorry I woke everyone up." Thankfully it's too dark for Carter to see my cheeks burn red.

"It's okay, babe. You sure you're good?" I can hear her underlying concern about Carter being in the room.

"Yeah, thank you."

"Ok, I'm going back to bed. Love you."

"Love you too."

The door closes and Carter brushes his hand along my arm. "You sure you're okay?"

"I am. Nightmares are nothing new for me. Probably freaked you out though, huh?"

"Not freaked out. Just worried about you."

"I appreciate you waking me up when you did. Truly. Thank you."

"Would you like me to stay? I mean, on the floor. I'll sleep on the floor next to you and keep you company."

"You don't have to do that."

"I want to. I don't want to leave you." His hand slides into mine and the warmth of it scatters the remaining edginess.

"Okay," I whisper.

His free hand strokes my cheek. "I'll be right back. I'm gonna grab my shirt, blankets, and a pillow."

He returns moments later, and I snuggle under the comforter, resting my head on the pillow as he creates a makeshift bed on the floor next to my side of the bed. With his arm behind his head, he lies on his back and covers himself waist high with the top blanket.

"Do you have nightmares every night?" he asks softly.

"Not every night, no. Just every once in a while."

My hand hangs off the edge of the bed wanting to feel his warmth again. I want those strong, protective arms around me that give me brief moments of false security. It's better than the desolation and loneliness I feel now. As if Carter senses my need, he raises his hand, intertwining his fingers with mine. The warmth of his hand quiets my mind and I drift off into oblivion. This time there's no nightmare.

CHAPTER SEVEN

—

ALEX

If I'm not at my desk in twenty minutes I'm going to be late for work. Tapping my fingers against my black, leather messenger bag, my patience wears thin. The line at the coffee shop is a mile long, at least it feels that way this morning. Unfortunately, my beloved Keurig machine bit the dust, and I'm now waiting in line for my morning dose. If I don't get it soon, I might just lose it.

The bell rings and more patrons enter the shop. I hold my gaze steady on the moving line, repeatedly inhaling the refreshing scent of coffee grounds to tide me over. Finally reaching the front of the line, I rattle off my order.

"Make it a large." I have a feeling it's going to be that kind of day.

The warm liquid instantly soothes the headache growing between my temples. As I turn to leave, I'm greeted with a gentle touch on my arm. I look up and nearly drop my cup.

"Todd."

"Alex."

It's my ex-fiancé, in the flesh, and he looks amazing. He's like a freaking clone of a younger Brad Pitt and the last year has apparently done him well. He's practically glowing with his sun-kissed skin, and the fancy black suit he's wearing does his athletic body justice.

"You've grown out your hair. You look beautiful."

Hearing him say that weakens my knees. I almost married this man, and you don't get to that point in your relationship without having deep feelings. If only he hadn't crushed me and ripped my heart in two. I was already broken before he left me, and when he abandoned me, that was the last straw. My view on life and myself took a dark turn after that.

His hazel-green eyes study my face, and I pull myself from my thoughts. I don't want him to know the effect he has on me. I only want him to see the confident, independent woman I've spent the last year becoming.

"It's good to see you too. You look great. Handsome as always."

"Thank you." A smile spreads his full lips. "How are you doing these days?"

What a question. I laugh to myself. No doubt he's wondering if I pulled myself together or if I'm still an emotional wreck. Truthfully, probably both.

"I'm doing good. I work for Kevlar and Kline as an operations specialist now." I glance at my wristwatch, fidgeting in my heels. I need to get going.

"Alex, that's great. They're one of my clients. Excellent business."

"Thank you. I'm sorry I can't stay and talk with you longer. I'm gonna be late if I don't leave now. It was great to see you."

As I turn away, Todd reaches for my arm. I don't shudder from his touch and that seems to please him. His perfectly straight teeth shine behind his charming smile.

"Maybe we could get together for a coffee or dinner?"

My stomach flutters. "Um, maybe."

"How about tonight?"

"I can't. I have a kickboxing lesson."

The statement surprises him. "Ok, how about tomorrow night? I can take you to that new Italian place that just opened up on Broad Street."

"I'll think about it."

He pulls a business card from his wallet. To be courteous, I take one out of my bag and we swap.

"It was really good to see you."

The sincerity in his voice pulls at my heartstrings. How can someone who devastated me emotionally still have such a strong effect on me?

I smile and bolt out of the coffee shop before I throw myself into his arms.

At my desk, I nibble on my pen and stare out the window as my mind takes a walk down memory lane. I thought Todd was the one. He was successful, charming, doted on me, and was incredible in bed, but after one torturous day, my life was ruined and all my dreams of a happily ever after came crashing down. Our love wasn't strong enough. It was all a lie. Love doesn't conquer all.

Glancing at my bag, I reach for the card inside. In embossed gold, his name shines across the front—*Attorney Todd Livingston*. It was his connections that set me up with a great attorney who kept my story out of the news and interview rooms. I was able to give witness testimony via written reports and never had to face the public with what had happened.

The day I found the letter Todd left me, I read it over and over for days. He had loved me but felt he had lost me.

He was right. He had.

I'm not the same woman he used to know. I was broken down to my core and had to rebuild Alexandria DeMarco. I had to discover who I was again with the demons I now carried.

My hand reaches for my phone and I dial.

"Hey, babe! What's up? You wanna do lunch today?" Jane's familiar and chipper voice instantly lightens my heavy mood.

"Yes, I do. Meet me at Zoey's Cafe in fifteen."

"What? He asked you to dinner?" Jane's long blond hair falls forward as she leans in for her drink.

"He did."

"What'd you say?"

"I said maybe. I was running late and didn't have time to talk."

"Do you want to go?"

"Kind of. Seeing him standing in front of me, it was as if time hadn't passed. Everything about him was familiar. His suit, his styled hair, the smell of his Armani cologne. If only my life hadn't been ruined, we'd be married by now."

"But he left you. Marriage means being there for one another, no matter what."

"He didn't leave much. I was broken and dead inside."

"Don't make excuses for him."

"I'm not. It's true. He was afraid I'd never come back from it."

"You just needed time and he wasn't willing to stand by your side and give it to you."

My phone vibrates on the table, but I ignore it as the waitress sets our food down.

"Enjoy ladies."

"Thank you."

Glancing at my phone, surprise sweeps over me. A notification displays a text from Todd. I swipe my finger across the screen and read it.

It was really good to see you. Is it terrible of me to say I miss you? I hope you'll say yes to dinner.

The expression on my face must be indicative of my shock.

"What is it?" Jane stares at me questioningly as she takes a bite of her chicken alfredo.

"Todd texted me. I can't even. Here," I pass my phone to her, "read it yourself."

"Are you kidding me right now?" Her eyes widen. "He misses you? Where was he for the last year?" Jane's face burns red. If Todd was here, he'd probably have a high heel in his ass by now. She hands the phone back.

"What are you gonna say? Don't you dare say you missed him too. If you're gonna go to dinner with him, I expect you to be aloof and make him work for every moment of your attention. I don't think you should even say yes."

My fork stabs around my plate aimlessly as my mind wanders.

"Part of me wants to go to dinner to show him how good I'm doing and to show him what he let go of."

"What about Carter?"

Guilt slams into my gut. Todd distracted me from any thoughts I might've had of Carter.

"We're just friends. There isn't much to say about him."

"Uh huh. And that's why you were kissing during the blindfolded coin search?"

"You saw that?"

"I may have snuck a peek to see what you were doing."

"Why didn't you say anything?"

"Why didn't you tell me you kissed?"

"It was the alcohol." My stomach churns. I don't believe my own lie. I wanted him to kiss me with or without the influence of alcohol.

"You're full of shit. I'm not blind, I saw the connection between you two. He stayed by your bedside all night. He cares about you."

I'm quickly losing my appetite. "It's too much too fast. I shouldn't have let him kiss me."

"What about the movie?"

"I agreed to go as friends."

"I think he's interested in more than that."

"I'm not sure I am."

"Because you're my best friend, and I love you, I'll be nice, but the mean girl in me wants to tell you that Todd is a dick and you should text back, *fuck off*, then go out to the movie with Carter and give into his kisses."

My lips part in amusement. "And what does the nice Jane think?"

"That you're gonna do whatever you want to, and I'm still gonna love you even if you do something stupid."

"I like the nice Jane better."

"Of course, you do."

CHAPTER EIGHT

—

ALEX

"You ready to kick ass today?"

I slip on my gloves and meet Carter on the mat. "I think so. My stomach is a little upset."

"Why?"

"I scarfed down something to eat before coming here. I was starving. I didn't eat much for lunch."

"We'll take it easy then. I don't want you getting sick."

Raising his mitts, he gives the instructions. I bury my gloves into the mitts, one after another. The day's events are on replay and my chaotic movements reflect it. Todd threw my mind into disorder, and now, Carter is in front of me, putting my body in a state of pandemonium.

"What are you thinking? You seem distracted."

"I ran into my ex today."

Carter's brows dip inward. "Where at?"

"The coffee shop near work."

"What'd he say to you?"

I stop punching and pull at my glove strap. Carter takes over and removes my glove.

"He said something that got to you, didn't he?"

I nod, embarrassed.

"You wanna talk about it?"

"No."

"You wanna kick the shit out of something until it doesn't bother you anymore?"

"Yes."

Carter motions toward the kickboxing bag. "Have at it."

I do as he's shown me before, starting low, then going high, then switching to the other side and doing the same. It's working. The frustration of Todd saying he misses me after all this time is wearing less on my emotions. Exhausted, I collapse to the floor and lay back, breathing heavy.

"I'm done. It's out."

Carter squats down next to me. "I think we should go see that movie tonight. You need a distraction."

I'm too tired to argue. "Only if you let me pick the movie."

"Deal."

The rest of our time is spent working on more core exercises. Carter definitely knows how to shape a body. Since coming to these classes, I feel stronger physically. Once finished, I put my gloves away and chug water. Sweat beads across my brow and trickles down my back. Carter hands me a towel.

"You did amazing today."

His praises always enchant me.

"You do a good job of motivating me."

Carter smiles, and I catch myself staring at his lips, remembering what it felt like to be kissed by him. Before my mind gets anymore muddled, I grab my bag and get ready to leave.

"You want me to pick you up or meet there?"

"Let's meet there."

Digging out my phone, we exchange numbers, then I search for movies at the local theater. I choose a comedy that starts at seven and he agrees.

"I'll see you there." I wave and head home to get ready.

When I pull up, Carter is already standing outside the theater waiting for me. He looks incredible in his jeans, boots, and button-up shirt with the sleeves rolled up. As I approach, his eyes light up.

"You look pretty as always."

"You look good too."

He puts his elbow out and I roll my eyes before giving in. Sliding my hand beneath his arm offers me that same warmth he always radiates and I fight the urge to tuck my whole body into his.

We approach the counter and provide our tickets. Carter pays for the snacks, we gather everything, and head into the theater. Picking a spot closer to the back, we settle in.

Carter flicks a piece of popcorn in the air and catches it in his mouth. I try to do the same, but it falls into my shirt and my cheeks get warm as I laugh and dig it out.

"That was fun to watch."

Tossing the kernel at him, he catches it, flicks it in the air and grabs it with his tongue as it comes back down.

"That was in my shirt."

Carter shrugs. "Maybe you should put more in there. I'll help you dig them out."

I shove his shoulder and he laughs. The previews start, drawing my attention to the screen. A sensation swims across my skin and I notice Carter staring at me.

"What?"

"Nothing," he says, "just looking at how beautiful you are." Sliding an arm around the back of my chair, he leans over and kisses my cheek.

"Smooth lines like that won't guarantee you a second date."

"So, this is a date?" he whispers in my ear.

My stupid mouth.

"A friend date, I mean."

"Call it whatever you want as long as I get to spend time with you."

Carter's eyes drop to my lips as I nibble the bottom one. I sense his desire to kiss me, and I quickly turn to the screen.

By the end of the movie, I'm laughing so hard, I'm crying. We glance at each other and our laughing settles. It's time to go and I don't think either one of us wants to.

"I'll walk you out." Carter takes my hand and we stay that way as we walk to my car. As we approach, I release his hand.

"I had a great time tonight. You were right. I needed the distraction."

"I'm glad you had fun. We'll have to do something else again soon, as friends."

Smiling, I reach for my keys. "Shoot, Carter, I dropped my keys in the theater."

"I'll help you look for them."

"No, really, it's fine. I know they're right where we were sitting. Have a good night. I'll see you on Saturday."

I jog off toward the theater. Once inside, I check the desk first. They don't have them. I enter the theater and start searching around the floor where we sat. My fingers find the key ring, and I lift them off the floor. Relieved, I return to the front desk and let them know I found them and head out of the theater, back to my car.

"Hey!" I turn to see a skinny, dark-haired guy ditch a cigarette and walk towards me. "Can I get a ride with ya? My friend left me behind."

Immediately, tension coils in my gut. "I'm sorry, I'm in a hurry. I'm meeting a friend."

"Come on. I don't live far. You really gonna leave me hanging?"

"You don't have a friend you can call?"

"My cell phone was in his car."

"You can use my phone if you need to."

Reaching for the phone in my purse, it slips from my hand as I'm shoved against the wall. Pain ripples up my back and into my head. I try to move, but he pins his weight against me.

"I'll take your phone and your wallet," he seethes.

With my head pounding, I hand over my phone without hesitation and slowly reach for my wallet. "Can I please take my ID out of it?"

Tilting his head, he grips my throat. "Maybe I wanna pay you a visit."

Vomit rises to my mouth and panic takes over my body. Tears pool in the corner of my eyes, and I whimper as fear seizes me. My trembling hand holds my wallet hostage. I don't want to give it to him. Dropping it back into my purse, I use my hand to shove at him instead. He slams me back against the wall and my head smacks the cement. My focus is obscured as disorienting pain throbs in my skull.

Reaching into my purse, he digs for my wallet. A figure move toward us, then a fist crosses my vision before the man's pressure on my body is released. My hand goes to my head and with my freedom comes clarity. I see Carter's fist slam into the guy's face, blood splattering from his nose onto the pavement. The guy isn't quick to give up. He fights back and lands a punch on the edge of Carter's jaw.

Without missing a beat, Carter grabs the guy, lowers him into a headlock and puts a knee to his face. Carter releases him, then swiftly turns his body, and dropkicks the guy. He collapses to the ground heaving.

Carter is at my side instantly, pulling me into his arms. Kissing my head, he runs his hand through my hair.

"I was waiting at your car for you. You were taking too long, so I came to check on you. Are you okay? How bad did he hurt you?"

I cry into his shoulder and he holds me close as he pulls out his phone and dials the police. Carter never leaves my side as the police officer asks questions and has us both fill out reports. The mugger is handcuffed and put into the back of a police car. Warrants for his arrest back up our statements. This wasn't his first assault and robbery. The officer releases us and Carter walks me to his car.

"I'm taking you home, I'm not leaving you." I nod as he opens the door and helps me in. When he gets in the driver side, he pulls me into his arms again. "I'm so sorry, Alex. I should've gone in with you."

"Don't even think that. You stopped him. That's all that matters."

Carter nods, his expression painful to see. He's consumed with concern for me.

"We'll get your car tomorrow."

Nerves rattled, I drop my keys at the door. Carter reaches down, picks them up, takes my hand in his and kisses it before he puts my key in the lock.

Walking in behind me, Carter closes the door. Setting my keys, phone, and purse on the entryway stand, I head right to the kitchen. Grabbing a shot glass out of the cabinet, I pop the top off a vodka bottle, pour it into the glass, and quickly swallow it down. Carter steps up behind me, takes the shot glass, pours more vodka into it, and drinks it.

"Another?"

I nod.

Pouring me another shot, I take it from his hand, gulping it down. His hands slide over mine then lifts them one at a time and kisses them.

"You should take a hot bath. I'll raid your movie collection I saw and pick one for us to watch."

His idea is perfect—something soothing, then something distracting.

"I like that idea."

Looking down at his hands, my eyes go wide. "Carter, your knuckles."

Moving his hand left and right, he stares at it as if he hadn't yet noticed it. Putting his hand under the sink faucet, he washes the blood off. The skin on his knuckles are cracked and fresh blood bleeds out.

"I have Band-Aids."

"It's fine," Carter says, grabbing a wad of paper towels, pressing them against his knuckles. "The bleeding will stop in a minute. Go enjoy that bath."

With his encouragement, I head to the bathroom and turn the faucet to hot. Stripping down to nothing, I slip a toe and foot in, then ease in the rest of me. Instantly, the warm water soothes the tension in my muscles while the liquor calms my mind.

After the bath, I throw my hair into a bun, and with fresh clothes, I join Carter in the living room. He's sprawled out on the couch, without his shirt, watching one of my movies. He sits up as I take the spot next to him.

"I'm sorry I took so long."

"As long as it made you feel better, I'm good."

"It did."

Carter reaches forward, takes me in his arms, and lays back on the couch. The sudden closeness tightens my muscles, but as soon as he pulls my hair tie loose and runs his fingers through my hair, my muscles give, and I relax against his chest. The movie plays in the background as I drift off to the soothing strokes of his hand.

The morning light shines through the window, warming my face. Lifting my head, I grimace at my stiff neck. Carter is sleeping peacefully with his arm still comfortingly around my back. Looking down at his tattoo, my curiosity gets the best of me, and I trace the outlines, mesmerized by the interlocking shapes.

Carter shifts and his eyes flutter open. Looking at me, he smiles, then raises his hand to my cheek and caresses it before leaning forward and kissing me. His kiss is warm and sensuous. Arousal swirls in my stomach, then travels south, between my legs. His erection presses into me, and I pull away as my nerves splinter.

"I'm sorry. I can't."

"Alex, wait." Carter adjusts himself before getting up from the couch. "I would never hurt you or push you faster than you want to go. Give me a chance. Give us a chance."

"I'm sorry, Carter, it's not you, it's me." Embarrassment prickles the back of my eyelids and tears take shape.

Turning toward the hall, I escape into my room. Tears trickle down my cheeks as I change into fresh clothes. Carter taps on my door, and I take a breath, wiping the tears from my eyes. Behind the door, his agonized expression nearly breaks me.

"I know what happened. I know why it's hard for you to let me in."

Shock slaps me in the face. "How?"

"I asked Kyle the night of the party."

"You have no idea what happened!" Fresh tears stream down my face. "No one knows what happened!" My head falls into my palms and my knees give out.

Catching me in his arms, he lifts me and carries me to my bed.

My broken words spew out. "Why did he tell you? He shouldn't have told you. It's not his past to tell."

"Alex," Bringing my attention to him, he wipes the tears from my face, "I don't know what you're feeling right now. Talk to me."

I look away from him. "I'm angry, shocked, embarrassed, humiliated."

Gently, he takes my hands in his. "Ssh, don't cry. It kills me to see you cry." He kisses my hands. "You can tell me anything. I want you to know you can trust me. I understand why you need to take things slow."

The pain, embarrassment, and humiliation swirl in my stomach like a whirlpool. I pull my hands from his.

"You should go."

"What? Why?"

"Please, just go."

Carter's expression morphs into confusion and frustration. "What about your car?"

"I'll have Jane take me."

"Alex."

"Please, Carter. I need to be alone."

I sit there numb as I listen to him gather his things then close the door behind him. As soon as he's gone, I fall into my comforter and sob.

Jane enters my apartment and stares at me, bewildered.

"It's ten a.m., and you're drinking?"

"He told him, Jane."

"Who told who, what?"

"Kyle told Carter what happened to me. Why I'm so fucked up."

Jane walks to my table and takes the wine glass from me. "You're not fucked up." Sitting across from me, she takes a swallow of my wine.

"When did Kyle tell him?" I can see the anger forming on her face.

"I don't know, but now he knows what that sick fuck did to me. Why I can't handle a relationship. Why I'm nuts. There's no point in giving it a shot. I'll freak out like I did before, and Carter will ditch me just like Todd did. No man wants a woman who's afraid to have sex. I'm hopeless. Meant to spend my life alone in misery." I pull the glass from her hand and chug the rest of it.

"You're not meant to live your life alone in misery. You need a good guy who is patient and understanding and I think that guy is Carter."

Raising my brows, I laugh. "Even good guys want sex."

Moving to the counter, I pour another glass, but Jane swipes the glass from my hand and dumps it in the sink. I grab the bottle and smirk before chugging it.

"You're not gonna do this to yourself."

"Do what to myself?"

"Backtrack, get depressed, close everyone off."

"What the fuck do you know? Your life is perfect, with your perfect house, and your perfect marriage."

Jane snatches the bottle from my hand and sets it top down in the sink. "No more alcohol! You've had enough!"

Traipsing to the living room, I fall onto the couch, and lay back, watching the back of my lids. "You should go."

"What about your car?"

I laugh at the irony of the repeat conversation.

"I'll figure it out later."

"I'm not leaving. You're drunk."

"So, what? It feels good to be drunk. It's better than crying, alone, in my bed."

"Get in the shower."

"No."

"Yes."

Jane pulls me off the couch and pushes me forward.

"I really don't like the mean Jane."

"Sometimes I have to be the mean Jane. That's what friends are for."

CHAPTER NINE

—

ALEX

Pulling out my debit card, I hand it to the receptionist at the massage parlor. I point to Jane. "I'm paying for hers and mine."

The sweet, round-faced receptionist politely nods and swipes my card.

"This is a good way to make up for being a jerk Sunday morning," Jane quips.

"It's the least I can do. I was a jerk. I hope you understand why I was so angry."

"Oh, I did, and Kyle got an ear full."

"I hope you weren't too hard on him."

"I was. He deserved it. He wants you to know he's really sorry and hopes you'll forgive him."

"Of course, I will, *eventually*."

Jane chuckles. "Kyle says you skipped kickboxing class this week."

I take my card back from the receptionist's outstretched hand. "How'd you know that?"

"Carter told Kyle. He came over to our house last night. They played Xbox and Carter asked me about you. He was worried and wanted to know how you're doing."

"You can tell him I'm fine."

"Why don't you tell him yourself?"

Tucking my card back in my wallet, I frown at Jane. "I'd rather not. Things were already getting complicated. I'll reimburse you for the classes or get another instructor."

The receptionist points to a door to the left. "You ladies can go back now."

I push the door open and a woman with blond, curly hair tied up in an up-do smiles at us. "I'm Connie. I'll take you ladies to your massage room."

As we enter, the scent of lavender and vanilla hits my nostrils, and I take a deep breath, letting it shed some of my tension.

"There are water bottles on the counter and a changing room to your left. I'll come back in a few moments with Lori and we'll begin your massages."

"Thank you."

Moving to the changing room, I hang my bag and strip down.

"You really gonna cancel the classes or get another instructor?"

"Yes. I told Carter from the beginning I didn't want things to get complicated and now they have. It's best I cut it off now."

Stepping out in the white robe provided, I hang the robe on the peg, then slide onto the bed. Jane comes out next and does the same.

"What about Todd? Did you text him back?"

"Nope. I never responded. My life is less complicated without men in it. I was doing fine before either of them started messing with my head."

The massage was just what I needed. Dabbing my hair dry, I step out of the shower. After a blow dry and fresh clothes, I go into the living room to relax and read a book. A knock at my door interrupts those plans.

Looking through the peephole, my stomach does a loop-the-loop. Opening the door, I stand between it and the outside.

"Todd, how did you find my house?"

In a gray tailored suit, he stands with a dozen red roses in hand and a smile that would charm the pants off any normal woman.

"Perks of being a lawyer. These are for you."

Taking the roses, I bring them to my nose and inhale their beautiful scent. My stomach flutters. The memory of how he used to do this when we were dating flashes through my mind.

"Why are you here?"

"I haven't been able to stop thinking of you since I saw you. I know I messed up. More than messed up. What happened between us wasn't your fault. It was mine. I couldn't handle what happened to the woman I loved."

"Coming to my house with roses and an apology doesn't fix the pain I went through."

Head lowered, he raises his eyes, searching mine, for any sign of empathy.

"I know it doesn't, but I'm hoping it can be a start to you someday forgiving me."

I glance at the roses, then his handsome face smeared with anguish. "It is a start."

Todd smiles and old feelings stir. "Have dinner with me tonight? I reserved a table at our favorite place."

My stomach grumbles. I'm starving and the food at Algino's is too tempting.

"I'll go, but it's not a date. You know how much I love their food. It's impossible to turn it down."

Todd's charming smile widens. "I'll wait while you get ready."

When I enter the living room, his eyes roam over my body then drop to my black heels. He always did have a thing for me in skimpy lingerie and tall heels.

"You look stunning."

His words affect me more than I want to admit. I ignore the sensation warming my body and go for my jacket. "Thank you."

Instantly, he's behind me, lifting the jacket over my shoulders, and brushing my hair out from under it. Goosebumps trickle over my shoulders and arms.

"You ready?"

"Yeah."

Holding the door open for me, I step out then lock it behind us. When we reach the car, he opens the passenger door for me and I catch his gaze follow the length of my legs. My cheeks grow warm from the desire I feel.

As we drive to Algino's his gaze catches my attention several times. His bottom lip slides between his teeth as he watches me.

"I meant what I said. I've missed you."

My reserve falters and the words spill out. "I've missed you too."

Todd places his hand on my knee and I try hard not to flinch. I don't want him to know physical contact from a man still startles me. I only want him to see my confidence. Holding my composure, I finally relax as his thumb caresses me.

When he smiles, it's obvious how happy he is I haven't jumped or brushed him away. He suffered through it so many times in the beginning.

We arrive at the restaurant and the valet opens my door. Todd joins me after his keys are handed over. We walk in together and are quickly seated.

"I'm guessing you're ordering your favorite?" Todd asks as the menus are handed to us.

"Of course, I am."

"Then I'm ordering your favorite dessert too."

Algino's is fine Italian and as much as I love the food I haven't walked into the restaurant since Todd left me. I take a moment to take it all in—the linen, fine china, the chandeliers, and marble floors. It's as exquisitely decorated as the food they prepare. Todd is attentively watching my movements and I take note of how much he's doting on me. It reminds me of what it was like before when we were together and happy.

"What are you getting?" I ask.

"You know I like to try new things."

Briefly, he glances over the menu then lowers it. He's made his decision. Always decisive and confident. Even if it's a façade, I want him to think I have that same confidence I once had.

"I'm getting the Pansotti Alla Genovese."

The waiter comes, and I order a glass of wine and Todd orders a Scotch and an appetizer for us.

With my nerves tense, I finish my glass of wine before the food arrives. I'm thankful when it does so I can fill my nearly empty stomach.

As we eat, Todd shares highlights of the last year and how his clientele has grown significantly. The news doesn't surprise me. He always was a shark when it came to getting what he wanted. The part that stings is when he tells me his younger sister is now married and they're expecting their first child. Elizabeth's now-husband had proposed around the same time Todd proposed to me. We could be in the same position expecting our first baby and it tears a hole right through me.

Todd must sense it and quickly changes the subject.

"What about you?"

Little does he know my life's been a rollercoaster of highs and lows and I'm thankful I still have my job. I was fired from my previous one, and the only new activities in my life are kickboxing classes and my friendship with Carter.

"I love my new job. I chose them for more than their excellent benefits. It gave me a chance to give back to the kind of officers who helped me that day."

Todd's expression darkens at the mention of my attack. He downs his Scotch and I can see I'm losing him as he drifts off in thought.

"But the newest activity I started is kickboxing lessons."

Todd's expression transitions and life comes back into his eyes.

"Oh yeah. How's that going?"

"It was going good, but I think I'm going to cancel the lessons."

"Why would you quit?"

His tone is disapproving. Todd doesn't understand quitting except for our relationship, but to him, it was probably more like a break while I got myself together.

I fiddle with my food. "Maybe I won't."

"You shouldn't. It's not good to quit. You should see it through. It'll be good for you."

I don't want him to think I'm unable to handle my commitments. It's something I know he sees as a weakness. "You're right. I won't quit."

Todd smiles. "How's dinner?"

"Just as delicious as I remember."

Todd reaches over the table and I see his hand is going to take mine. I steady myself in anticipation. Taking hold of my hand, he runs his thumb over it.

"I like this. Seeing you again. How about we have dinner again tomorrow?"

"I have kickboxing tomorrow."

"I'll come over after. What time should I be there?"

"Seven-thirty."

"Where are you taking your lessons at?"

I hesitate and Todd narrows his brows.

"Raise the Bar."

"I know that place. Kyle and I went there a few times."

My chest tightens wondering if he knows Carter.

"What's your instructor's name?"

I hesitate again and Todd frowns. He's far too observant of my body language.

"Carter."

Todd shrugs. "Don't know him."

I let out a breath of relief.

The waiter brings the highlight of my evening, the flaming custard. It's ignited and served to our table. Watching the flames jump wildly, I glance at Todd. I know what he's thinking. The last time we had dinner here, we had the same dessert that night. We couldn't even make it home. He pulled his Corvette over and I slid into his lap.

I'm aroused at the thought of it and how amazing it felt to have him inside me. The flames die down as the liquor is burned off and Todd hands me a spoon.

"Eat slowly. I want to watch you savor it."

Spooning a bite, I slowly lick it clean. His gaze is carnal as he watches me. His voice is low and sensual as he takes a spoon and slides it into the custard.

"Remember the night I licked the whipped cream off you?"

My nipples harden to peaks. "I do."

"Remember what we did after?"

His hand grazes mine as I dip the spoon. Taking hold of it, his thumb caresses across my hand. The memories of how he explored my body in new ways that night flash through my mind.

"I do."

"Would you let me do it again?"

Desire burns between my legs and I shift uncomfortably. I swallow the lump in my throat. *Don't let him know. Be brave.*

"Yes, but not tonight."

A grin splits his lips and he strokes my hand. "Of course, baby. I have to earn it."

Surprise sweeps over me at the sound of my old nickname. It feels good to hear him call me it, but I'm not sure I'm ready for it.

Todd releases my hand when the waiter brings the bill, then hands him his card.

When the waiter returns, Todd pulls out my chair and holds my jacket as I put it on. His lips touch just behind my ear, the exact spot he knows makes me weak in the knees. Pleasure spreads from head to toe.

"You ready to go?"

"Yes."

The familiar touch of his strong hand and the delicious scent of his Armani cologne has me angling my body toward his. He raises his arm and puts it around my waist. Leaning over, he kisses my temple.

"I miss this," he whispers.

So do I.

I lean my head against his shoulder as the valet brings his Corvette around. On the ride back to my apartment he places his hand on my knee and I'm proud of myself for how relaxed I am with it.

With his Corvette parked outside my apartment, he walks me to my door and we stop outside of it.

"I'm glad I get to see you tomorrow."

"I am too."

Todd steps closer and gently moves me into his arms. Hand grazing my hair, he holds my neck and brings me in for a kiss. The familiar strength of his desire overwhelms me. I'm moved against my door, and he presses into me, moaning into my mouth and roaming his hands over my back. His hand cups my ass and squeezes.

Putting my hand on his chest, I gently push him back as panic seizes me.

"Not so fast, stud." Thankfully my voice doesn't betray me.

Todd chuckles and places a lighter, gentler kiss on my lips before releasing me.

"I can't help it. You know what you do to me."

Staring back at his hungry hazel eyes, I do my best to hide my fear. "Tonight was wonderful. Thank you for dinner."

He takes hold of my hand, caressing it. "You sure you don't want me to come in?"

"You have to earn it, remember?"

Todd smirks. "Night, baby." He kisses my head and turns to leave.

Gathering my breath, I watch him walk back to his car. He enters it and waves. Digging my keys out, I push through the door, and lean my head against it for several minutes, calming my nerves. I'd spent so many nights wishing to have Todd back in my life, and now that he is, I'm terrified.

CHAPTER TEN

—

CARTER

Wiping my neck and chest with the towel, I greet Rachele at the counter. "Did my five o'clock, DeMarco cancel again?"

Rachele shakes her head. "No, she didn't cancel."

The tension in my chest lightens. I hoped she would come to her session. I owe her an apology for being an insensitive prick. I understood why she canceled the last two. I had no right to bring up what happened to her as a reason for not letting me in.

I head to the mats and prep, hopeful she shows. When I see her walk across the gym several minutes later my heart skips a beat. Seeing her reminds me of how much I've missed her.

Not a day didn't go by this week that I didn't think of her. If only I hadn't acted like a tool, she still might be speaking to me.

She approaches with that same shy smile and lust filled eyes she has every time she sees me and I can't help smiling.

"I'm glad you're here. I was afraid you weren't going to come back."

"I want to keep coming, but I need to make sure it's not gonna be complicated between us."

"Alex, I'm sorry for how I acted. I never should've said what I did. I acted like a douchebag, and I know it's not an excuse, but I had just woken up with you in my arms, and it felt incredible. I didn't mean to act like a tool."

Her face twists into an expression of anguish. "I can't give you anything more than friendship."

A brick hits my gut. "I understand. You want me to get you another instructor?"

She shakes her head, tears pooling at the corners of her eyes. "No. I want to continue to work with you. I'm comfortable with you."

Comfortable. I've landed in the damn friend zone.

"We better get to work then."

Starting her out on stretches, I discover I'm not completely in the friend zone. Her eyes watch me like a curious cat and glance away when she's realized she's stared too long. She's a little rusty from missing two sessions and I place my hands on her hips to adjust her stance. She doesn't flinch at the contact and I'm surprised. She's gotten used to me touching her and that brings me a hell of a lot of satisfaction. Maybe being the friend she needs is the best way to go about this.

"How was your week? Anything new?"

It's clear that question hit a button. Her body language changes. She's obviously uncomfortable.

"It's been a busy week. I did go to the massage therapist you recommended, and you were right, she's ah-mazing. We picked up a new account at work and..." she pauses and throws a couple punches in silence. "My ex took me out to dinner."

Hearing that affects me more than I want to show. "So, he's back, huh?"

"We were engaged. That's not something you let go of easily."

As the tension builds in my chest, I now understand why I've been friend zoned. The bastard who left her when she was at her worst wants her back at her best. *Asshole*.

"Just be careful. Guys are supposed to be there for the women they love, not run out on them when it gets hard."

Her punches increase in speed and she continues in silence. I can see I've hit a nerve.

"Let's move onto a core circuit."

Pushing her body to the limit, I make up for her missed sessions and I'm proud when she doesn't whine or give up. She wipes the sweat from her brow and makes sure to regulate her breathing.

"Did you play any sports in high school or college?"

"I ran track and did pole vault. Played soccer too."

It's no wonder athletics come easily to her.

"Have you been running to loosen the lactic acid build up?"

"I have."

"Good. I want you to start adding protein shakes after your workouts even on rest days. It'll optimize muscle repair and growth."

"Got it, Boss."

"You're gonna need it. Your workouts are going to get more intense, and soon, I'll add self-defense lessons."

Her expression morphs, I can see her getting lost in her own thoughts. The last thing I want is for her to go back to those memories.

"Time."

She drops the ropes and steps off the balance ball. The darkness I saw overcast her eyes a moment ago is gone.

"Get some water, then we'll stretch." Grabbing a towel for her, I meet her at the bench. She takes the towel and guzzles her water.

"You did damn good today."

"Thanks, Coach."

I lean in and nudge her shoulder. She smiles, her gaze lingering over me.

"You sure about this guy?"

Her smile flips to a frown. "Are you mad at me?"

"No, I'm jealous." Her eyes light up, clearly surprised by my honesty. "Part of me hopes the asshole fucks up because we never got a chance to explore what's between us. But the other part of me wants to see you happy."

"You make it difficult."

"I make what difficult?"

"Just being friends."

I brush a stray hair from her face, and her eyes soften, staring at me affectionately. "I'd suggest dating us both, but I couldn't share you. I prefer to have you all to myself."

Nudging my shoulder, she nibbles on her bottom lip. "I gotta go."

"Will you be here for your next session?"

"I will."

Watching her head to the front door, my chest constricts when I see a pretty boy in a suit approach her and kiss her cheek. I squash the urge to drop kick the fucker and get back to gathering my shit.

In my periphery, I see the guy walking toward me. When I look up, I get a better look at him. Damn, he looks familiar.

"Hey man, it's been a while."

Shit. Her ex is Kyle's friend, Todd.

"Yeah, it has."

"So you're Alex's instructor?"

"I am. You got a problem with that?"

"I don't give a fuck you're her instructor. What I got a problem with is you touching my girl. I suggest you keep your hands to yourself or I'll have your ass fired."

Is this asshole for real?

"I don't think so, bud. Do that, and I'll tell Alex about the time I saw you walk out of here with the blonde. Pretty sure you and Alex were together then, am I right?"

"Go ahead. She won't believe you. She'll think you're selfishly trying to sabotage what we have. And by the looks of it, you wouldn't want her to think that, would you?"

"Get the fuck out of my gym."

"Glad to see you understand me."

The asshole walks off and I see Alex looking back at me as he nearly drags her out of the gym. Her expression tells me she's worried about our conversation. She should be. Her ex is a cheating prick.

CHAPTER ELEVEN

—

ALEX

"Todd's going to be here any minute."

Jane sways her foot as it dangles over her other leg. "I know. That's why I'm lingering. I don't like that you've let him back in your life or that you're going out of town with him."

"It's his sister and brother-in-law's baby shower. It's one night and we're staying at their house. Todd said I could have my own room."

"Uh huh. I still don't like it."

Todd knocks on the door and I nervously let him in. He glances at Jane sitting at my table. She forces a grimace into a smile.

"Jane." He nods.

"Todd. How are you these days?"

"Can't complain."

The awkward tension can be cut with a knife.

Rubbing Todd's arm, I get his attention. "You mind taking my bag out to the car?"

He looks at my bag next to me. Moving closer, he kisses me on the cheek and grabs it. "Yeah, baby. I'll be outside waiting for you."

The moment the door closes behind him, Jane jumps out of the chair. "Did he just call you baby?"

"Yes."

"Alex!"

"Jane!" I mock, as the fumes escape her head.

"I don't trust him."

"Stop worrying. Taking this trip is important to me."

"I want you to be careful, and if you need me, *for anything*, I don't care if it's in the middle of the night. I will drive to where you're at and bring you home."

Approaching her, I wrap my arms around shoulders. "I love you."

"I love you too. Be careful, okay?"

"I will. I'm excited about the getaway. It should be a fun weekend. Oh my gosh, I almost forgot."

Running back to my room, I gather his sister's gift. I spent almost my whole day off shopping for it and would've felt terrible if I forgot it.

"Okay, I'm good. Let's go."

Walking outside, Jane gives Todd the evil eye as she saunters past him to her car.

When he sees my gift bag, Todd gets out and smiles. "You're always so thoughtful. It's one of the things I love about you."

His words send butterflies flapping through my belly. My smile widens when he comes to my side and kisses me.

Taking the bag, he puts it in the trunk before opening the passenger door for me.

"It's going to be a fun weekend. I'm glad you decided to come."

Pulling up to the colonial home, my nerves bunch. I haven't seen Elizabeth or James since before that night. She tried to reach out to me, but I couldn't face her. I'd closed off everyone. How I treated her brother makes me feel ashamed. *Will she blame me for the breakup? How does she feel about me after all this time?*

The touch of Todd's hand on my leg turns my attention to him. "Baby, you okay?"

"Yeah, I'm nervous about seeing your sister and what she thinks of me."

Placing his fingers under my chin, he lifts it so I meet his gaze. "You have nothing to worry about. No one would dare disrespect you knowing how I feel about you."

Warm lips pull my lust to the surface. My breath gets heavy as Todd caresses my inner thigh.

"Have I told you how good you look?" His hazel-green eyes are filled with desire.

"No, you haven't."

"I'm slipping then, 'cause baby, you look good enough to eat." Tongue sliding between my lips, he moves with erotic efficiency. His caresses continue up my thigh and I struggle with a mix of arousal and uneasiness.

"Todd."

"Yes?"

"We need to go in before someone sees us."

A heavy sigh expands his chest. "You're right." Taking my hand, he rubs my palm with his thumb before bringing it to his side of the car and laying it over his erection. "It's hard to stop when you do this to me." Having my hand guided in rhythmic strokes, my body goes into a neurotic frenzy between heightened arousal and jumpy nerves.

"Come here."

Pulling me close, he covers my mouth with a heated, needy kiss as he shifts my hand into his jeans. My mind goes blank as his kiss warms my body and the sounds of his moans give me as much pleasure as they do him.

"Baby, you make me hard as a steel pipe."

Unbuttoning his jeans, he gives me better access. "Harder, baby."

The words fill my mouth as his grip tightens on my hair and his kiss turns rough.

"Put your mouth on it. I'm gonna cum."

My body tenses.

"Fucking now! I'm gonna cum."

Forcing my head down onto him, he fills my mouth until he hits the back of my throat. Tears pool at the corner of my eyes as I control my trembling emotions. Hot cum shoots down the back of my mouth and into my throat.

"That's it, baby." Letting out a moan of pleasure, he eases his grip. I must look like I'm in shock. His expression twists and he seems angry. "What's wrong?"

I'm stunned into silence.

Letting out an annoyed breath, his brows furrow. "I don't know what your problem is. You used to gobble my dick like it was a gourmet dessert."

Zipping his jeans, he gets out of the car. I sit there, holding back tears, trying to find composure before entering Elizabeth and James' home. Todd opens my door and puts out his hand for me to take it. Stepping out, he pulls me into his arms and caresses my cheek.

"I'm sorry for snapping at you. I thought you wanted it as much as I did."

"I did. I'm sorry. That was the first time since—"

"It's okay. That probably wasn't the best time to do that, it's just, I've wanted you to touch me like that for the last few weeks. I shouldn't have rushed you." With tenderness, he kisses my lips, nose, then forehead. "You okay? Ready to go inside or do you need more time?"

I shake my head. "I'm ready."

"If it's any consolation, you're just as good as I remember." Smiling, he lifts my chin for another kiss.

As soon as we enter, Elizabeth squeals then runs to her brother. Being his twin, she's just as gorgeous as he is but a female version. She outstretches her arms as far as she can to make room for her round belly. Todd's smile goes ear to ear.

"Okay, okay. Enough of that."

She tilts her head and frowns.

"Elizabeth, you remember Alexandria?"

"I do. It's so good to see you again. I'm so glad you came."

To my surprise, she leans forward and pokes me with her big belly as she hugs me. Raising the gift bag, I ease out of her embrace.

"I brought you something."

"That's so sweet. Bring it out back. That's where everyone is hanging out." She motions for me to follow. I glance at Todd and he bobs his head.

"I'll be there in a minute. Elizabeth will take care of you."

Taking off into the kitchen, I hear several male voices greet him.

"How are you?" she asks, guiding me through their massive house. Sadly, my apartment could easily fit inside their family room.

"I'm good." My voice betrays how nervous I am.

"You look incredible. I love the long hair and you look really fit."

"I've been taking kickboxing classes twice a week."

"It shows. I miss my toned belly. As soon as this baby is out, it's gonna be back to the gym."

"I'm sure it won't take long. I remember you were always super fit before."

She opens the sliding door onto a patio and my nerves bunch at the number of people spread throughout the three-story deck with a bar, catered buffet, cake table, seating areas and a giant swimming pool. I feel more out-of-place than a freshwater fish in the ocean. Anxiety creeps along my neck, and I wish Todd would've stayed by my side, at least until I was introduced to a few people.

Elizabeth guides me to the gift table and I set the present down next to at least fifty others. Taking my hand, she pulls me along and introduces me to several of her friends, then leads me again to a couple who look like older copies of Elizabeth and Todd, their parents. It's too late to flee as Mrs. Livingston's eyes are already locked on me.

"Alexandria." Her expression is indiscernible, and I can't tell how she feels about seeing me. "You look well."

Really? I suppose the last time she knew, I wasn't well, so seeing me now must be a huge surprise for her.

"Thank you. It's nice to see you both again."

Mr. Livingston, having always been the nicer of the two, takes my hand and places his palm over the top of it. "You look lovely dear. It's a pleasure to see you here. Where is my son?" He glances behind me, and as if by cue, Todd steps up behind me and places his arm around my waist. Everyone watches me, no doubt expecting me to freak out, but instead, I lean further into Todd's embrace.

Mr. Livingston and Elizabeth smile with approval and what seems like genuine delight, but Mrs. Livingston's mouth contorts before she looks at her son.

"How's work, darling?"

"Good as usual. After the weekend I have a client I need to meet with, but if he follows my instructions, his zoning compliance should come through fine."

Todd's father smiles proudly. He always did love that his son had become a lawyer like him, keeping the trade in the family. As they talk business law, my mind drifts off.

I've always found these conversations boring. Mrs. Livingston seems to notice and strikes while she has her opportunity.

"Alexandria, why don't you come with me." Taking my hand with an uncomfortably tight grip, she guides me to the bar. "You look like you could use a drink to loosen up. I'm sure Todd would like it if you brought him one too."

I can't argue with that logic, even if it did sound condescending.

"What do you do these days?" Without having to say anything, she raises her hand and the bartender starts making her a drink. Damn, she's got him trained already.

"I'm an operations specialist for Kevlar and Kline."

"That's a man's field. What on earth are you working there for?" She takes her drink and sips from her pretty pink straw.

The bartender looks to me. "I'll take a Scotch and a glass of Moscato." My attention returns to her look of disapproval. "They have great benefits and I feel like I'm giving back to those that helped me."

As she leans in closer, her expression twists into one of discontentment. "While you're here, try not to mention anything about that incident. I want my daughter's baby shower to be pleasant and joyful."

She might as well have punched me in the gut. It would've been less painful. "My *incident* isn't something I discuss with anyone. Don't worry. I won't ruin your daughter's baby shower."

She's more vile than I remember. Taking my glass of wine and Todd's Scotch, I leave immediately. I have no interest in having another conversation with her anytime soon.

Todd notices my change in mood instantly. He takes his Scotch and kisses me, then leans into my ear. "Baby, what's wrong?"

"I'm pretty sure your mother thinks I'm a freak."

"What'd she say?"

"She wanted to make sure I didn't talk to anyone about my *incident*, so I didn't bring down the mood of your sister's baby shower."

Todd rolls his eyes. "For fuck's sake. Go find us a place to sit and eat. I'll join you in a moment."

I watch as Todd pulls his mother and father aside. I feel like garbage for already starting family drama. Mrs. Livingston glances my direction and scowls. It's clear she's not happy about whatever Todd said. All three of them come to my table, and I sit upright, nervous and unsure of what to expect. Todd sits next to me, then his parents take the seats on the other side of me, with his mother taking the seat directly next to me.

She forces a smile my direction. "I apologize, Alexandria. My comment to you was inconsiderate. I may have had a few too many margaritas."

Blame it on the alcohol. Nice game plan.

"I appreciate the apology. I'll forget you mentioned it."

"Thank you, dear."

With his arm around the back of my chair, Todd slides me closer. He kisses my temple. "Feel better?"

Not at all.

"I'm sorry if I caused any problems."

"Never, baby. You ready to eat?"

Any appetite I might've had left me, but I don't want to drink on an empty stomach, so I nod and follow him to the buffet. Placing a few items on my plate, I return to my seat.

In an attempt to rid my anxiety, I quickly nibble on my food and drink more wine. The music quiets down for an announcement. After everyone is done eating, James and Elizabeth are going to cut the cake and reveal the baby's sex. My stomach knots. The invitation had been in blue and I assumed that was on purpose. My gift was intended for a boy. I now have a fifty-fifty chance that my gift will be a disaster.

Raising the wine glass to my lips, I finish it off, feeling miserable and alone even though Todd is sitting next to me caressing my leg. Thankfully, he's busy chatting with extended family and unaware of how terrible of a time I'm having.

Plates are taken away before the cake is rolled out to the center. Elizabeth and James look ecstatic as they hold the knife together. I'm envious of their bliss. The knife slices through, then squeals of joy erupt before the cake slice is raised revealing; *pink*.

Tears prickle the back of my eyelids. This trip couldn't be going any worse.

The party dies down, and as expected, a cleaning crew comes in and returns the deck to its former glory. Presents are carried into the home and taken to the nursery. Evening has turned to night and Elizabeth slinks upstairs to sleep. Following her to the room I'll be staying in, she hugs me goodnight and thanks me again for my present even though I know the basket I made with all boys clothes, hats, booties, mittens, and toys won't be used. Well, maybe the toys will be.

Setting my luggage bag on the bed, I dig through it for PJ's. Todd enters the room with his bag over his shoulder.

"I'm sorry, baby. We're sharing a room. My cousin Dallas is too drunk to make it home. I gave him my room to sleep in. I hope you don't mind if I bunk with you." His smile couldn't get any wider and I'm too exhausted and tipsy to argue.

"That's fine." Entering the bathroom, I get cleaned up, then change into my silky shorts and tank top.

When I walk out, Todd is already laying under the comforter. Lifting it, I slide under and see he's stripped down to his boxers. He outstretches his arm for me to lay against him. Wrapping his arm around me, he holds me close, and I lay there, breathing in his scent. Beneath my hand, his chest is muscular and smooth, but the image of Carter's tatted chest is what slips into my mind. My cheeks flush, but I have no time to think on it. Todd raises my chin and kisses me.

Sliding his hand down my stomach, he lifts the top of my shorts and continues further down. My body heats up as he caresses me, numbing my mind with his kiss. Heat and need burn between my legs. Soaking wet and breathing heavy, I moan into his mouth, igniting his own need. He slides a finger in and strokes as his palm presses against my clit.

"You feel incredible, baby."

With his arm holding me against him, he turns us, putting me on my back. Sliding in and out against my wet folds, he moves faster, thrusting deep. "Will you come for me? I want you to come for me."

Tension builds in my abdomen, but it's just out of reach. Todd strokes harder and faster. When I don't reach my orgasm, his strokes ease and he withdraws from me. Tears sting my eyes as I hold them back.

"What's wrong?"

"I just, it's been an overwhelming day, and it's been a long time since I've…and we're at your sister's house. I'd feel better if we were at my house or yours."

"It's okay. As soon as we're back home, we'll pick up where we left off."

Lying on his back, he pulls me into his arms. "Get some sleep."

Tucking myself into the nook of his arm, he kisses my hair. I lie there, my mind and emotions in a whirlwind. I can't understand how even when I'm with him, I still feel so alone.

CHAPTER TWELVE

—

CARTER

Jane walks out the sliding door with two fresh beers for Kyle and me, sets them on the table, then takes a seat for herself.

"So, how's Alex's weekend getaway going?" I press.

"Awful. She texted me and said everything that could go wrong did."

Part of me is relieved to hear she didn't have a wonderful time with her ex, but the other part feels bad that she's miserable.

"Does that mean they're done?" I ask, hopeful.

Jane frowns. "No. They're still seeing each other. I don't understand why. He broke off their engagement and left her. I don't know how she's able to forgive him."

"Because he's a manipulative son-of-a-bitch."

Jane's brows pinch inward. "What do you mean?"

I tug on my beer. "Nothing."

Jane leans forward over the table. Her expression heated. "If you know something, you better tell me, right now!"

"I have no proof of anything, only what I saw."

"Start talking."

I point my beer towards Kyle at the grill. "Kyle and Todd used to come to the gym together. There was a chick that had been coming too. I thought she was cute. Thought about asking her out. Well, one day I see Todd flirting with her, then the next day he comes to the gym alone, without Kyle, and an hour later he's walking out with his arm around her. That was over a year ago, so I assume he was still with Alex. And I have no proof that anything happened between them."

Kyle glances at Jane who's fuming at this point. He looks uncomfortable with what he's about to say. "Her name was Lana."

Jane's eyes bulge and she glares at Kyle. "You *knew* about her?"

"Todd started seeing her right after he and Alex broke up. I didn't tell you because I didn't want you to tell Alex. She was going through enough already."

"I'm calling her, right now!"

Kyle steps forward and takes her phone. "No, you're not."

"Kyle's right," I tell her. "I already told Alex I hope Todd fucks up. He was right when he said she wouldn't believe me. She'll think I'm trying to sabotage their relationship for selfish reasons."

"She's my *best* friend! She deserves to know what a dick Todd is."

Jane snatches her phone back from Kyle and he wrestles it from her and shoves it in his pocket. "Calm down. I don't know if he cheated on Alex. All I know is he started dating the chick right after they broke up."

"How in the hell could he be over Alex that quickly? They were engaged!"

"She was a rebound, Jane. Someone to get his kicks with."

"Because Alex wouldn't give him any, he found it somewhere else?"

"I'm not defending him."

"Sounds like you are!"

"Calm your ass down. I'm not the problem here."

Jane sits back in her chair and huffs, then snatches the beer from Kyle's hand and chugs. "She deserves to know what he did."

"You need to stay out of it is what you need to do. Let Alex decide what's best for her."

"What do you think?" Jane's gaze cuts directly to me.

Sitting back in silence, I chug my beer, not wanting to antagonize the dragon waiting to spit fire at me if I speak.

"So, you agree, I should tell her?"

Isn't she clever?

"Of course, I want you to tell her. I hate seeing her with him, but I want Alex to be happy. What happened between them is in the past. Maybe he really wants their relationship to work and who am I to ruin that?"

Jane's foot swings over her other leg anxiously. "He's a dick," she mumbles, before chugging more of Kyle's beer.

CHAPTER THIRTEEN

—

ALEX

As I enter my office, I see my assistant, Melanie, leaning over and smelling a vase full of red roses sitting on my desk, next to a white box wrapped in a gold bow.

"A delivery guy dropped these off for you this morning," she explains in her sweet, sing-song voice.

Pulling the little card from its clear holder, I read it.

Thinking of you. Hope you'll wear this for me tonight. Todd.

"Who's it from?" she asks enthusiastically.

With rosy cheeks, I grin. "My boyfriend, Todd."

"Are you gonna open it?"

With a mixture of curiosity and apprehension, I pull the bow and unravel the box. I tip it open privately, unsure of how risqué the contents may be. Seeing something black, I slowly open the top. Moving the tissue paper to the side, I lift the black dress out of the box.

"Oh my gosh! It's stunning!" Melanie raves.

My cheeks swell as I admire the soft, fine fabric of the strapless, knee-length dress.

"It is. He must be taking me somewhere tonight."

Melanie stares at the dress mesmerized. "I'm envious."

A knock on my office door turns our attention to the entrance. A young man walks in with a smaller box similar to the one I just opened.

"Miss. DeMarco?"

"Yes?"

"Delivery for you. Please sign."

I scribble my signature on his clipboard, and he hands me the small box. I glance at Melanie and grin as my anticipation builds.

"Hurry! Open it," she beams.

Tugging at the bow, I open the box. Inside is two tickets to a play at the theater.

Melanie peeks into the box. "Oh, my gosh, Alex! This is so romantic!"

Our weekend trip wasn't as good as we both hoped, but Todd is obviously trying to make up for it. Butterflies flap in my belly as I giggle with excitement.

My office phone rings and I wave at Melanie. It's time to get to work. I answer, and Todd's voice carries through the phone, tickling my skin across my neck and shoulders.

"Hey, baby. Did you get my gifts?"

"I did. Thank you."

"I'll see you tonight, then?"

"Yes, you will."

"Good. Can't wait to see you."

He hangs up, and I spend the rest of my day trying hard to focus on my work, but it's useless. Todd has me so distracted I'm getting nothing accomplished. When lunchtime arrives, Melanie calls my desk.

"Hey Mel, what is it?"

She giggles into the phone. "There's a really hot guy here to see you."

My stomach flutters. "That's probably Todd."

"Uh, nope. His name is Carter."

The fluttering in my stomach halts, then repeats their circular spin. "Oh, okay. Send him in."

I feel foolish. I can't focus on anything while waiting for Carter to walk in. When he does, he instantly brings a smile to my lips.

"Hey, beautiful."

Crossing his arms, he leans against the door frame and surveys my office with those captivating eyes of his. "Nicely decorated and that view is fantastic."

I smile appreciatively. "What are you doing here?"

"Jane said you had a rough weekend. I thought I'd stop by and coax you out to lunch, as friends of course."

Irritation tickles my neck. *Apparently, no one can keep my secrets from Carter.*

"What did you have in mind?"

"I was thinking the Greek restaurant on Whiskey River Street. It's not too far from here."

"Okay, I'm game."

"Great."

Gathering my purse, I lock my office behind us. "Melanie, I'll be back in a while. Want me to bring you anything?"

"I'm good, thanks for asking."

We step outside my office building and Carter strolls over to a green Kawasaki street bike. He picks his helmet off the seat and outstretches his hand for me to take it. A thrilling sensation swims through me. I'm jazzed at the idea of getting to ride the bike. My grin spreads ear to ear. Carter looks at me and smiles.

"Now that's the smile I like to see. You gettin' on?"

I nod, taking the helmet. I'm sure I look ridiculous in my blouse and dress pants, but I don't care. Bikes have always fascinated me—the speed, freedom, riding the edge of danger. I slide on and wrap my arms around him. His abs are rock hard, and the warmth of his back presses into me, relaxing my own body all the while my emotions are abuzz.

We weave through traffic and I watch in amazement as everything whizzes past us. Carter controls the bike like it's an extended limb. He owns the road and my attention. The thrill of the ride has my energy high. My body's numb of anxiety, too exhilarated to feel anything otherwise.

We arrive at Little Greek and he parks the bike. Climbing off, I remove the helmet, practically bouncing on my heels. Carter takes the helmet and sets it on his bike.

"Did you enjoy that?" he asks, a smirk curling the corner of his mouth.

"Uh, yeah. That was awesome."

"I'll have to take you on a longer ride sometime."

My exhilaration is butchered as I think of Todd. "We probably shouldn't."

Carter frowns. "I forgot about him."

For a few moments, I did too. Guilt gnaws at my insides as I follow Carter into the restaurant. He pulls out my high-top chair and I take a seat.

"What are you gonna get?" I ask him as we look over the menus.

"I have a bad habit of always getting the same thing everywhere I go, and it usually is something that has chicken or steak in it."

I laugh. "Me too. I'm terrible at trying new foods. When I know something is good, I want to keep getting it."

"Should we try something new today?" he asks. We both look at each other before he makes a face and I shake my head. "Nah."

The waitress comes. We both order the same thing—chicken gyros and Sprites.

"Do you like to cook?" he asks.

"I do, actually. My grandmother was Italian, and she made amazing dishes. I picked up some of her skills. Do you?"

"I can cook a few basic things to get by. I do love Italian," he winks.

"Maybe I'll have you, Jane, and Kyle over one night for some authentic Italian food."

"I'd love it."

Carter's beautiful blues lock on me and study me. My body warms from the lustful look in his eyes. Pulling my gaze away from his, my cheeks flush.

"Alex."

I look back at him, nervous. "Yeah?"

"I have my first MMA fight coming up. I've been training for it for a while now. I'd like it if you came. I could use your support."

My stomach tightens. "An MMA fight?"

He nods.

The thought of him getting hurt causes my stomach to coil. "I'll come, but I don't know if I can watch it. I can't stand the thought of you getting banged up and bleeding."

"The goal is to be the least banged up and bleeding."

I frown. "Carter."

"Will you come? It would mean a lot to me."

The way his gaze meets mine, begging me with those soft blue eyes, melts my reserve. "Yes, I'll come."

"Thank you. It'll help to have you there."

"Why is that?"

"No doubt I'll feel awful by the end of the fight. Seeing you will be my consolation."

A peculiar sensation runs through me. I know his comment shouldn't be making me feel as good as it does and that leaves me with lingering guilt.

"I'll be there with aspirin and a bottle of whiskey in hand."

"Good. I'll probably need both."

Our food arrives, and we settle into eating and talk about some of the upcoming training he'll be doing with me. After we're finished, he tries to pay, and I ask the waitress to split the bill. Carter frowns at me. "Now I owe you something for that."

"No, you don't. You brought me out to lunch to make me feel better. That was enough."

We get our bills and head back out to his bike. That same exhilarating feeling rushes through me.

"If I'd known you would react like this, I would've taken you out on it sooner."

He hands me his helmet and I slide on behind him. The breeze cools the heat warming my body as I lean against him. Something about him has always felt comforting to me. Knowing he'll be leaving as soon as we get back fills me with overwhelming disappointment.

When we arrive back, he helps me off the bike and out of his helmet. His gaze lingers over me and I feel hypnotized as he studies me.

"It was good to see you today. Maybe I'll pop in for lunch again sometime."

"I'd like that."

"I'll see you tomorrow, beautiful."

Turning away, he puts on his helmet as he climbs onto his bike. I watch, mesmerized by how attractive he looks atop his motorcycle. I head back to my office in a daze.

Melanie grins at me as I return. "How was lunch?"

"I got to ride a motorcycle to lunch. Best. Lunch. Ever."

She laughs and hands me my missed messages.

"Um, Todd called a couple times. I think he wanted to see you for lunch. I told him you were with a client."

"Thank you." Rubbing my hand across my temple, I attempt to ease the headache forming.

Back in my office, I fiddle with my phone before finally dialing Todd back.

"Baby, where were you?"

"Melanie told you I was with a client, right?"

He sighs. "I wanted to give you your last present during lunch, but it's fine, I'll bring it with me tonight."

"Another present?"

I can hear him smile into the phone. "It completes the outfit."

As soon as he says that, I know—he bought me high heels.

"I look forward to seeing them."

Todd chuckles. "See you tonight."

CHAPTER FOURTEEN

—

ALEX

The dress Todd got me is skintight and reveals my cleavage. It's like he bought the dress one size too small on purpose. My hair is curled and partially pulled back, makeup done, and I'm sipping wine to shed my edginess. Todd knocks on the door and I walk to it barefoot.

Standing on the other side in a black tux is Todd, looking incredible, and in his right hand, he has a pair of black stilettos dangling from their tiny straps.

The shoes are sleek, sexy and suicide on spikes. His gaze rolls over my body and his eyes glimmer with desire.

"It's a good thing I already bought the tickets, or we wouldn't make it there at all. You look hot as hell, baby." He steps into my apartment and holds out the heels. "Let me see it all together."

Taking the heels, I smirk at him. He leans against the door and watches my ass as I walk to my sofa.

I sit and slide the heels on and buckle them tight. Slowly, I stand and make sure I'm balanced before walking toward him. He runs his tongue across his bottom lip then releases it between his teeth. "Come here."

Meeting me in the middle, he pulls me to him. The length of him grows hard and goosebumps form across my skin. Placing his hand in my hair, and the other around my waist, he holds me steady as he kisses me, his tongue venturing in and out with raw intensity. Hand lowering down my back, he squeezes my ass. Pressing his erection against me, he moans into my mouth.

"We need to go now, or I'll say fuck it and throw you over this couch."

My hand goes to his chest, stopping him as that thought causes panic to set in.

"We should get going. I don't want to miss the play."

Taking my hand in his, he moves it over his erection as his kisses travel along my cheek, neck, and ear. I let out a breath as arousal warms my core.

"Are you sure?"

My ass hits the couch and his hand slowly slides up my inner thigh. Wet kisses and his warm breath mingle against my ear as his hand pushes past my underwear.

"'Cause baby, your body is telling me otherwise."

His finger slides into my wet folds and I tilt my head back as pleasure rushes through me. Todd nibbles at my neck and works in swirls against my clit. Continued kisses cover my moans as my body trembles and my orgasm builds.

"That's it, baby. Come for me."

Raising my knees to his waist, I give him better access. Arm rested on my back, he holds me on the edge of my couch.

"Fuck, baby. You feel so good."

Whimpering, I push my hips against the stroke of his hand.

"Yes. That's it."

With his other hand in my hair, he tilts my head back and kisses me rough and passionately. Releasing my hair, he uses both hands to secure my legs around him before lifting me off the couch. He presses me into his erection, and I try to jerk back, but his lips cover my mouth and my body relaxes into his kiss.

He carries me to my room, covering me with kisses and nibbling my neck. My breath is heavy, and my desire is pulsing between my legs. Todd lets my legs down by the bed and pulls my dress up and off. He glances down at my black, strapless bra and lace underwear. A grumble escapes his chest.

"I've waited so long to have you."

Before I can say anything, his lips lock on mine as he sheds his jacket and unbuttons and removes his shirt.

"Climb on the bed for me."

Taking his lead, I ease onto my comforter, my stomach tight with anticipation and unease. He kicks off his shoes, unzips his pants and folds them down, exposing his boxer briefs. With one hand he pulls his erection out and strokes it.

"Take your bra off slowly, then the sexy lace underwear."

Nervously, I follow his instructions. His strokes quicken as he watches me. I'm now lying on my back in full view for him with nothing but the heels. Moving forward, he touches me, rubbing my clit, making me wet with desire.

"Have you had anyone, but me?"

Shaking my head, I let out a pleasured breath.

His hand grips my thigh. "You're so perfect, baby. Just for me."

The tip of his erection presses into me and my body instinctively jerks back. His grip on my thigh tightens. "It's gonna hurt a little at first. Relax."

He pushes forward again, and my body locks up. "Todd stop, I'm not ready."

"Yes, you are. Relax."

He pushes into me and I try to pull back from him. With his grip tight, he holds me steady. "Damn it, Alex. I'm not going to hurt you!"

Tears pool in my eyes. I want him to stop, yet I'm ashamed I feel this way. I shouldn't feel like this. I should be accepting him, letting him make love to me, but my body is trembling, and tears are running down my cheeks. It's too late. I've made a mess of everything.

Letting out an angry breath, he shoves away from me. Pulling his pants up, he zips them, then grabs his shirt and jacket in quick, abrupt movements, indicating how pissed he is.

Turning onto my side, I cover my breasts as the tears stream down my cheeks.

"I thought you'd changed, gotten over it. We can never move forward if you can't handle us having sex."

I watch his back as he walks out. Moments later, I hear my front door slam behind him.

CHAPTER FIFTEEN

—

CARTER

Alex arrives for her lesson and she looks tired and worn down. Her eyes are somewhat puffy as if she cried not too long ago. My chest tightens at the sight of her sorrowful expression.

"Alex, you okay?"

She steps forward and I can see the emotional weight pressing down on her. Tears fill the corner of her eyes and I open my arms for her as she moves into them. Running my hand over her neck and back, I try to soothe her tears. I want to know why she's upset and I want to fix it now.

"Alex, talk to me."

"Todd…last night…he…" More tears dampen my shirt as she sobs into my chest.

"Did he hurt you?"

Her head moves against my chest and anger courses through me.

"Alex." I lift her head and look at her as I wipe her tear-stained cheeks. "How bad did he hurt you? Did he…"

She shakes her head no and some of the tension eases out of my shoulders. "Fuck the training. I'm taking you home."

Placing her hand on my chest, she shakes her head. "No, I want to stay. I want to work out everything I'm feeling."

"We'll do a half hour today, how about that?"

She agrees, laying her head against my chest. "I'm such an idiot."

"No, you're not. He's an asshole."

"He is."

I rub along her back. "You sure you're ready to do this?"

Her tears have stopped, and she sounds more confident. "I am."

I put her through a circuit, and she gives it all she's got. I can see by the end that her stress has lessened, and I even get a smile out of her.

Handing her a towel, I sit next to her on the bench as she drinks her water.

"I don't want you to be alone at home. I have a dinner thing with my family tonight. How about you come with me?"

She studies me, her beautiful green eyes softening. "I don't want to impose if it's a special family dinner."

"It's fine. I think you'll have a good time if you come."

"Okay. I'll come."

"I'll pick you up in an hour."

She smiles and nods, waving as she leaves. "Thank you," she mouths silently.

When Alex opens her door and glimpses my bike behind me, her face lights up, and I'm thrilled to see it. She steps out and I hand her the extra helmet I brought her.

"Brought one just for you."

Her bright, green eyes have lost their puffiness and are now filled with intrigue. Satisfaction spreads through my chest. Making her happy brings me more joy than I anticipated.

Taking the helmet from me, she tucks it into her arm and walks with me to my bike. I help her onto it and caress her arm. She doesn't flinch and I'm relieved.

"You ready?"

She climbs on and I make sure she's settled with her warm hands around my waist and nestled against my back before I take off.

The road beneath me gives my body a feeling of utter freedom. It's better than the release I get at the gym or the adrenaline rush of a fight, but having Alex cling to me as I slip through the breeze and increase speed is just as pleasurable as an orgasm. A woman's warm body and the power of a high-speed machine is intoxicating. The only thing better would be if I could make love to her as she leans over my bike and looks back at me with those pretty, lust-filled eyes.

The dude down south makes himself known and I cool my thoughts. The last thing I want to do is give her a reason to shut me out again. I was the one she came to when Todd hurt her and that tells me she sees me as the man in her life who can soothe her troubles. I want to be so much more than that for her, but it's a start, and I'm not going to ruin it.

When we make it to my mother's home, I see my brother has already arrived. His shiny red mustang is parked along the side of the road. I pull into the drive and hold the bike steady so Alex can climb off. I set my helmet on the bike and take hers and do the same. Her expression tells me she's nervous about this dinner. Gently, I take her hand and she grips it tight. She's more nervous than I thought.

"Everyone is gonna love you."

Leaning down, I kiss her head and feel her tense muscles ease slightly. She gives a forced smile and I squeeze her hand a bit, letting her know I'm here for her.

I knock, and voices reach the door before opening it. My mother's round face swells with a grin. Her black, bouncy curls swing as she motions us in.

"Come in, come in. Carter didn't tell me he was bringing a date!"

She reels Alex in for a hug and squeezes her tight.

"Not a date. Alex is a friend."

Alex's eyes dart from my mother to the food on the counters.

"I'm sorry. I would have brought something. It was last minute that I was able to come."

My mother waves her hand in the air. "Don't you worry yourself one bit. We have *plenty* of food to feed these men. Welcome to our home. I'm glad you could join us tonight. I'm Sandy, Carter and Kevin's mother."

"It's a pleasure to meet you. I'm Alex."

"Well, I hope you came hungry because I've made enough food for a feast. Would you like something to drink? I have beer, wine, soda, or water."

"I'd love a glass of wine."

"Ah, my kind of gal already? What kind? Red or white?"

"White would be great."

"Hey C!" My brother's boisterous voice rings through the house. He walks into the kitchen dangling a beer in his hand. "Get in here. The fight is on."

"I'll be there in a minute. Kevin this is my friend, Alex."

Eyeing her, he moves in and lifts her in a bear hug. She's too shocked to react and goes limp for a moment until he releases her. He ruffles his giant hand over her head and hair, and she laughs, wiggles free, and backs up to me for safety.

"Welcome to the family, little bird."

She glances at me, confused. I caress her arm and she moves into my chest.

"Everyone is little to him."

"Carter Maxwell!"

"And that would be his wife, Carrie. Be prepared for another hug," I whisper.

114

"Oh!" Carrie's mouth makes the shape and her big, brown eyes narrow in on Alex. "Gimme, gimme." She stretches her arms out for Alex. Alex slides into them and she laughs as Carrie rocks her back and forth. "Carter never brings anyone to dinner! He must like you."

My cheeks get warm, but Alex doesn't see. My mother hands her the glass of wine and Alex drinks enthusiastically. No doubt my affectionate family is already overwhelming her.

"What is going on in here?"

My younger cousin, Phillip walks into the kitchen with my aunt, Annalise behind him. They look at me, then Alex, and back to me. Before they can say anything, my mother breaks up the crowd. "Everyone out of the kitchen. We're overwhelming her. She hasn't even got her jacket off yet."

My eyes meet my mother's. "Thank you," I mouth.

She winks and takes Alex's jacket and hangs it by the door, as I do mine. Alex hugs her glass of wine and lingers, unsure of what to do with herself.

"Would you like to help me with these biscuits, hun?"

"Yes." Alex sets the wine glass down and awaits instructions with an expression of relief. I lean against the kitchen island and watch her and my mother interact.

"C, get in here man. You're missing this."

"I'm good. I'm gonna chill here for a minute."

Alex looks over her shoulder and smiles. Her eyes soften as she notices me watching her.

"You can join them. I don't mind."

"I'm enjoying this view better."

Her smile widens, and her cheeks flush. She joins me at the island and sits on the stool next to me, placing the biscuits on the cookie sheet. Moving closer, I take a couple biscuits and help her place them. Her gaze raises to me and I can see the attraction in them. I can't stop myself from leaning in and kissing her cheek. She giggles and nudges me with her shoulder before taking the cookie sheet to the oven.

With her wine glass in hand, my mother is grinning ear to ear as she watches us.

Alex retrieves her own glass. "Go on in. I'm gonna hang with your mom for a while."

"All right. I'll be in here if you need me." I grab a beer from the fridge and pop the top before heading into the living room. I glance over my shoulder and catch her staring. With rosy cheeks, she looks away.

CHAPTER SIXTEEN

—

ALEX

"This is my sister, Annalise." Sandy points to her look-alike with the same jet-black hair but in a pixie cut.

"It's nice to meet you, Alex."

She shakes my hand and joins us at the kitchen island as Sandy pours her a glass of wine.

"Are Carter and Kevin twins?"

Sandy shakes her head. "They're a year apart but might as well be twins. Been inseparable since Carter was born."

"They seem to have a special bond."

I watch Carter and his brother chat and laugh like they're best buds. Every once in a while, Carter glances up to check on me and gives me that sweet smile of his that makes my heart flutter.

"How long have you and Carter been friends?"

"A little over a month."

"How did you meet?"

"He's my kickboxing instructor. My best friend paid for me to have private lessons and hand-selected Carter as my instructor since he's friends with her husband."

"She made a wise choice," Annalise chimes in. "Carter is very disciplined. Always has been. If only Phillip was as focused."

Carter walks in and grabs a chip and dunks it into the melted cheese. "Don't you worry, Phillip will find his way."

"I appreciate you being there for him and motivating him. You've been a great influence on him."

"It's not easy without a father figure around. He's doing good. His grades have improved. I'm proud of him."

Carter gently caresses my shoulder as he moves past me to the fridge and a warm sensation spreads through me. Grabbing another beer, he pops the top and glances at his mother. "Need any help setting the table, ladies?"

"Yeah, that'd be great."

"I'll round up the boys."

Carter leaves the room to get his brother and cousin. Sandy leans closer to me. "Don't tell Kevin, but Carter is my favorite." She winks, and I smile before raising my glass to my lips.

I hand the mashed potatoes to Carter, and he carries them to the dining room table. It's the last of the dishes and he returns to retrieve me. Sliding his hand into mine, he walks with me to the table and pulls out a chair for me, then sits in the one next to me. Everyone takes a seat around us, and Sandy raises her glass for a toast.

"I'm thankful to have my family together once a month for dinner. I'm thankful for my boys and all the laughter and joy you bring into my life. I'm thankful Alex could join us this evening, and I hope she'll join us again. Cheers everyone."

Our glasses clink against each other's and Carter smiles at me with glistening blue eyes. Our moment is broken when Kevin passes a dish of meatloaf his direction. Carter places some on my plate, then his and passes it on. The food makes its rounds, and before long, the room is filled with chatter and laughter.

With our stomachs full of delicious food, we quickly clear the table and move into the living room to relax. On the couch, I fill the empty seat next to Carter, and he reaches behind me and rests his hand on the cushion. His fingers graze my hair before he finds a loose strand and winds it around his finger repeatedly. He doesn't seem to notice he's doing it, and it feels so good, I have no desire to stop him. My lids get heavy, and I nearly purr with every gentle tug of his fingers. My body eases into his, desperate for his warmth to surround me. He places a soft kiss on my head and I rest my eyes as my body slips into complete relaxation.

"You tired? Want me to take you home?" he whispers.

I shake my head. "Yes, but I don't want to leave."

Carter smiles against my temple before kissing me. "Then we won't."

Unsure of how long it's been, I startle awake with a couch pillow on Carter's lap and my head against it. Carter caresses behind my ear and I quickly settle. "I'm sorry I fell asleep."

"It's okay. You weren't out long. Fifteen minutes maybe."

Turning on my back, I look at him. He searches my face, staring at me affectionately.

"I'm glad you came tonight."

"Me too."

Looking around, I notice no one is left in the living room, but us. "Where'd everyone go?"

"Outside. They're gonna start a fire in the fire pit."

"Why didn't you wake me?"

"Because you looked too peaceful to wake up."

"You wanna go outside with them?"

"Only if you do."

I rub my hand along his hand and wrist. "Why are you so sweet to me?"

"I think you know why."

"Because you're a nice guy."

"I am," Carter chuckles, "but that's not the only reason why."

"Because you think I'm pretty?"

"I don't think you're pretty. I think you're gorgeous." Carter caresses my hand. "And you're still wrong."

"Because I'm crazy and entertain you?"

"You're not crazy, but you do entertain me." He takes my hand in his and raises it to his lips. "I'm sweet to you because I care about you. I want to spend all my spare time with you and kiss you as much as you'll let me."

His words and the affectionate touch of his lips against my skin sends a tingling sensation through me.

"Do you want to kiss me now?"

"I do."

"Will you?"

"Yes."

Placing his hand under my head, he raises me into his arms. His kiss is tender and passionate, warming me head to toe. Our kiss lasts for what feels like minutes and I'm filled with a yearning desire that numbs my mind and throbs at my core. With his hands caressing my body, I feel myself drifting into pleasured bliss. I don't want his kiss to end and neither does he it seems. When his lips part from mine, my breath is heavy and my need for him excruciating.

He rests his forehead against mine. "I want this. I want us, but I don't want to be your second choice. I want to be your only choice."

His gaze lingers over me. The weight of his question slows my heavy heartbeat. Before I can answer, Kevin walks in, and a grin smears his face.

"Looks like I have shitty timing."

"You do, bro," Carter laughs quietly, "but it's all right. You guys waiting on us?"

"Yeah, mom sent me in to see if you guys were joining or leaving."

Carter looks to me for an answer.

I kiss his cheek and smile. "We're staying."

CHAPTER SEVENTEEN

—

ALEX

Jane pokes her fork at her chicken salad and glances at the dozen roses in my office trash can. "Have you heard from him?"

Finishing the bite of my sandwich, I nod. "He started texting me after I ignored his calls."

"What's he saying?"

"He's sorry. Really wants to talk to me in person and explain. I replied there's nothing for him to explain that will change my mind, and I don't want to see him. I told him it was over."

"I'm proud of you. Todd is an insensitive prick. You deserve better."

Dropping my sandwich into the styrofoam container, I sigh as my emotions form a tight knot in my stomach.

"He's not as terrible as you make him out to be. He wants intimacy back in our relationship, but I wasn't ready, and that upset him. I get that he felt rejected, but what broke me was how he handled it. He walked out on me again like I meant nothing to him, and I didn't hear from him for *two* days. I thought we were done, that he'd left me just like last time, and I refused to let it crush me again."

Jane tosses her empty container into my trash can and covers the broken roses.

"And that shows how far you've come. The old Alex would have locked herself away and fallen apart. You got through it. You didn't even need me." Jane pouts, and I smile, but it quickly fades.

"I turned to Carter, and I'm not sure that was the right thing to do."

"Why not?"

My stomach swirls in response to my confused emotions. "He's made it clear he wants more. He kind of gave me an ultimatum."

"And the problem?"

"I'm not sure I should jump into something with him when things between Todd and me are still muddled."

"You just said you told him it was over between you two."

I rub at the headache forming between my temples. "I know, but…"

"You still have feelings for Todd."

I nod, and she frowns.

"It doesn't feel right to start something with Carter when I'm not sure I'm completely over Todd."

"How do you feel about Carter though?"

My cheeks heat up, and Jane grins. "He's incredible. Every time I'm around him I feel comfortable, relaxed, but also worked up."

123

"What do you mean? Oh!" Her lips form the word, then she giggles. "That's a good thing. Does he get you more excited than Todd does?"

"The last time we kissed, yes, but thankfully we were at his mother's house, and it couldn't turn into anything more than a kiss because that's the part you know I'm worried about. I couldn't relax and give myself to my ex-fiancé. Why put Carter through the same thing? Why lead him on?"

"Carter isn't Todd. I don't think he'd push you if you're not ready." She glances at her phone. "I gotta get back to work, babe. We on for tonight?"

"Is Carter coming?" My stomach flutters, hopeful he is. Jane grins. "He is. So, you'll come?"

"Yes."

My bathing suit is hidden under my shorts and tank top, my towel over my shoulder as I walk out onto the deck. Jane jumps out of their swimming pool as soon as she sees me.

"Alex!" She opens a cooler and grabs Jell-O shots on her way to me. She hands me one. "I made your favorite flavor this time."

She hugs me, then walks with me to the pool as I slurp down the shot. Anna's boyfriend, Joe is trying to pull her off her floatie, and Kyle and Carter are both holding beers, chatting. When I approach the pool, Carter's eyes lock on mine, a smile curling the corner of his mouth. My stomach flutters. I'm about to strip down to my bathing suit in front of him and it's causing a mixture of excitement and unease. Smiling, I wave back, and he continues his conversation with Kyle.

Jane leans in close as I remove my shirt. "He's been anxiously waiting for you to get here."

"Really?"

"Yes, asked me twice if you were for sure coming."

My lips part into a wide smile. Sliding off my shorts, I can see Carter watching me in my peripheral. Jane and I climb in, and Kyle is like a water ninja waiting to attack. He grabs both our ankles and yanks us under. I pop back up like a bobblehead doll and splash water at him.

"You girls needed to get wet. Jane's been laying on that floatie thing since we got in here."

"I didn't want my hair wet," Jane pouts.

Carter looks at me and there's an awkward tension between us. It's been a couple days since his mother's dinner, and it's obvious we're both unsure of the other's thoughts or feelings. I gather my courage and swim over to him. He puts his arm up on the pool edge and I move into it. Gaze lingering on my face, I feel as though he wants to kiss me but doesn't want to make the wrong move. Instead, he reaches forward and smooths a few strands of wet, sticky hair off my face.

"Thank you." I touch his hand as it lowers, and he keeps hold of it beneath the water. "I had a really good time with you and your family Tuesday night."

"That's good because my mother is already asking when you'll be back."

The corners of my mouth raise. "Your family is amazing. I wouldn't mind having dinner with them again."

Carter's eyes glisten and he adjusts our hands so our fingers intertwine. "Yeah?"

"Yeah."

"What about dinner with just me and you? Would you be up for that?"

His eyes search mine carefully, worried he's treading water in my own emotional pool. I push my nerves down into my gut. This is a moment I need to decide if I'm going to open up to Carter and give him the chance he's asked for twice or slink back into my shell and make excuses. I take a breath.

"I think I owe you an authentic Italian dinner."

Carter pulls me closer and gently places my hair behind my ear. "Is tomorrow too soon?"

I chuckle, and Carter smiles unabashed.

"No, it's not too soon. It's perfect."

Thumb caressing along my cheek, I lean into his touch as he nears for a kiss, then jump when cold water splashes my direction. Carter's hand releases mine and he catches the beach ball before it hits my head.

"Sorry," Anna says with a scrunched face.

"It's okay."

Carter tosses the ball back to her and looks to me. "I think that was our cue to join in."

"I think so."

Propelling forward, I feel Carter's hand graze along my leg. His grip tightens, and I'm gently pulled beneath the water. His hand holds me by the neck and brings me to his lips. I've never been kissed beneath the water and it sends a thrilling sensation through me. The kiss is quick and tender before he releases me. My head lifts from the water and I suck in air. Carter comes to the surface with his handsome smile spread wide. Winking at him, I swim off to join Jane and Anna.

With the evening light gone, Kyle stacks a couple more logs onto the bonfire as we all relax around it, full from our hotdogs and s'mores. Jane nestles into Kyle's arms when he returns to her on the blanket. Anna has her head in Joe's lap, staring into the fire, watching me roast my marshmallow. I'm waiting for it to get burnt and crispy on the outside.

"Any longer and it's going to be crisper than the logs."

I glance back at Carter's playful grin.

"I like it crispy like a log."

Pulling it back from the flames, I scoop it into my fingers as it melts off the roasting stick. Carter laughs at me as I tilt my head to catch the dripping marshmallow. I gobble it down and Carter raises his hand and wipes at the corner of my mouth. Bringing his finger to his lips, he licks it clean.

"You taste good."

"I taste like marshmallow goo," I chuckle.

Carter leans back on the blanket we share, resting on his bent elbow. "I like marshmallow goo."

Laying on my side, I face him, leaning on my own bent elbow. "Nah, I think you'd like whatever flavor I had on my lips."

Carter grins mischievously. "You're right, and if everyone wasn't here now, I'd want to kiss those lips."

Fingers linking with mine, he stares at me, his gaze hypnotizing. I wish we were alone. Kisses from Carter always leave me breathless and feeling sexy and desired.

"What are you thinking?"

"How good it feels to be around you."

"We can make this a permanent thing."

I glance down as my nerves tickle the back of my neck.

Carter raises our hands and kisses my fingers. "Or we can take one day at a time."

My lips pull back into an appreciative smile. "I'd like that."

CHAPTER EIGHTEEN

—

ALEX

The table is set with wine for me, beer for Carter, and a fragrant, white candle in the center. On the stove, the lasagna cools while the garlic bread finishes baking. Pouring some wine into my glass, I raise it to my lips and sip, easing my jittery nerves. To my surprise, I'm more excited than edgy. I'm anxious to see Carter's expression when he sees the effort I've put into our dinner. I know he'll appreciate it and that means a lot to me.

The sound of his bike engine roars to a stop, and I take another sip of my wine before heading to the door. His smile lights up my entire entryway as soon as he walks in. Wearing a nice pair of jeans, a button-up shirt with rolled-up sleeves, and his unruly hair haphazardly falling over his head, he has my belly stirring with an unfamiliar fire.

He leans in and kisses my cheek. "It smells delicious in here. I thought I was hungry before. Now I'm starving."

"Good, because it's ready."

Taking his hand, I lead him to the dining table. His gaze sweeps over my intimate set up, then he steps forward, using my hand to pull me close. His kiss is gentle, yet passionate. The fire in my belly becomes a blaze and burns right to the center of my core. When his lips part from mine, I catch my breath and stare up at him in a daze.

"This is perfect. Thank you."

Elation bursts through my chest.

"I thought you'd like it."

"I do. You keep surprising me."

"How have I surprised you?"

"From the moment I asked you to join me at my family dinner, I expected you to say no, but you didn't. I thought the dinner was going to be a one-time thing, that you'd still only want to be friends after, then you came to Kyle and Jane's, and you surprised me again. Then tonight, this dinner. I feel like you're giving us a chance." He takes my hand in his. "And I hope I'm right."

Caressing my thumb along his hand, I smile. "You are."

Carter pulls me to him, hugging me against his chest, kissing my hair. His body is warm, and he smells intoxicating—a mixture of soap, masculinity, and cologne.

"You don't know how good it feels to hear that."

Looking at him, I can see the emotion just beneath the surface of his gaze. He kisses me again and my body tingles. *This*…is how I want to feel.

"What can I help you with?"

"Nothing." Standing up on my toes, I kiss his cheek. "Get comfy and be prepared for the best lasagna you'll ever eat."

"Yes, ma'am."

Carter sits while I pull the garlic bread from the oven then plate his food with a slice of lasagna. Adding the garlic bread to it, I bring it to the table, then repeat with my own plate. As soon as the first bite is taken from the fork, Carter lets out a sigh.

"This is good, really good."

Glancing up at him, I smile appreciatively. "I just might have to cook for you again."

Carter looks at me, trapping me in his dark, blue gaze. "I'd love it. Anytime you want. Anything you want to cook."

Leaning back in his chair, he looks content and utterly satisfied as he drinks the last of his beer. I carry our empty plates to the dishwasher and cover the lasagna. Carter takes the pan from my hand and puts it in the fridge for me. Just as I lift my wine glass from the table, I feel his warm body press against my back. His hands caress my shoulders and arms as his lips gently kiss just behind my ear. Goosebumps rush across my skin and I let out a breath as my knees get weak.

"Thank you, beautiful. That was amazing."

Turning in his arms, his hand raises and caresses my cheek.

"I should probably get going before it gets too late."

The thought of him leaving creates a tight knot in my stomach.

"I don't want you to go."

Carter rubs his thumb along my hand, still holding me in his gaze. "I'll stay if you want me to."

131

"I do. I want you to stay."

Removing the space between us, Carter places his hand on my neck as he kisses me slow and soft. His affection seeps through his kiss into every limb, snuffing out my anxiety and replacing it with incredible warmth.

Our lips part and he places his forehead against mine. "You're so beautiful. Every part of you, inside and out."

Moving forward, I lean my head against his chest as he wraps his strong arms around me, holding me against him. I have nothing that needs to be said. All I want to do is feel as I bury myself in his loving embrace. Carter's silence is a symphony of emotions and my heart is his audience.

Moments later, I pull myself from his arms with tears prickling the corners of my eyes. Carter's kiss is sweet, and I'm lifted higher, more euphoric than I can ever remember feeling. He gently strokes my cheek.

"What would you like to do? I'll hold you all night if you want me to."

Looking up at his deep blue irises, I smile. "We can watch a movie if you want?"

"All right. Let's see what we can find."

Wiggling into Carter's arms, I nestle in with the popcorn bowl. Tossing a couple kernels in the air, he catches them and winks.

"Show off." I nudge his arm, and he laughs before he leans back, pulling me with him onto the pillows of my bed.

"Good choice on the movie," Carter praises.

"I knew you'd like it."

"You did, huh?"

"I'm figuring you out."

"I'd like to think I'm not complicated."

"That's good because I am."

Running his hand through my hair and over my shoulder, he sends exhilarating chills down my arms. "Maybe I like my woman complicated."

Leaning my head onto his chest, I grin like a fool as his words linger. *His woman.* Those two words send fluttering wings through my belly.

When the movie ends, Carter takes the bowl to the kitchen. I sneak away to the bathroom, brush my teeth, remove my makeup, and change. I open the door, and with the bed lamp illuminating his body, I get a glimpse of his bare back and his curved ass in his jeans. Sliding in next to him, his eyes open. A sweet smile parts his lips.

"You look gorgeous."

My stomach does a swirl and a cheeky grin spreads my lips as I pull the comforter over me.

"Thank you."

Laying on my side, I slip my hand into Carter's. He brings my hand to his mouth and kisses it.

"Goodnight."

Closing his eyes, he holds my hand close to him. I lay still, admiring him and his long, dark lashes, strong jawline, smooth shaved face, and the curve of his full lips.

The corner of his mouth raises and his eyes slowly open. Lifting my fingers, he kisses them softly.

"Can I hold you?"

Desperate for his warmth, I nod. Standing from the bed, he raises the comforter and joins me under it, placing his arm around me as I nestle into his chest. His fingers stroke my hair as I follow the circles and lines of his interlocking tattoo.

He glances down, watching me trace it with my finger.

"You like it?"

"I do. There's so many designs and directions. Every time I look at it, I find something new. Does it have a meaning?"

"This part does." He points to the section across his chest and shoulder. "My father died in a motorcycle accident. It's in memory of him. I added to it as time went on."

The memory is clearly painful, I can hear it in his languished tone.

"How old were you?"

"Seventeen."

"That's so young to lose a parent. I imagine it was really hard on you."

Carter's long, smooth strokes continue as he looks off, expressionless. "It was. Kevin and I were close to him."

I rest my hand on one of the feather-like designs on his chest. "I lost my mom six years ago."

134

Looking at me, his expression is empathetic. "What happened?"

"She died of cancer. After she passed my family drifted apart. I haven't spoken to my sister in a few years and my father isn't the emotionally loving type. He's remarried and lives in Europe."

Placing his hand under my chin, he gently lifts my face to meet his gaze. "You're like me. Tragedy doesn't break you down, it builds you up."

My heart explodes into a million tiny fragments of emotion. Carter is seeing me for who I truly am. I'm not damaged goods to him, I'm a woman who's overcome the tragedies in her life and become stronger because of them. Inside, I feel the deep wounds of Todd's impatience and his astringent criticism closing, replaced by Carter's patience and understanding.

Pressing my lips against his, I wrap my leg around his waist. With a steady hand, he holds me close, loving my lips with his. My abdomen tightens with arousal and beneath, my core aches with need.

Carter breaks away. "Alex," he says, his voice low and breathy. "I'm...we should slow things down."

Under my knee, I can feel the length of him stretched and pressing against his jeans. The desire to touch him and feel him twitches my eager fingers.

"Can I ask you something?"

His thumb strokes my cheek as he looks at me tenderly. "Anything."

"Can I explore you, without being touched?"

Eyes wide, he swallows a breath. "Is that what you want?"

Running my finger along his chest, I assure him, "Yes."

Kissing me slow and sensually, he leans back and slides his hands under the comforter. Moments later, his jeans and briefs hit the floor. His hand takes mine and soothes the jittery nerves dancing in my belly. He brings my hand to his lips.

"You can stop at any time if it's too much. I won't be upset." Kissing my fingertips, he lets them go and places both hands behind his head.

"As hard as it's gonna be. I promise to keep my hands here." His fists lock around the twisting bars of my headboard.

My lips curve before I lean forward, kissing him. Pulling away, I notice the anticipation in his eyes and lower my gaze to his chest. Slowly, I run my finger along his tattoo, tracing the outlines. My heartbeat thuds in my ears as my stomach kinks with a mixture of excitement and uncertainty. Following the center line of his hard abs to his stomach, I caress along the tattoo that crosses his lower abdomen.

Glancing up at him, he meets my gaze with desire resting just beneath the surface. Seeing that desire, knowing it's because of me, gives my body a tantalizing rush. With the added courage, I reach down and take him in my hand.

The size of him shocks me and I fight back my nerves as I run my hand from base to tip. The corner of his mouth raises, then fades as he leans his head back, giving into the pleasure of my strokes.

With my other hand, I toss the comforter back, and Carter lifts his head to see my reaction. My eyes widen, but my strokes don't ease. The heat between my legs is igniting a fiery need. I want to please him. I want him to feel as good as he makes me feel.

Moving my body lower, I lick across the head and he sucks in a breath just as I fill my mouth with his erection.

"Alex," he mutters. My headboard creaks as he tightens his grip.

Holding him steady at the base, I lick along the outside, then take him back in my mouth, sucking hard and rhythmically stroking the lower length of him. As desire erupts at my center, I increase my pace, eager for him to reach his climax. Desperate for my own release, I reach into my shorts and caress my clit. Moans burst from my lips.

"Alex." His voice is grated, edgy. "You're fucking incredible."

The headboard creaks louder and his abdomen flexes. One more pump into my mouth and hot cum bursts from his tip. A breath escapes him, and he lets out a low, sensual moan as I lick across his head. With heavy lids, his gaze meets mine and he releases the headboard.

"I didn't expect that. That was…damn, Alex." He outstretches his arms. "Come here."

Settled on his lap, I lean forward. He holds my lower back and caresses his thumbs along the top of my shorts.

137

Bringing my lips to his, I give several slow, sensual kisses before pulling his bottom lip between my teeth.

A growl escapes his chest. "You are...so fucking beautiful." He rests his head against mine. "You have no idea how much I want to make you feel as good as you just made me feel."

"Save those thoughts for the next time we're together."

"That's tomorrow. You have training."

"Lucky for you then," I smile.

Sliding down the bed, he lays back, taking me with him. "It can't come soon enough."

He rolls me to my side and I giggle from the surprise of it. Gentle kisses sweep across my cheeks, nose, and chin.

"Goodnight, beautiful."

I kiss his jaw, then nibble. Light laughter escapes him as he closes his eyes. His arm is wrapped around me and my body is sensitive to the fact he's nude. I pull the comforter over us and turn to my other side. Carter tugs me against him and places a soft kiss behind my ear, sending waves of pleasure over my shoulders and arms.

"Thank you for tonight."

Thumb caressing my abdomen, his arm tightens around me. "I'm the one that owes you a thank you. It's the best time I've had in a long time."

As the warmth of him presses against my back, elation spreads through my chest.

"Me too."

CHAPTER NINETEEN

—

ALEX

"You were a good girl."

His breath scorches my ear before the weight of his body lifts off me. Tears burn my cheeks and drip onto my wet pillow.

The sound of his belt buckle jingles as he hitches his pants over his hips and zips them.

"I'm gonna find me a drink. Then we'll have some more fun."

My arms writhe and my body trembles. "No, please, no."

Strong hands shake me awake. "Alex."

Tears pour out of me as I curl into a fetal position inside Carter's arms. He holds me protectively against him.

"I'm here. I got you. You're safe." His hand strokes my hair and caresses my back. "I have you. You're right here with me."

My hand clutches desperately at his arm, tucking my body inside his protection. My breathing calms and the last of my tears trickle down my cheeks.

"Do you need anything?"

"Please, don't let go."

Kissing my head, he holds me close. "I won't let go."

His thumb caresses my hand as I lay still, trying to work through the excruciating memories.

"What can I do for you?"

My words jam in my throat. Fresh tears slide down my cheeks. Turning in his arms, my leg brushes against his jeans. Sometime after I fell asleep, he redressed. The thoughtfulness creases the corner of my mouth.

"Just having you here is helping. I feel safe with you."

Tender lips touch my forehead. "As long as I'm around, no one will ever hurt you. I promise you."

His words touch deep, soothing me. I lean my head forward, desperate for the contact of his lips again. He kisses me, then tucks me into his arm and lies on his back. My head rests against his chest as he brushes his fingers through my hair.

"Will you stay with me again tomorrow?"

"Yes."

My heavy lids descend as his loving strokes lull me back to sleep.

Sweat drenched fabric clings to my warm skin. Blinking away my drowsiness, I realize Carter's absence. My sorrow is instantly squashed by the delicious fragrance of sausage and eggs. Flipping the comforter off my legs, I climb off the bed and enter the shower to lift the remnants of last night's nightmare.

With my damp hair twisted over my shoulder, I put on fresh clothes and meet Carter in the kitchen. The table is already set, the dirty dishes gone. Shirtless, the deep recesses of his muscles flex as he moves around the table. My eyes drop to his toned abdomen, then lower to the knot in his jeans. Heat builds between my legs at the memory of his erection sliding between my lips. My cheeks flush and Carter glances at me and grins.

"Morning, beautiful. I thought I'd surprise you this time."

Awakening from my arousal, I step forward and kiss him. "Thank you."

He pins me with his desire-filled gaze and eases his hand over my ass. With a squeeze, he winks and gives me a nudge toward the chair. "Enjoy."

Carter may not cook a lot, but he sure has a handle on breakfast. It's cooked just right, and I savor every satisfying bite.

Taking a fork full of egg covered toast, Carter chews then asks, "You ready for your lesson today?"

"I am. You gonna take it easy on me since it's my first self-defense lesson?"

The corner of his mouth tilts. "What do you think?"

141

"I think I'm gonna be sore after training."

"I'll give ya some knee and elbow pads."

"Seriously?"

"No." Sapphire circles light up his face and his cheeks swell as he laughs. "But I'll draw you a bath and massage away the aches and pains."

"Bring it on then." I smile before sliding a bite of eggs into my mouth.

"What would you like to do tonight?"

"Do you have something in mind?" I ask.

"I do. There's a small Carnival on the Boardwalk downtown. It opened up last night. I thought you might like to go."

"Only if you promise to win me something big and stuffed."

"Deal."

Setting my plate into the dishwasher, I head to my room to change. A moment later Carter taps on my door. "I'm gonna head home to shower and change."

"Okay, I'll see you in a bit."

Another tap raps on my door.

"Alex."

Dressed in my workout gear, I open the door. "Yeah?"

"I wasn't gonna leave without saying goodbye."

Moving into his open arms, tender lips meet mine, igniting that fiery need between my legs. His kiss deepens, and his fingers get lost in my hair. With a heavy breath, he quickly reins himself in.

"Alex…" He pauses, then sighs, his thumb gently swiping my chin. "I'll see you at the gym." Whatever thought he had is gone.

I watch him leave and my heart aches as soon as he's out of sight. Placing my gear in my gym bag, I eagerly prep, then settle on the couch to call Jane.

"He stayed the night?" Her shocked and enthusiastic tone spills through the receiver.

"He did. It was incredible falling asleep in his arms."

"I'm sure he loved the oral too."

A giggle escapes me. "He did."

"This is a huge step, babe. I'm proud of you."

"He's taking me to the Carnival tonight. You and Kyle should come."

"No! He only invited you. He wants to spend more time alone with *you*."

"I know, but it'd be nice to have you guys there too."

"Nope, I'm not being your crutch, babe. Tonight, you're on your own."

"Fine."

Jane laughs into my ear. "Maybe we'll see you there."

"I better."

"Have fun, babe. Give into lots of Carter kisses."

"I will."

"That's my girl."

143

Seeing Carter as I walk into Raise the Bar has my stomach somersaulting. Once I approach him, his eyes light up, and he kisses me, there in front of everyone. Several gazes turn our direction, and I lower my head, suddenly feeling shy from the attention. Carter raises my chin and rubs his thumb across it.

"I want everyone to know how I feel about you."

A smile swells my cheeks. "I think everyone does now."

"Just as long as the most important person knows." He kisses my cheek, then takes my bag from my arms and sets it to the side.

I follow him to the mats as my chest becomes light with an amorous sensation.

"Today, I'll teach you how to defend while standing, then we'll move into ground techniques. Those will be the most important techniques to learn. That's when you're the most vulnerable."

Perspiration bubbles on my neck and heat builds throughout my body. Flashes, quick and aggressive, rip through my mind. I sway, and Carter reaches out for me, stabilizing me.

"Alex, you okay?"

Tears burn my eyelids as I close them, forcing the memories and pain back into its box. Carter brings me in close and wraps his arms around me, locking me against his chest.

"That nightmare…it's still fresh on your mind, isn't it?" My head moves against him. He kisses my hair. "We can cancel today's lesson. I'll take you home and start that bath and massage."

"No, I want to do this." I wipe the stray tears away. "I *can* do this."

"I know you can." Releasing me, he sets his hands on my shoulders and rubs them. "You're incredible, Alex. Your strength is limitless."

His words penetrate deep, helping me gather my strength. "Let's get started. How do I stand?"

Giving a tender caress across my arm, he steps back. "You sure?"

"Yeah."

"All right. First, I want you to be the attacker, so I can demonstrate what you should do, then we'll switch."

"Okay."

"The first thing I want to teach you is to block someone from trying to tackle you and get you to the ground. When someone is being attacked, we do what is called the reflex response. We put our arms up like this," he raises his arms, "to block our face. You want to use that same reflex response as defense and offense. If you do what is called, the spear, and move your arms and hands forward, you can knock someone back and stop them from getting you to the ground. Now, come at me like you want to tackle me."

Spreading out my arms, I apprehensively charge toward Carter. He puts his arms up, forward, and into my chest and neck. Resistance keeps the momentum of my body from moving forward, then he adds his own momentum, and I'm thrown back, quickly moving my feet to catch my fall.

"You see how that works?"

145

"I do, yeah. That worked better than I expected."

"Good, now let's switch."

Instinctively, I put my hands up like he taught me in kickboxing, and as he attempts to tackle me, I lunge my arms forward against his chest and neck and his efforts to tackle me are blocked, knocking him back a couple steps.

"See how that works?"

"Yes!" My enthusiasm tilts the corner of his mouth.

"The next thing I'm gonna teach you is how to respond if you know you're going to be tackled."

Before long, I'm flipping Carter over my head, and as he lands on the mats, my adrenaline and excitement pump wildly.

"Oh my God! I did it!"

"You're doing great. You're picking this up quick. If you're ready for it, we'll move onto ground techniques." Nervously, I nod. He takes my hand in his. "If at any moment you need to stop, just say so and we'll be done for today."

My nerves mix with my adrenaline, but I want to continue, unwilling to let the awful memories inhibit me. "Okay, let's do this."

"All right. Lie back with your feet on the mats and your knees up." Carter gets on his knees and settles between mine. Rubbing his hands over my legs slows the hard thumping in my chest.

"The first technique will be how to respond if I'm on top of you, trying to punch you and knock you out. I want you to grab my shirt, pull me in close, head to chest or shoulder, and keep me against you, then start wailing on

146

my head, face, and side. When I squirm to get free that's when you kick at my stomach and knock me completely off."

Several rounds of this have me breathing heavy but concentrating on the moves keeps my mind from going elsewhere. When Carter stops, my arms collapse, and I lay there, exhausted.

Lying on his side, facing me, he raises his head and rests it on his hand, not even breathing heavy. "How do you feel?"

"Drained. Ready for that bath and massage."

"You did great today. It was a good start. I have several more techniques to show you, but we'll do them in the next session. You ready to go home?"

"I am." I turn to face him, resting my head on my own hand. "What time are you coming over?" I ask, a little too zealously.

"Now, if you want. I brought a change of clothes and some of my things."

"Let's not waste any more time then."

CHAPTER TWENTY

—

ALEX

A sheen of moisture lingers on Carter's hard muscles and bare chest from his shower. My gaze is frozen on him, and the wanton need plaguing me does nothing for my willpower. Through the mirror, his eyes lock on mine. Arousal hardens his expression, and he watches me, waiting for my response. I didn't mean to catch him like this. I thought I'd get in and out before he was done with his shower, but now my body is moving on its own accord, drawn to him like an energy force needing a connection.

My hand grazes the door frame, and I cross the threshold, committing to my endeavor. Carter slips his fingers through mine as I reach for him. Turning me, he leans me against my sink counter, giving me a sensual kiss. His lips move against mine in slow, passionate motions. The need that plagued me, now burns between my thighs, begging to be sated.

Large hands take hold of my ass and raise me onto the counter. Moans erupt from my mouth between eager flicks of his tongue. Carter's hand is placed at my waist, the other tangled in my hair as he holds the nape of my neck, gripping me with such intensity, I tingle from his touch.

There's no place for words in this moment. I want this sensation, this desire and total loss of control to last as long as possible. My fingers slide into the waistband of Carter's towel and pull it loose. Carter begins to pull away. Leaning forward, I claim his mouth and reach for him. His erection fills my hand, and a subtle moan escapes him as I continue to stroke the length of him.

Releasing from our kiss, his breath is heavy. "Alex…" His hands take hold of the counter as he gnaws his bottom lip and closes his eyes, giving into my touch. Bold, blue sapphires flick open and narrow in on me.

"I need to make you feel as good as you make me feel."

His lips slam into mine and he lifts me from the counter. Legs instinctively wrapping around his waist, he carries me to my bed and lays me on it.

"I won't let things go too far, I promise, but I need to taste and touch you. Do you want that? Do you want my mouth here?"

Gently, his hand rubs against me and heat bursts from my core. My head tips back and I let out a desperate, needy moan.

"Yes, please touch me, *everywhere*."

My clothes can't get off fast enough, but Carter insists on undressing me slowly. Each article of clothing slides off, followed by a trail of kisses. Lying bare beneath him, he admires me as he places his hands on my waist and slides me to him. With my legs spread, he lowers himself.

The moment his tongue touches my clit and begins rhythmically twirling and sucking, my body tingles, and my orgasm builds, ready to erupt at any moment.

Soaking wet and jerking my lower half against his face, Carter manages to still slide a finger into me and I cry out in pleasure. His skilled licks and strokes take me right over the edge. My body trembles, exploding into a sensation of euphoria.

It's the first orgasm I've had from a man in over a year, and I lay there basking in the incredible feeling. Carter eases onto the bed next to me and raises his hand to my breast and kneads it in his palm, flicking his thumb over my hardened nipple. Covering it with his mouth, he sucks, pulling it between his lips. Arousal shoots up my abdomen and back down.

Placing my hand on his cheek, I raise his lips to mine, ready to devour him just as he did me. With my hand to his chest, I push him onto his back. Reaching down, I take his hardened erection in my hand and stroke him several times as I kiss him.

Pulling away from his kiss is a struggle, but I'm eager to please him and give him relief. I lower myself and take him into my mouth. Laying his head back, he lets out a breath. His hand lovingly strokes my hair as I move my lips and tongue up then back down.

A pleasured groan escapes him and his hand finds my breast and massages it as I take him to his climax. I know he's near when he thickens then pulses. Hot cum fills my mouth and I swallow and lick every bit of him clean.

Carter takes me in his arms and lays me down on top of him. His erection presses against me and I don't panic or shudder. I lower my hips to his, enjoying the feel of him against my wet folds.

Tenderly, his hand strokes my face, his thumb running along my bottom lip. Bold, blue eyes are fixed on me, and I can see the affection in them, but I know it's more than that. Something has grown between us, and it's happened so quickly, I was too slow to catch on to it.

"There's something about you that makes me want to have you in my arms every night and wake up to you every morning. I want you to be mine. I want you to know I'm serious about us. I want a committed relationship with you."

Hope brightens his eyes and before my mind can think my heart is already speaking for me. "I want the same."

Carter's smile lights up his face. His kiss parts my lips and his tongue caresses mine, and with his kiss, I feel it— I'm falling in love with him.

His hand strokes my hair. "We better get moving before the man down south perks up again."

Giggling, I wiggle off him. He kisses my nose, cheek, then lips. As I turn away from the bed, Carter slaps my ass cheek. Laughter escapes me, and I glance over my shoulder to see him looking at me with a giant grin on his face.

Bright lights from the Carnival cast glowing shades of color across the horizon. The Ferris wheel spins and blinks as the delicious fragrance of funnel cakes and fair food meet my nostrils. Carter's arm drapes over my shoulder.

"What do you want to eat first?"

"Mmm, taco in a bag, chili dog, barbecue pulled pork, pizza, and fried chips."

"We'll see how many of those you actually get through," Carter laughs, grinning at me. "Just make sure to save room for the funnel cake."

"Oh, I will. Don't you worry."

Moments later, my sticky, barbecue covered fingers feed Carter the last of our shared pulled pork sandwich. He smiles and winks at me and I use the napkin to gather the bit of barbecue sauce on the corner of his mouth.

"Taking care of me already?"

I blush, and Carter smirks before kissing me. "I like it." His arms slide around my waist.

"Where to next?" I ask.

"I think it's time I win you something big and stuffed."

Handing me my own set of darts, Carter's gaze sweeps the stuffed animals. "Which one do you want?"

I point to a fuzzy, cream-colored bear. "That one."

Carter nods. "That one it is."

Nine darts later, the vendor is handing me the bear I chose. I take the big, fluffy thing with black, button eyes and tuck it in my arm. It's silly that something as trivial as this stuffed bear gives me butterflies, but it's a symbol of something more. Carter displays time and again how important it is to him that I'm taken care of and happy. His fingers find their way between mine as we walk through the crowd and the verbal coaxing of game hosts. It's a cooler night, but my body is humming with heat—all because of him.

Glancing at the flashing lights and swaying seats of the Ferris wheel, I look to Carter.

"You want to ride?"

"If you do, then yes."

The line moves quickly, and we're tucked into the bucket seat with my bear smashed into the corner for its own protection. Carter places his arm around me and I nudge closer to him. A soft caress of his fingers brushes my hair behind my ear, sending a ripple of pleasure across my shoulders and arms.

The seat jolts forward as the operator shifts the power mechanism. Blinking lights fill the corner of my eyes as I look out over the dark backdrop and the colorful specks of vendor stands scattered across it.

A graze of Carter's thumb along my neck returns my attention to him and his handsome face.

"Would you like me to stay the night again?"

"Yes."

"Would you still like the bath or massage?" His comforting touch caresses my arm as the Ferris wheel brings us up toward the top once more.

"If it's on the table, I'll take both." I wink, and he squeezes me close before kissing me.

Leaning into his nook, I indulge in his affectionate strokes along my arm and side while we watch the painted

153

horizon rise and fall with each rotation of the old, squeaky, romantic carnival ride.

As we descend the Ferris wheel stairs, I get a glimpse of Jane's blond hair swishing back and forth as she waves her arms with enthusiasm. Moving through the crowd to find her, I reach her and am instantly pulled into her embrace. Her cherry blossom fragrance envelops me, snuffing out the scent of fried dough for only a moment until we separate.

"I'm glad you made it!"

"We arrived a bit ago, just finished messaging you when I saw you both."

My phone vibrates in my pocket and I laugh. "Just got your message."

The corner of her mouth creases as she looks at the fuzzy bear tucked in my arm. "Having fun?"

"I am."

"He staying over again?" Jane tilts her head toward Carter who's deep in conversation with Kyle.

"Yes."

Jane's toothy grin spreads wide. "I'm proud of you."

Rolling my eyes, I place my hand inside her arm. "Help me find a bathroom."

Jane waves her hand over her shoulder. "C'mon hot cheeks, Alex needs a bathroom."

Kyle and Carter follow a few steps behind as we weave through the crowd. They stop at a game booth to shoot guns at stars while Jane and I slip into the bathroom just ahead of the stand.

As I turn the corner my body jolts in response to seeing Elizabeth, Todd's sister.

"I'm so sorry." Nerves bunch in my stomach as I place my hand on her arm to steady her.

Her bright, hazel-green eyes dart between me and Jane. "Alex. How are you?"

We all move out of the path of women trying to get to the stalls. "I'm doing good. How are you? I'm surprised to see you here."

Her hands rest on her swollen belly. "I'm very ready for this gal to arrive. Eight more weeks. We're counting down. We came to visit Todd for the weekend, but he had some paperwork to catch up on tonight and couldn't make it out with us."

Relief sweeps over me.

"Congrats," Jane tells her, pointing to her belly.

Elizabeth studies her. "Jane, right?"

"Yeah, it's been a long time."

"Time flies, doesn't it?"

My foot shuffles from the awkward conversation, I'm ready to dodge her scrutinizing gaze. I'm sure she senses my discomfort, it's practically emanating off me.

"He misses you, Alex."

And there it is.

"He's been torn up ever since your fight. He wants to work things out. He loves you."

"He has a funny way of showing it," Jane chides.

Elizabeth's smooth voice develops an edge. "What's that supposed to mean?"

"He walked out on her *again*."

155

"He didn't walk out on her. They had a fight. That happens when two people love each other." Her eyes shift to me. "He said he gave you a couple days to cool off, and when he called to talk, you broke up with him."

"Your brother neglected to share a few crucial details with you." Jane's eyes narrow. She's about to unleash and Elizabeth is an unsuspecting innocent caught in the mix.

"Jane." She glances at me and I shake my head. Her shoulders roll back.

Elizabeth stares at me with pleading eyes. "You should call him. He really does miss you." She affectionately touches my arm as she retreats.

Jane huffs. "Clearly Todd doesn't tell his sister *everything*."

The conversation has my mind and emotions equally rattled. I grab Jane's arm and pull her farther into the bathroom, glancing over my shoulder to ensure Elizabeth is out of earshot.

"What's wrong? Don't let what she said get to you."

"Of course, it got to me! He said he was letting me cool off. What bullshit is that?"

"He's a douche. Have an amazing night with Carter and forget about that conversation."

Letting out a breath, I hand Jane the stuffed bear before storming into the next available stall.

When we walk out, my eyes scan the crowd for Carter. He gestures at me and I head right into his arms. He caresses his hand over my hair, instantly soothing my anger and frustration.

"Everything all right?"

156

"We ran into Todd's sister," Jane explains.

Carter releases me and gently strokes his thumb across my cheek. "She say something that upset you?" I nod, and Carter puts his arms back around me and kisses my hair. "You wanna head home?"

"Yeah, I think I'm ready to call it a night."

Taking the bear from Jane's outstretched hand, Carter tucks it in the opposite arm while wrapping me in the other.

"We'll see you later. We're gonna head out," he says to them.

Jane moves in and hugs me. "Have fun tonight," she whispers before kissing my cheek.

CHAPTER TWENTY-ONE

—

ALEX

Looking at the big, bug eyes of the silly bear as I place it on my nightstand has joy filling my chest. My smile widens as the warmth of Carter's body meets my back. His arms wrap around me as he nuzzles into my neck.

"Feeling better?"

Putting my hands on his arms, I rub along them.

"I always feel better when you're around."

An affectionate kiss sends goosebumps over my skin. His warm breath meets my ear. "I'm gonna start the bath."

Those words alone cause a tightening, needy heat to build at my core. His tongue flicks the lower part of my ear and that heat pulses just before his warmth leaves me. The sound of the tub faucet pouring water reaches me and my body tingles with anticipation. Knowing in moments I'll see Carter naked in all his glory reignites that fading heat between my legs.

With his bare chest taunting me, he fills the frame of my bathroom, and with one curling finger my legs move to him, reeled in by the sexy desire in his eyes.

I stop before him and with slow, sensual movements his hands lift my sweater. Calloused thumbs graze my sensitive skin and brush across my bra, lingering on my hardened nipples. Carter's gaze drops to my full breasts held up by a platter of black satin and lace before raising and meeting my eyes with fierce intensity.

"You're incredibly beautiful."

Gently pulling me to him, his lips meet mine in a loving, slow kiss. The back of my bra clasp comes undone in his hands. His fiery lips leave mine tingly as the bra flutters to the floor. Stepping back, he admires me. The lascivious look in his eyes doesn't cause me to shy away. No, it excites me and gives me confidence that he appreciates what he sees and won't hurt me to have what he wants.

Taking my hands in his, he kisses each before lowering them and meeting my lips as his fingers work to unfasten my jeans. Slipping my thumbs into each side, I slide them and my underwear, down and off. I leave his lips for only a moment to kick away my jeans before returning to what I crave more of.

My hands reach for his jeans and lower them off his hips as his mouth molds to my lips in sensuous, devouring motions. Carter pulls away for a breath when my hand takes hold of his erection. His hand rests against the wall as I repeatedly stroke the length of him.

"Alex," he breathes.

Lowering onto my knees, I take him into my mouth. He reaches for the faucet and turns it off before resting one hand on my head and tangling his fingers in my hair. A low moan escapes his lips as my hand grips his ass cheek. I hold the base of his cock and push him to the back of my throat, sucking hard with each stroke.

"Fuuuck, Alex, you destroy me."

Minutes later, the salty taste fills my mouth and I swallow before licking at the last bit lingering at his head. Heavy-lidded eyes meet mine as I stand. He pulls me to him and rests his forehead against mine.

"You don't know what you do to me."

Brushing my finger across his lips, I grin at how satisfied I make him. "I like knowing I make you feel good."

"You do, beautiful. So damn good." His hand squeezes my ass. "Get in there. My turn to make *you* feel good."

The fragrance of my vanilla body wash fills my nostrils as I slide into the warm, silky water. Behind me, Carter sheds his jeans and briefs and eyes my ass as I lower myself beneath the water. My gaze lingers over his solid abs and Adonis belt pointing to his trimmed hair and semi-erect gorilla of a cock.

Jittery nerves bunch in my stomach at the thought of how he'll feel stretching me, then those thoughts turn to arousal at how good I know he'd feel inside me.

With a gentle grip on my waist, he slides my ass to him, molding me to his chest. A tender kiss skims my collarbone, across my neck, then the shell of my ear.

"Do you want me to touch you?" His hot breath on my ear does quick work stirring my arousal.

Leaning back on his chest, I take hold of his hand and lower it beneath the water to where I want him to touch.

"Yes."

My ear is sucked between his lips as he places one finger on my clit and rolls against my nub. Two fingers slide into me, and I gasp at how good it feels to have him working me this way. Sliding in deep, curving his fingers and rubbing at just the right angle has the bath water thrashing against the tub as my hips jerk in response.

"Carter…"

His lips touch my neck, nibble, and suck against my skin as his palm rubs against my clit, his skilled fingers stroking mercilessly. With the tingling of my body and curling of my toes my orgasm builds, mounting, eager to erupt.

With his free arm, he holds me close to him as I come undone. Trembling, my head tilted back, forming an O on my parted lips, I revel in the high coursing through my body.

Fingers sliding out, he caresses along my sensitive clit, then abdomen as I lay against his chest, basking in the glorious sensations he created. His hardened erection presses between my ass as he gives tender kisses to my cheek and neck.

"Is it selfish of me that I already want to make you come again?"

Laughing, I intertwine my fingers in his. "Not selfish at all, from my point of view."

"Good, because that right there was so damn sexy." Cheek rested against my hair, he caresses along my arm. "You mean a lot to me. I hope you know that. You've shown me incredible trust, and it hasn't gone unnoticed."

A smile forces its way across my face as my body grows warmer with increasing affection. "I do know. You're patient with me and show me how much I mean to you every time we're together. The more time we spend with one another, the more I'm falling in love with you."

With a gentle caress of his hand along my neck, he adjusts his position so he can tilt my head to his. With his kiss, his tongue dives in and out with such intensity and desire, my whole body ignites with incredible need for this man. Pulling away, his eyes center on mine, and I can see the adoration in them.

"Don't stop falling in love with me because I've fallen hard for you, and I want to spend every day making you as happy as you make me."

Sitting up, I turn my body to his. Placing my hands on the sides of his face, I lean in and press my lips to his in a long, sensuous kiss, sharing as much of my emotions as I can. I want him to feel an inkling of what I feel, to know how much he's become the man I needed.

Touching his thumb to my cheek, he caresses gently as his eyes tell me what he's feeling, that I'm it, I'm the one he wants, I'm his choice, and he'll be as patient as I need him to be.

"Let's get you clean, beautiful. I want you in my arms and on that bed in there."

CHAPTER TWENTY-TWO

—

CARTER

The sun's rays peek through the curtain, warming the side of my face. My eyes slowly open and tucked in my arms is the most gorgeous woman I've ever laid eyes on, and her heart belongs to me. It's what I've wanted since shortly after meeting her, and it's a bit surreal I finally have her to myself.

Last night turned me from a man to mush. The fact she's become so comfortable with my touch and even needy for it has me losing my hard exterior and willing to do anything to keep her happy and to continue building her trust.

The changes I've already seen from the moment she walked into my gym to now amaze me. She's incredibly strong, and I've come to admire that strength. It's a part of why I'm in love with her.

My biggest problem now is I don't want to leave her side. Leaving her is going to be agony—I'm totally addicted to the dimple that forms when I make her smile, the sparkle that lights up in her eyes when I make her laugh, the satisfaction on her face when I make her come, and those breasts of hers—I'm fucked for sure. She owns my heart and cock, and for the first time in my life, I'm happy as shit about it. She's the first woman who's ever inspired the *I do* thoughts. *And that* tells me—she's the one.

Her pretty green eyes flutter open when I stroke her cheek. That dimple appears and my heart skips a beat.

"Good morning."

"Good morning, beautiful. How'd you sleep?"

Wrapping her leg around the outside of my thigh, she scoots closer to my chest.

"Best night of sleep I've had in a long time."

Pulling her to my chest, I lie back. Kissing her slow and soft, she presses down on me, and my fading erection springs to life. She doesn't panic and pull away. Instead, a moan escapes her lips, and she lowers her hips farther down, putting my cock tight against her clit.

With her tongue diving in and out of my mouth, she rides against me, giving little whimpers of pleasure. My cock swells, aching to be inside her, to feel her walls clamp down on me as I thrust deep into her and bring her to orgasm. My breath heavy, I pull away from her luscious lips, eager to give her what her body is craving.

"Want me to make you come?"

"Don't ask anymore. The answer is always yes."

Flipping her onto her back, I thrust against her clit. Her head tilts back, and a breathy moan seeps from her perfect, full lips.

"Carter…"

"Yes, beautiful?"

"I want you."

Another thrust and her fingers are a vice grip on my biceps. "I want you too."

My lips slam down on hers, smothering her next moan as her hips buck upward driving me against her harder. Through her shorts and my briefs, I can feel her soaking wet for me. My hand slides down her abdomen and lifts her shorts and underwear out of my way. Finding her this aroused for me is tipping me toward absolute insanity.

"So damn sexy," I mouth to her lips.

"Don't stop," she pleads.

"Do you want me inside of you?"

"Yes."

"I won't hurt you, I promise you."

"I know you won't."

Gently sliding her shorts and underwear down her legs and off, I follow with kisses along her inner thigh before putting my mouth on her clit and tonguing it in rhythmic swirls. Her hips rise toward my face as I tongue fuck deep and add my fingers to stretch her for my swollen, aching cock.

Her fists clench the tangled bed sheets as she spews a run-on sentence of *ohmygoddon'tfuckingstop*. Her body arches and her orgasm fills my mouth and hand. She's Absolute. Fucking. Perfection.

Glossy eyes meet mine as I sit up and lower my briefs off my hips and toss them. Her gaze falls to my erection. Her eyes go wide, and I'm concerned she's not ready, but

165

my doubts are squashed when she licks her bottom lip and her eyes fill with desire.

"Do I need a condom?"

She shakes her head. "I'm on the pill."

Those four miraculous words mean I get to feel every bit of her as I make love to her. A smile lifts the corner of my mouth.

"I'll go slow. I want you to enjoy every moment."

She sits up and removes her tank top then lowers herself as I move between her legs. Holding my tip, I move it against her clit, and her eyes close as I'm covered in her silky wetness.

"Open your eyes, beautiful. I want to see everything you're feeling."

Bright, green eyes meet my gaze as I slowly slide my head into her. She's tight as a fist, and I move ever so gently, readying her to take me fully. Lowering myself, her breasts press against my chest, and I place my hand to her neck, holding her close to me. My lips press against hers in a slow, affectionate embrace. She laces her fingers in mine and I hold her hand above her head as I ease the rest of the way into her.

Pulling out, I give her walls a chance to adjust before thrusting into her again. I can't stop kissing her and loving on her as her incredible warmth surrounds me. She's heaven on earth, ecstasy in a tight package. Now that I've experienced her, felt her take me with such need, I want to bury myself deep inside her, over and over.

And for the next several thrusts, I do just that, and her pleasured moans tell me I'm doing it right.

"Carter…you feel incredible."

My lips sweep across hers. "You do too, beautiful, so damn good."

"Please don't stop loving me like this."

The friction of her tight walls is pumping the blood from my head to my cock. The recognizable tingle is at my tailbone—any second and I'm gonna lose myself in her.

My thrusts grow more eager, and she's riding right along with me, her moans growing louder, her nails digging into my skin. Head falling back, her hips drive into mine. Two more thrusts and her orgasm covers me as I fill her.

Laying above her, I kiss her continuously as we both come down from our high. My fingers caress along her cheek as I look her in the eyes and see satisfaction and affection in them.

"I didn't hurt you, did I?"

"No, I wanted you so much it eclipsed the soreness at the beginning."

Still inside of her, I don't want to pull out. Holding her like this, knowing how big of a step this is for her and that we took it together has me falling even deeper in love with her.

I kiss her lips, slow and tender. "I already want to make love to you again."

She nuzzles her nose against mine then kisses me softly. "Please do."

CHAPTER TWENTY-THREE

—

ALEX

As I soak in the hot bath water, Carter's fingers brush along my scalp, spreading the shampoo through my hair. I'm sorer than I want to admit to him, but it was worth it. Having Carter make love to me twice was glorious. He was attentive to my needs, careful, and yet gave me amazing pleasure. And now the way he's treating me—drawing me a bath, washing my hair, and offering to make me breakfast while I relax—I can't even begin to express how much it all means to me and how thankful I am to have him in my life.

"You're an amazing man."

Tilting my head back, he kisses my forehead. "Remember that when we have our first fight."

"All you have to do is say, 'yes, beautiful, you're always right,' and the fight will be over." I grin, and Carter laughs so hard his eyes crinkle.

"Is that right?"

"Yep."

The pressure of his fingers brings my head back to meet his gaze. "I think I could soften that heart of yours with this…" Warm lips brush across mine softly, teasingly, before his tongue slides in and swirls in passionate motions.

His fingers tangle in my hair as I raise myself from the bath water and place my hands to his chest. Heat builds at my center and wanton need spreads through my body. In a kneading caress, his hand massages my breast as the tip of his thumb strokes back and forth over my hardened nipple.

"How do you feel?" He mouths against my lips.

"I'm okay." More than okay actually. Needy desire is burning between my legs and I want him to stoke that fire before bringing it to a satisfying climax.

With swift movement, his hands take hold of my hips and raise me from the bath. My body soaks his shirt and jeans, but he doesn't seem to care as he lays me on the floor beneath him. Raising himself, he removes his shirt and rolls his hips out of his jeans and briefs.

Taking the length of him in his hand, he moves forward between my legs and places his head against my wet folds.

"You sure?" he asks, concerned.

"I am."

Wrapping my leg around him, I pull his hips forward, and his eyes go wide as he slides in deep. His head hangs back, and he bites into his lip before tilting his head forward and meeting my gaze. Blazing desire fills his eyes as he lowers his chest down to me. Holding me close, his hips rhythmically rock against mine, and I ride out the euphoric sensation as it courses through me.

Music sounds in the background as I place my hands around Carter's rock-hard abs and lay my tank-top covered breasts against his warm back. Taking my arm, he moves me against the kitchen counter as the bacon sizzles in the skillet and the scent of it taunts my nostrils. With a tender kiss, he caresses my side.

"Still feeling good?"

A satisfied smile spreads my lips. "Yes, all because of you."

Thumbing my bottom lip, he smiles, lighting up those beautiful blues. "Does that mean I rocked your world?"

"More than rocked it. Might need to put that prince of pleasure on a pedestal."

Carter's laugh bursts from his chest. An affectionate kiss is placed on my forehead. "Go relax. I'll bring you breakfast in a few."

Clicking on the remote, I settle into the couch cushions and flip through the channels while inhaling the delicious fragrance of eggs and bacon. The TV does little to keep my attention when I notice Carter's hips bouncing to the left, then right. With his fitness regimen, he's got an ass that would make most women jealous. Eggs flip in the air and his backside goes in rhythm with the vocals he belts out.

I'm pretty sure I've died and gone to heaven. The sexy never ends with this man.

I giggle, and he glances over his shoulder, shining a grin, then winks. That does me in. Arousal tingles at my center and I nibble my lip and watch the more entertaining show in my kitchen.

"Over easy?"

"Yes."

Grabbing his phone, he turns up the music. Kane Brown's "There Goes My Everything" pours out of the speaker. Carter's voice is an unanticipated match and that sexy voice of his shoots electricity straight through me. Singing along, he carries the plates of food to me and sets them on the coffee table. His doesn't miss a beat as he takes my hand and raises me from the couch. Placing his other hand around my back, he moves our hips. Staring into my eyes, with playful affection, he sings the lyrics to me.

As the song ends, his movements slow and he cups my face and kisses me with incredible passion. I'm left breathless and mesmerized.

"It's true, beautiful. I can't believe you're mine."

Tears pool at the corner of my eyes. The emotion emanating off him reaches deep in my core and leaves me with my own feelings of intense adoration.

"Believe it, because I am."

"That's what I've wanted since I met you."

Lips pressed to mine, he ends the moment in a tender kiss. Taking my hand in his, he leads me to the couch and hands me my plate. With my legs dangling over his lap, I dig into the delicious breakfast he prepared.

171

"What's on the agenda for today?" I ask.

"I'd love to spend the whole day with you, but I've got work to do for my upcoming MMA fight. You still coming to that?"

"I still don't want to see you get hurt, but yes, I'll be there to support you."

Carter's hand touches my knee and rubs affectionately. "Good, it means a lot to me to have you there."

Taking my empty plate, he returns the dishes to the kitchen. Knowing he's leaving soon, already has my stomach in a knot. "I'm gonna miss you today."

"Yeah? You wanna come over to my place tonight?"

Sitting up on the arm of the couch, I watch him as he comfortably moves around my kitchen. "Yeah, I do. I haven't got to see your place yet."

"I'll give you the address. Wanna come over around six?"

"Works for me. I'll bring dinner."

Carter joins me at the couch. I take his outstretched hand and he pulls me into his arms. As he brushes a stray hair behind my ear, his eyes settle on me, admiring my face. The affection I see looking back at me fills me with immense joy.

"You make it hard to leave."

"Then don't."

"Got to, beautiful."

My lip juts out as he gathers his things and puts a t-shirt on. Returning to me, his finger swipes my chin and raises it slightly.

"This morning was incredible. I'll miss you too."

172

His goodbye kiss causes a tantalizing sensation to rush over my skin. "See you tonight."

CHAPTER TWENTY-FOUR

—

ALEX

With my legs outstretched beneath my desk, I twist my pen in my fingers and laugh at Jane's high-pitched squeal through the receiver of my office phone.

"You little hussy! Twice?"

"Yes, and that was just yesterday morning. Jane, he's amazing."

"You owe me something big. I found him and knew right away he would be perfect for you."

"I do owe you. You know me better than I know myself sometimes. You've been an incredible friend and sister to me this past year."

My conversation is cut short when Melanie pops her head into my office.

"I'm sorry to interrupt. Your eleven a.m. is here."

"Gotta go, call you later."

Disconnecting, I wave my hand, indicating she can let them in. Standing to greet them, my stomach quickly churns with nausea. Todd, with his usual confident swagger, walks into my office. He looks impeccable in a black tailored suit, his hair perfectly gelled, and there's even a sparkle in his eyes when his gaze sweeps over me.

"What are you doing here?" My tone sounds sharper than I intended.

"It seems an appointment is the only way to get you to talk to me."

"You made an appointment under a fake name to see me?"

"Alex, baby—"

My hand goes up. "I'm not your baby."

Todd's shoulders slump. "Alex, I'm sorry. I'm sorry for everything. I made the mistake of thinking we could pick up where we left off. *I* made the mistake of pushing you too soon. I want you back. I haven't stopped thinking of you. Not a single day in over a year. The last couple of weeks…" The emotion in his voice is raw. "I feel like I'm losing you all over again."

The dejection in his eyes is tearing me apart. I remember seeing the same broken-hearted stare when I turned him away time and time again after my attack. My exterior is shattering to pieces.

Todd steps closer and takes my hand in his. "You know no other woman has ever meant as much to me as you do. You were going to be my wife—Mrs. Todd Livingston. Do you remember how happy we were?"

Reaching into his jacket pocket, he removes a white gold, diamond engagement ring. He bends to one knee, and the hopeful emotion in his eyes penetrates me deep.

"I love you, Alexandria DeMarco and I believe you still love me. We can still have the future we planned. Will you give us another chance? Will you be my wife?"

CHAPTER TWENTY-FIVE

—

CARTER

Raising the bouquet of assorted lilies and daisies to my nose, I take in the fragrance of the colorful flowers that reminded me of Alex the moment I saw them. The elevator to her floor dings and I step off, carrying our lunch in my other hand. I'm arriving a bit early, hoping to catch her before she takes off for her own lunch.

After waking up to her in my arms, in my bed, I want her to know how much this weekend meant to me. Hell, if I'm really honest with myself, I want an excuse to see her again, to kiss her delicious lips and hear her giggle when I squeeze her ass.

I nod to Melanie when she comes into view. Melanie looks at me frightened. Her gaze switches to Alex's office, then back to me. She jumps out from behind her desk.

"Alex is with a client right now. Take a seat. I'll let her know you're here."

Her tone startles me and I glance in the direction of Alex's office. What I see through the window has an all too familiar ache burrowing its way into my chest. I set the flowers and bag of food on Melanie's desk.

"Mr. Maxwell."

Melanie's voice is distant compared to the pounding in my ears. With heavy thuds, my feet cross the floor and I swing the office door open. Alex's tear-filled eyes raise to me and she withdraws her hand from Todd's.

Todd stands and barely gets a chance to speak before my fist is slamming into his face.

"Carter!" Alex screams.

"You think you're gonna walk your ass in here and win her back with a proposal? Stay the fuck away from her."

"Do I need to call security?" Melanie's small frame is shaking in the doorway.

Alex waves her hand. "No, it's ok, thank you, Melanie."

Todd moves his jaw and his hazel-green eyes darken as his glare attempts to slice through my exterior.

"You're gonna pay for that."

"Todd!"

Knuckles rap the door behind us. "Alexandria, is everything all right?"

Alex's eyes widen and she swallows before composing herself in front of an older, gray-haired man in a suit. "Yes, Mr. Kline. Everything is fine. These gentlemen were just leaving."

Mr. Kline nods, eyes us both, then departs as silently as he came.

That confidence she displayed moments ago fades the moment she looks at us. "Our conversations will have to wait until later. Right now, you both need to leave before you get me fired."

Eyeing Todd with contempt, I motion for him to walk out first. He pockets the engagement ring and looks to Alex. "Think about what I said. I love you."

Once he's out the door, I turn to Alex. "What the hell was that?"

Palming her face with her hands, I can see her fighting back tears. "Carter, I can't do this right now. *Please*, can we talk about what happened later?"

"You really want me to leave after what I just saw?"

Tears pool at the corner of her eyes. She hesitantly nods. "I can't do this, not here, not now. I don't want to argue. *Please*, Carter. We'll talk when I get off work." She retreats closer to her desk and I follow.

"If I hadn't interrupted, what would you have said?"

The tears escape her eyes and trickle down her cheeks in slow droplets.

Behind me, I hear shuffling feet and turn to see Melanie looking at us with a concerned expression.

"Alex, Mr. Kline would like to see you."

Alex wipes her cheeks and straightens her shoulders. "We'll finish this later. Melanie, please see him out."

CHAPTER TWENTY-SIX

—

ALEX

My foot is bouncing anxiously as I await Jane to meet me at Louego's Bar. The high-top table I chose gives me a perfect view of the front door. As soon as I see her walk in, I lower the wine glass from my lips and wave to get her attention. Still in her work attire, like I am, her blond locks are in a tight up-do and her black skirt hugs her thighs and stops just above her knees. Hanging her black leather purse on the chair, she slides into it.

"What is going on, Alex? Carter is blowing up Kyle's phone, so of course Kyle's blowing up mine." Her brows pinch inward as she awaits my explanation.

"Order your drink, then I'll explain."

Twenty minutes later, she finishes her mimosa as I finish sharing what happened during work earlier in the day.

"He seriously proposed?"

"Yes, and the look on Carter's face...he flipped. He punched Todd, demanded I tell him what I was going to say. He looked horrified. Mr. Kline heard the yelling. He gave me a warning that my personal life needs to stay out of the workplace."

"What are you going to do?" Jane slides her empty drink to the center. "Why haven't you answered Carter's calls?"

I thumb my nearly empty glass before meeting her gaze. "They both started calling me incessantly since I got off work. I had to turn off my phone so I could be alone to think."

Jane's forehead develops wrinkles. "What do you need to think about?"

I let out a breath. "How to handle this situation."

"What do you mean? You want to be with Carter, right?"

My fingers pinch the bridge of my nose together as I close my eyes and try to settle my whirlpool of emotions. Lifting my head, I return my gaze to her worried expression.

"I do. I'm in love with him. He's swept me off my feet, but I feel guilty. When Todd was confessing what I mean to him and how much he wants to be with me, when he pulled out the ring and asked me to marry him, I had a moment, one single moment where I thought about it. How can I face Carter now? He asked me what I was going to say? I know why he asked me that. He walked in the very moment I had that thought. I know he saw it in my eyes and it was more than that. He looked crushed. We just had an amazing weekend where he made me feel beautiful, safe, and desired, and the very next day this happens. I'm afraid he'll harbor doubts now. I'm afraid he'll walk out on me too. Why did Todd have to do this?" Tear droplets slowly slide down my cheeks, and I wipe at them, feeling lonely and scared.

Jane reaches over and rubs my hand. "You and Carter took major steps forward this weekend, and I know that alone has created significant emotions. Then Todd's confession, his proposal, then Carter's outburst, you're emotionally overwhelmed. I get it. I understand why you needed time to clear your head."

Thankful, I meet her gaze. "I am overwhelmed, and I want to talk to Carter, but I'm emotionally exhausted, and I feel the longer I go without talking to him the more upset he's going to get."

"I think you're right. He finally got you, and the threat of you being taken away by another man you have major history with probably terrifies him. You need to call him soon."

Letting out a breath, I tip the remaining wine to my lips. Swallowing it down, I let some of the day's tension go.

"I know, I'm going to go to his house and talk to him."

"What about Todd?"

"I don't know," I shake my head. "It's like he has a hook so deeply rooted in my heart, all he has to do is tug on the strings, and I'm reminded of the feelings I have buried away."

Jane's eyes narrow on mine. "After all he's done to you, how can you still have feelings for him?"

My finger runs along the rim of my glass as the memories dance across my mind. "For the longest time, it was always him. He was my everything."

"What about now? What about Carter?"

A smile raises the corners of my lips at the thought of how he makes me feel. "Each time I'm with him, he puts the pieces of my shattered heart back together."

CHAPTER TWENTY-SEVEN

—

CARTER

I'm pacing. Actually, fucking pacing. Pretty soon I'm going to wear a mark through my hardwood floor. She's not answering my calls or texts. It's going straight to voicemail. I glance at my phone again. Nothing. My temper unleashes and I throw my phone toward the couch. It bounces off the arm and disappears somewhere on the other side of the room. "Damn it!"

Every fucked up thought possible is going through my head. Did that son-of-a-bitch say something that pulled her back to him? Does she want to give them another chance? Is this why she's not answering my calls? I stop pacing and grip the edge of the bar in my kitchen. My knuckles are shining white. This can't be happening again. Alex is different. She's not Lindsey. Lindsey was the kind of woman that would stab a man in the back and twist the blade right through his heart.

It tore me to shreds when I discovered she'd been dating another man while she was dating me, and it was his proposal that won her heart. The memories flood me and the heavy thuds of my feet pound the floor as I walk to my fridge and pull out a beer. Popping the top, I down several swigs, trying to shake the sting of what that bitch did three years ago.

It's like it was yesterday, walking up to her house, the night black, the stars bright, the cool breeze easing the heat prickling across the back of my neck when I see his car in her driveway. Reaching the stairs of her porch, the light in the living room is on. On the other side of the window, he's on his knee, holding a ring. She jumps into his arms and kisses him before he puts the ring on her finger. A year and a half of my life spent loving a woman who never loved me the way she'd made me believe.

Lindsey I could let go of, but Alex—I can't let go of her. I won't let go. And one thing I'm not is a coward. I've fought for everything I've ever wanted in my life and I'm not going to stop now. Slamming the beer on the counter, I head to my door, grabbing my motorcycle keys and jacket on the way. Swinging the door open, I nearly knock Alex over as I charge out.

"Carter."

"Alex." I grasp her elbow to steady her. Her pretty green eyes shyly lower to the ground then raise to meet mine.

"I'm sorry I haven't answered your calls. I needed some time to decompress and deal with everything that's happened in the last few days."

The last few days. Does she regret the weekend? Does she regret sleeping with me?

185

Standing in jeans and a sweater, I notice her shiver, so I pull her inside. Closing the door behind us, I toss my jacket on the nearby chair and drop my keys on the end table. She nibbles her lip and shifts her feet. She's nervous. *Fuck. This can't be good.*

"Please don't be mad at me."

Here it goes. Back into the friend zone. Not. Fucking. Happening.

"Today was overwhelming. I'm sorry—"

Closing the distance between us, I gather her by the waist, pull her to me and crash my mouth to hers. She stiffens for a split second, then melts into my kiss. A moan escapes her between our breaths. Sliding my tongue between her lips, I dive in and out, putting the need I have for her into the kiss. She moves with me as I back her to the couch. I place her on the cushions and lay above her only removing my lips for a moment to adjust myself.

Her hands roam beneath my shirt and trace along my abs and chest. My fingers get lost in her hair as I hold the nape of her neck and place my other at her waist. Her hips push against my hardening erection and I growl into her mouth.

"I want to be inside of you."

"Then stop talking and fuck me."

My cock is now upright and rigid at the sounds of her whispered words. Wasting no time, I tear at both our clothes, removing everything in my way until she's laying bare beneath me. Those bright green eyes watch me with seductive want as I lower myself down to her soaking wet folds. With my thumb, I rub along her clit, and her head falls back.

"Look at me, beautiful. I want to see it all."

My eyes stay locked on hers as I lower myself and place my tongue where my thumb was. In circular licks, I toy with her clit and suck the little nub until she's sputtering profanities in her sweet voice.

Her body arches when my tongue lowers and dips inside. She bucks against my face and I can see her orgasm building. Sliding my hands under her ass, I hold her steady as I tongue-fuck her into ecstasy.

A pleasured chorus of moans and words spill out of her mouth, she claws at my chest, pulling me to her. With one gentle thrust, I fill her tight, wet hole. Bending her knee, I hold her leg in place for me to go deeper in. The sounds of my thrusts mingle with our satisfied moans. I can't get enough and the incredible feel of her is taking me over the edge. One more thrust and we both ride our high, one after the other.

Kissing her lips, I lay above her, holding myself up enough so I don't crush her. She pulls my bottom lip between her teeth, then nibbles my jaw. I laugh at her playful bites and kiss her again.

Taking a satisfied breath, she looks at me confused. "You're not mad at me?"

"I am mad at you. I'm pissed you kicked me out of your office. I'm pissed you didn't answer my calls. I'm pissed the lunch I had planned for you was ruined by that douchebag thinking he could propose to my girl. Now I'm waiting for you to tell me your answer was no and you came here to tell me that."

The light in her eyes dims. She pulls away from me and we both instinctively gather our clothes. My gut wrenches into a knot. I'm getting angrier by the second.

"What was this? A goodbye fuck?"

Her eyes widen. A scowl forms on her face. "No!"

"Then talk to me. What's going on?"

Redressed, she sits back on my couch. I want to pull her into my lap and turn this night into how I had originally imagined it to go, but I can't fight this feeling of dread— that it's all been too good to be true.

Her eyes have the pre-tear glisten in them.

Go ahead, just rip the damn band-aid off already.

She hugs herself, folded up into a ball in the corner of my couch. She looks miserable. I want to fix the pain I see in her eyes, but I'm not sure I can.

"I came here tonight to tell you it's you I want, but today when Todd proposed, he brought back old memories and feelings." She closes her eyes tight. "For one moment, I thought about the future we had planned when we were together." She opens her eyes and I see a mixture of guilt and hope in them. "But that future is no longer what I want. I want you."

The tears she was holding back are now trickling down her cheeks. Hearing she thought about his proposal stings my chest, but right now, she needs to know how much I want her too. Moving in closer, I wipe away her tears before pulling her into my lap. She buries her head into my neck and releases all the emotions she'd clearly been

188

holding onto all day. Stroking her hair, I soothe her until she calms down.

"I'm so sorry I didn't call or come over sooner. You were so angry. I thought I was going to lose you after today."

Taking her face in my hands, I look into her sad and hopeful eyes. "You're not going to lose me. I'm all in. I'm yours, and you, beautiful, are all mine."

Putting her legs around my waist, I lift her off the couch. As I carry her into my room, I place tender kisses on her lips, cheeks, and neck.

"We have more to talk about, but it can wait until after I make love to you."

CHAPTER TWENTY-EIGHT

—

ALEX

The beach is quiet as I walk along the sandy shore. Coming here after work has given me time to think before meeting with Todd. Ahead of me, the boardwalk is now empty, void of the carnival that bustled with life two days ago. The only remnants are a bit of litter the county staff are diligently clearing off. After walking to the steps, I stop and sit, waiting for Todd to arrive.

At the sound of footsteps, I turn and stand. Hazel-green eyes settle on me, and that same hope I saw in my office is vibrant in his irises.

"Alex."

"Hi, Todd."

He points to the beach. "You want to walk together?"

I nod, and with my flip-flops dangling in my hand, I turn, then step down into the sand.

"I'm glad you called me. I've been hoping you would."

My eyes look off into the distance at the gray sea and the white birds diving for the fish below. Their calls echo as loudly as the thudding in my heart. I don't want to hurt him and see the pain in his eyes again. Gathering my courage, I take a breath and return my gaze to him.

"You surprised me with your proposal."

Todd stops and faces me.

"I meant it. I want us to have a fresh start. I've done nothing but screw this up since we got back together. I pushed too hard, too fast, and I realize that now."

"I've started seeing Carter." The words spill out of my mouth, shocking me as much as they do him. His handsome face contorts into a grimace.

"I had a feeling that was the case when he sucker punched me."

"I'm sorry about that." I suddenly notice the slight discoloration on the side of his jaw.

"You sure you want to be with an aggressive man like that?"

The memory of Carter sharing what happened with his ex, Lindsey, flashes through my mind. "He's not aggressive. You were… It doesn't matter. He walked in on something that, yes, he could have handled better, but he had his reasons."

"Alex, I know you. We were together for four years. Carter can't give you what you need. I can. I can take care of you and give you a great life. Carter is a man who's chasing an unrealistic dream and will become a washout, unable to provide for you."

Anger festers and stirs in my gut like an angry bees nest. "You *don't* know what I need and you don't know Carter."

191

"You don't think I've seen men like him before? I know his kind all too well. You're a beautiful, intelligent woman who needs someone who can offer you the life you deserve. Carter will struggle to achieve what he wants and he'll take you down with him when he fails."

A shiver runs down my back. "How can you be so cold?"

"I'm not cold and you know that. I don't want to see you end up with the wrong man. I love you and I'm trying to get you to see how much I care for you. I've never stopped loving you."

I look away as tears sting my eyes. The anger has turned to frustration and confusion. Todd's fingers gently swipe my windblown hair behind my ear. His thumb erases my stray tear.

"I know you still love me too, or I wouldn't be affecting you this way."

His warm touch brings back the memory of how much love we used to share. Guilt pangs my stomach and I remove his hand.

"I think it's best that we don't see each other or communicate anymore. I'm with Carter now."

Todd's jaw tenses. "You're making a mistake."

"Goodbye, Todd."

I turn to walk away, and his hand takes hold of mine, pulling me back to him. Fingers caress along my cheek then disappear in my hair. His lips come down on mine, filled with an emotional pull that makes my head spin.

"I'll wait for you to realize it's me you belong with, but I won't wait forever."

192

With tears falling down my cheeks, I pull away from him. His hand slips out of mine, and I move my feet faster, wanting to flee from this situation as quickly as possible.

When I enter Raise the Bar, I instantly find relief when I see Carter clearing exercise gear off the mats from his last class. Sweat gleams across his shoulders and toned back, and my body tingles at the sight, reminding me of our intimacy from the night before. He turns when I approach, and the way his eyes light up when he sees me peels away the emotional distress from my meeting with Todd.

"Hey, beautiful." His kiss is soft on my lips before he pulls me into his arms. The familiar scent of his heated body and fading cologne fills my nostrils, taunting my senses. Holding me like this relaxes the last of my frayed nerves. "How was your day?"

"Work was good. Afterward, I met with Todd."

The muscles in his arms tense. "Yeah? How'd it go?"

"I told him we're together, and that he and I shouldn't communicate any longer."

His eyes glisten with what I assume is relief.

"That means a lot to me to hear you say that."

I kiss him affectionately then move to the bench and set my bag on it. "What are the plans today, Coach?"

Carter steps up to the bench and rubs along my arms. "As long as you're up for it, I want to have you practice a few kickboxing moves, then we'll do more ground self-defense lessons."

Removing my gloves from the bag, I place them on and join him in the middle of the mat. He raises his boxing mitts and gives the instruction. "Right, Left, Right, Duck."

We proceed through a series of these before he tosses the mitts and grabs the kicking pad. Ensuring my form is correct, he sets the bag down and places his hands on my hips. His breath is warm when his lips graze my ear.

"I wanna take you out for a special dinner tonight."

My body ignites, craving more of his touch. "I'm all in. What time?"

"Carter."

Both our heads turn in the direction of the boisterous voice. Carter adjusts his hands, placing one behind my back and guiding me with him as he walks to meet the man who called out his name. He points to me, then the tall, muscular man with gray-peppered hair, tan skin, and age lines on his attractive face.

"Alex, this is John Hawkins, my promoter. John, this is my girlfriend."

John extends his hand, revealing a fancy silver watch beneath the sleeve of his stylish button-up shirt.

"Pleasure to meet you, Alex." His tone is neutral, no emotion, and all business. His attention returns to Carter. "Are you available this evening?"

Carter glances at me then back to John. "What do you need?"

"I'd like to take you out to dinner tonight. Allan will be coming too. We have a lot to go over before your fight on Saturday."

"You mind if I bring Alex?"

John seems to force a smile. "Sure." He glances at me. "We'll be discussing a lot of fight business. Hopefully, you won't get bored."

"No, I'm very interested to learn more about MMA fighting." Until now, my experience was non-existent. Can't even remember seeing a fight on TV before, but I'm about to get a fast lesson in all things MMA. I want to understand this part of Carter's life. If it's important to him, it's now important to me.

"Let's meet at the Riverview Lodge at six p.m."

John leaves as quickly as he came and Carter pulls me into his arms and hugs me. His hands play with the end of my ponytail and tug, lifting my chin up to meet his troubled gaze.

"I'm sorry we have to change our plans. I had something special prepared for tonight. Do you mind coming to this dinner instead? I'd like you to be there."

Caressing his back, I smile. "Yes, I'd love to come. I want to learn everything I can about this part of your life."

"I'm really glad you're coming tonight."

I stare up at his warm, blue eyes filled with adoration. "Me too."

"Let's finish up your session, then we'll get ready."

The Riverview Lodge is a glamorous restaurant nestled along the beach of the Atlantic Ocean. After the sun sets, the normal turquoise water is black as night save for the glistening moonlight sparkling across the waves. In my knee-length, black dress and heels, I glide in front of Carter to our seats on the balcony. Covered in white linen with flowers in the center of the table, I imagine how romantic this setting could be if it was just Carter and me, but my thoughts are scattered by the arrival of his promoter, John and who I assume to be his trainer, Allan.

Standing to shake hands, Carter puts his arm around me and rests it on my lower back as he reaches his hand out to take Allan's, then John's.

"And who's this lovely lady?" Allan's cheeky grin is charming. It brightens his round face and detracts from the unsightly scar across his brow.

"My girlfriend, Alex."

Allan outstretches his hand, and his bright, brown eyes widen further as he looks me over. "Carter here has been holding out on us. He didn't tell us he had such a stunning girlfriend. Can't blame him. I'd hide you away too."

My cheeks flush, and Carter tightens his grip and winks at me, giving me the impression Allan is being playful. My nerves settle.

"Nice to meet you too," I reply cordially.

John waves his hand toward the table. "Let's have a seat. We need to get this man fed."

Sliding into my seat, I take the white napkin and set it on my lap as our young male waiter approaches and fills our glasses with water.

"What can I get you all to drink?"

"A round of scotch and whatever the lady would like," John tells him, then looks to me for my decision.

"A glass of Moscato."

"You're finest," John adds, then smiles at me.

Minutes later, the waiter delivers our drinks and takes our orders. As soon as he leaves, John and Allan jump right into discussing the upcoming fight on Saturday. I learn Miami is the location, only a couple hours from where we are in Villa Heights.

Carter's hand on my knee is taken away when Allan references a fight card and who Carter's opponent is. Suddenly Carter's expression turns serious and he's clearly focused in on the tips and instructions Allan is sharing with him.

Leaning forward, Allan's hands are moving in the air as he talks to Carter. "Reggie has a better ground game. You'll need to keep the fight on your feet. If he gets you down, it's gonna be tough for you to get back up."

"How many wins does he have in?"

"Two," John shares.

Watching Carter, I can see how serious he takes this. Every time he mentioned the fight before dread filled me, but now, hearing him and his trainer go over moves has me feeling more confident about his ability to win and even a little excited to see it happen.

The waiter interrupts their discussion about fight techniques and Carter sits back and places his hand on my knee and caresses me affectionately before the food is served.

With only one bite in, I'm practically moaning at how delicious the duck breast is. Carter winks and takes a bite of his braised beef and I can see him holding back his own moan of satisfaction. John is clearly pampering Carter and showing him the good life. As happy as I am for Carter, John's efforts to impress him leave me with an odd feeling of apprehension.

With the conversation returning to Saturday's fight, my attention drifts to the balcony and lingers over the royal blue sky surrounding the silver moon. The water is no longer calm and smooth as when we arrived. The wind has picked up and sweeps across my legs, sending a shiver down my back. John catches my body's reaction and stands, removing his jacket from the back of his chair and offers it.

Startled by the gesture, I shake my head. "I'm okay, thank you."

Carter stops talking to Allan about pre-fight activities, his attention turning to John and me. "Thank you, but it's time I get her home."

After thanking John for dinner, Carter listens to a few last-minute words of advice and preparation, then says his goodbyes.

Exiting the restaurant, the evenings chill raises the hair on my skin. Carter places his arm around me and pulls me close, giving me the comforting warmth of his body.

"What did you think?" he asks as we walk to his car.

"The food was delicious, the company was great, and I'm utterly fascinated by how much goes into preparing for a fight. Are you nervous at all for Saturday?"

Opening the door for me, he helps me in, then settles in the driver side.

"I am some, it's my very first fight, and two sponsors will be watching. I want to impress them and you," he quickly adds.

"You don't need to impress me." Taking his hand in mine, I kiss his rough knuckles. "I already adore you. Just don't get hurt and that will be enough for me."

"I'll do my best to come out the least scathed."

His soft lips press against my forehead and the tender affection increases how loved I feel by him.

When we arrive at my place, I ask him in, and his smile spreads wide in appreciation. I only have a few days left with him until Saturday's fight and I'm going to take as much of that time spoiling him as I can.

CHAPTER TWENTY-NINE

—

ALEX

Tall, silver buildings fill the horizon as we drive into busy Miami. Pulling up to the elegant Hotel, the valet opens my door, then walks to the trunk to retrieve our bags. John and Allan are waiting for us in the lobby. Peering through the clear glass doors ahead, I wave as I pull my suitcase alongside me. Nerves tickle my belly knowing tomorrow is the big day for Carter and winning this fight is a big deal for his career. He's gone into what I call—fighter mode. He's mentally focused and equally nervous. He hasn't admitted it, but I can tell by the puckered brows and unusually long amounts of silence.

After getting settled into our room, I'm going to make sure he has a relaxing evening. John said Carter needed a good meal, a swim, time in the hot tub or a massage. No alcohol and no strenuous physical activity. I guaranteed John that Carter would receive all of those things. With a prior call to the hotel, I booked a massage for this evening, following our dinner and his swim in the hotel pool.

Approaching John and Allan, Carter places his hand at the small of my back and brings me closer to him. Reaching out a muscled arm, he shakes John and Allan's hands.

"Thank you for the hotel arrangements."

The crease of John's mouth turns upward. "My pleasure. Enjoy your evening, relax, get a good meal, then tomorrow the fun will begin."

"You're going to be a star, Carter. I know one when I see one," Allan adds, tipping his head, his lips creased.

"Thank you for everything you both have done for me. I hope to make you proud tomorrow and to impress the fuck out of the sponsors."

The men chuckle in unison.

"You're already checked in." John hands Carter a wallet size envelope with room keys inside. "Room 218. See you tomorrow."

Taking the envelope, he tucks it into his pocket. "I'll be ready."

With a pat on my shoulder, John tips his head at me, acknowledging me and I'm sure the duties I promised him I'd fulfill.

"Have a good evening, Alex."

Allan waves before falling into step with John.

With the swipe of the hotel key, Carter pushes the hotel room door open for me to enter before him. Rolling my bag inside, I set it by the king size bed and take in my surroundings. The room is a suite, fitted with a kitchenette, living room, large bathroom, and further in, the bedroom with a second TV mounted on the wall across from it.

Carter rests his bag by the dresser, then stops in front of me. Taking my hands in his, he raises them and kisses each hand.

"It means so much to have my girl here with me for my first fight. I feel calmer with you here."

"I'm glad I'm here too." Wrapping my arms around his neck, I massage at the base. Tilting his head back, he closes his eyes and lets out a sigh.

"I just want to lay in bed and have you rub on me all evening."

"I promise to do that, but not until later. I have a few surprises planned for you."

Gaze snapping to mine, one brown brow raises in curiosity. "Surprises?"

"Mmm, hmm, I made reservations at a highly recommended steak and seafood restaurant, then we'll come back here and swim in the pool. Afterward, I booked us both massages in the hotel spa."

Arms fastened around my waist, resting at my lower back, he rubs one hand up and back down, caressing me with an affectionate touch.

"You planned all that for me?"

"Yes."

Lips, soft and tender brush against my mouth. His forehead lowers, resting at the peak of mine. "You're amazing. Thank you."

Looking into his sapphire eyes, I see the adoration I feel emanating from him.

"You're going to do great tomorrow and I'll be there when it's all over to kiss every bruise and massage your tired muscles."

With the graze of his thumb, his hand settles at my jaw. "How much time do we have before dinner?"

"An hour."

"Plenty of time for me to make love to you."

A kiss, masculine and greedy steals my breath. With his hand on my back, he pulls me on top of him as he falls to his back on the bed. Fingertips caress along my cheek and neck, keeping rhythm with the pace of his smoldering kiss.

My bare feet dangle over the edge as I watch Carter take his fourth lap across the distance of the pool. With each powerful stroke, his muscles flex, revealing his toned back. I've noticed the difference these last couple of weeks have made on his body. He's pushed harder, increased weights, running, increased his carbs. There's no doubt the ladies will swoon over him tomorrow. He's a stunning work of art, packaged in hard contoured muscles beneath a set of gorgeous blue eyes. And lucky for me, those eyes look at me as if I'm the most precious possession he owns. It's true though, he owns my heart—completely.

Carter accepts my flaws and doesn't punish me for them. With him, I feel free to be me, free to be scared, happy, or sad. He's the kind of man who will wipe my tears and hold me through the pain. The kind of man who will make me laugh when all I want to do is frown. He makes me stronger, not just physically, but emotionally. With his patience and love, he's repaired the shredded pieces of my soul. I no longer feel broken—he's made me whole.

"What are you thinking about, beautiful?" Carter swims between my legs and rests his arms on my thighs, looking up at me with sparkling blues.

"Thinking about you."

"Yeah? Good things?"

My giggle is involuntary. "Of course, good things. I'm sitting here thinking about how much you mean to me. How much I've fallen in love with you."

Strong, wet hands take hold of my waist and pull me into the warm water with him. My back rests against the wall, my legs snug around his hips. His hands cup my ass cheeks as his lips close in on mine.

"I don't think there's anything in this world that can make me happier than you."

Slipping between my lips, his tongue mingles with mine, a sensuous kiss toppling me, head over heels. I once believed Todd was it for me. How foolish I was.

A messy bun holds my dark hair atop my head while my feet are pampered by soft, white spa slippers. Between Carter making love to me and the tranquilizing massage, my body is in complete relaxation. Just before stepping into the shower area I see Carter exit the door to his massage room. I witness his relaxed expression before he raises his head, takes note of me, and winks. Relief fills me he enjoyed his massage. Short of being able to ensure he wins tomorrow, I feel I've done well helping him prepare and relax before the important fight.

Showered and redressed, I meet Carter in the waiting area. Standing, he reaches out his hand, and I take it. His smile lights up his eyes, and for the first time in days, I feel a sharp and sudden concern about tomorrow's fight.

"You okay?" Carter raises my hand to his lips and kisses it.

The last thing I want to do is make him worry. "Yes, it's been a great night. I'm ready to cuddle in bed with you though."

"Me too."

Releasing my hand, his arm curls around my waist as we exit the spa.

CHAPTER THIRTY

—

ALEX

Sitting in between Sandy and Kevin, my ass is wiggling as my nerves and excitement topple around my belly like a tumbleweed. The last I saw Carter, he had headphones on while shadow boxing. The trainers kicked us out moments after we said our good lucks and praises. He's going to do great, I know it, but I can't fight this jittery feeling.

The pulsing of bright, moving lights fills my gaze as the main lights are dimmed. The eager attention of every viewer goes to the entrance. A microphone clatters before a voice booms.

"Are you ready for the show tonight?" The announcer's excited voice riles the audience. A chorus of whistles and hoots surround me as my eyes dart anxiously between the entrance and the announcer.

"Fighting out of the red corner with two wins and zero losses, weighing in at one-hundred-seventy-one pounds, Reggie Renegade McMillan!"

Layered in lean muscle, tall, tatted, and sporting red shorts, Reggie owns the walkway. Confidence exudes from his solid frame. If he's nervous at all, it doesn't show. Fans stand in unison. Cheers and hoots echo through the casino's arena. The excitement is alive, a buzz moving through the crowd, heavy in the warm atmosphere. The audience is here for bloodshed and brutality. Reggie looks eager to feed their desires, using my Carter as the means.

Throbbing in my ears, my heart pounds against my chest. Reggie enters the ring and the announcer riles the crowd for the next announcement.

"Fighting out of the blue corner with zero wins and zero losses, weighing in at one-hundred-seventy pounds, Carter Maxwell!"

Jumping to my feet, I scream and cheer until my throat feels raw. I'm not alone. Around me, Carter's family cheer just as passionately. Eyes focused on Carter's, I wait for him to glance our way. It's brief, but our eyes connect and my lips crease into a smile. The nerves I witnessed earlier in the day are washed away, concealed by confidence, buried below his determination.

Worry etches across my brow. Realization of what I've feared all along is Carter won't quit this fight until he's broken and can no longer see or stand. He wants to win as much as he wants to breathe, so he's determined to succeed. Fear, palpable and harsh, tightens my gut.

The crowd awaits as the lead trainers say their piece. With shoes and shirts removed, mouth guards are slid in, Vaseline wiped over their brows, followed by slaps on the backs before they position themselves in the center of the ring.

"Fuck him!" Kevin shouts next to me.

Reggie is already sending a message by refusing to touch gloves. The arrogant asshole has a reputation to keep. Carter shrugs it off. The referee shouts, "Let's do this!"

Wasting no time, Reggie swings, clocking Carter in the upper cheek. Carter takes the hit, and quickly rebounds, sees the opportunity, and slams a fist into Reggie's unshielded ribs. Then another, a third. Reggie goes in close, intent to take Carter down on the ground where he will have the advantage. Leg folded over Carter's calf, Reggie goes for the takedown. Carter jumps back and counters with a flying knee.

Carter's not going to stay on the defensive. A skin to skin slap echoes in the air. Carter's just gained points for the leg kick to Reggie's calf. Bouncing on their feet, they dip and side step, calculating their next attack and each other's next move. A fist whizzes through the air, Reggie makes contact with Carter's face and I wince. Instantly, Carter punches back. Reggie takes a step, putting space between them. Carter doesn't hesitate and kicks the exact same spot on Reggie's calf.

Reggie is fueled, he leans forward, one swing, then another, knocking Carter against the cage. My hand shoots to my mouth and Kevin rubs my back.

"Don't worry, Little Bird, Carter's got this."

Carter comes back swinging. The testosterone is off the charts. The men are circling each other like lions going in for the kill. With a spin, Carter raises his leg and kicks at

Reggie's upper body. Reggie is pissed and charges with two more swings, making contact. Carter gets another kick in and the crowd goes wild as Reggie throws up his arms mouthing something inaudible to Carter.

Carter shocks the viewers when he charges Reggie, grips his hips, wraps a leg around his calf and takes him down. Reggie clearly wasn't expecting Carter to make such a bold move, but he still handles the takedown, punching and kicking his way out.

Back in the center, Reggie throws punches and Carter alternates dodging and swinging. Sweat beads off their swollen, red backs. From the stand, I can see Carter's puffy left eye and discolored cheek. The first round is nearly over. I'm not sure I can take two more rounds of this.

On the attack, Reggie moves forward, punching at Carter over and over, making Carter back step into the cage wall. Turning his body, Carter moves away from the fence, placing himself on the outside and lunges, swinging twice. Both men back step, watching the other, analyzing the other for their next move. Carter kicks twice, goes for a third and Reggie traps his leg, using it as leverage to overtake Carter. My muscles tighten, I know Reggie is stronger on the ground. Bouncing on his leg, Carter stays upright, and I let out the breath I was holding when the bell rings.

"You doing all right? Carter told me to keep an eye on you. No passing out on me."

The enormity of Kevin's hand feels odd when he gently touches my arm, stabilizing my shimmying knees. Releasing my weight against him, I ease into the seat.

"Two more rounds of this, Kevin. He's already beaten up."

The hungry crowd around me feverishly shift on the edge of their seats awaiting the break to end.

Back on my feet, I lean left and right, trying to get a good view of Carter as he and Reggie bounce and bob around the center of the ring. Clammy hands clench at my side as I inhale and exhale shallow, fearful breaths. Carter swings first and Reggie's body thrusts to the side. The hit to his upper face must have been hard, he sidesteps and takes a second to rebound. Carter doesn't give mercy. Moving his feet forward, Carter swings, again and again. Reggie seems rattled but returns swings just as fiercely.

Scarlet red dapples the floor. My chest constricts as I search for the source. It's Reggie's blood. Above his left eye, red tears leak down his face. Carter punches at the same spot and Reggie takes a step back. Relentless, Carter punches Reggie into the fence. Interlocking limbs rock from side to side as they fight to overtake the other.

The tussle moves away from the fence. Arms fly free as they realize neither is going down. A blue glove meets Reggie's face once again, and this time, Reggie stumbles. Blood spatters smear the floor as his knee buckles. Adrenaline coursing through his body, Carter seems ready to engage, to continue the pummeling, but the referee steps forward and places a hand on Reggie.

A technical knockout. The referee approaches Carter and raises his hand as the doctor and Reggie's coach move in and help Reggie to his corner. A blood trail follows Reggie to his side of the ring. The crowd roars in waves.

All my bottled fear escapes my body as I raise my arms and scream in celebration.

Allan joins Carter and hugs him, patting him on the back. The triumphant expression on Carter's face is burned into my mind. This is where he feels alive.

CHAPTER THIRTY-ONE

—

ALEX

Flashing blue and white lights have been traded from the excited buzz of the casino MMA ring to the dim, blue and white lighting of a Miami hotel suite. Inside, an array of fighters, friends, and groupies form several small energized crowds. With each inhaled breath, the aroma of beer, chocolate, and an overabundance of perfume consumes me. Upon the insistence of a fellow fighter from Knock Out Champions, Carter and I joined the after party.

Within a few steps past the door, Carter's embraced by two other fighters and quickly encased by a herd of legs and breasts. Grip tight on my hand, Carter pulls me close to him like a shield against the caressing hands and requests for signatures. Smiling cordially, I know he's being pleasant for his reputation. He signs a few memorabilia items then excuses himself from the overly affectionate women.

The last thing I want is to become the publicity blocker. Brushing my thumb over his hand to get his attention, I tilt my head toward the bar. "I'll get us something to drink."

"Thank you," he mouths, caressing my hand. My arm raises as he reluctantly lets me go.

Twisting and turning through the crowds, I make my way to the bar. Behind the cream marble top is a tall, light blond-haired guy in a black, fitted t-shirt and black slacks serving a variety of liquor to the waiting hands. He winks at me, mouth tilting.

"What can I get ya, pretty girl?"

"Sweet tea and whiskey, and a beer."

"Coming right up," he replies, reaching for two cups.

Arm resting on the bar, my gaze returns to Carter and the small crowd surrounding him. There's a generous number of pats to his back, smiles, and two pretty women inching as close as he'll allow. Seeing him do his best to dodge their advances pulls at the corner of my mouth. Stress creases form across his brow as he anxiously awaits my return.

"Here you are."

The bartender's voice breaks my gaze and I toss cash onto the bar top. "Keep the change."

"Thanks." A toothy grin spreads as he swipes the cash off the counter.

Drinks in hand, I turn toward Carter's direction and nearly drop both cups as a brush of cool, wet marker swirls across my moderately exposed cleavage. My breath catches as the wielder of this marker winks at me, his tongue darting across his bottom lip as if he likes what he sees.

213

Humiliation and discomfort compete for hierarchy. Before dumping my drink on him, I glance around me and discover I've stepped into a line of eager women, vying for this fighter's attention and signature. Happily, he's giving it to anything placed directly in front of his face, which unluckily for me, were my breasts.

Just as quickly, he moves onto the next female who thinks my idea is genius and lowers her shirt and bra, so the fleshy pink skin surrounding the nipple is visible. Immediately, and thankfully, I'm forgotten as the fighter encourages her to lower the shirt more. Giggles ensue just before a nipple pops from beneath her bra. Bolting with far less dignity, I find Carter where I left him.

Instantly, Carter's gaze drops to my left breast, and his brow dips in the same confusion I had moments ago.

"Wrong place, wrong time. I was mistaken for a fangirl. Not my finest moment."

Carter breaks into a humored laugh and the heat in my face lessens as I chuckle along with him. "I need to find a bathroom and wash this off."

"Yes, please. I'm finding myself dangerously jealous that another man's name is on my beautiful girl's body. Dangerous, because I don't have the energy to pummel him."

"Pummel who?"

A playful, cocky voice chimes next to me and my eyes follow the tats along the arms to the culprit of my embarrassment. Almond brown eyes drop to my breasts and that damn tongue darts out of his mouth licking his bottom lip.

214

"You're a fan?"

Carter places his arm protectively around my waist and brings my side to his. "Crank, this is my girl, Alex. She was getting me a drink and unintentionally ran into your marker."

Warmth spreads to my cheeks just before Crank laughs.

"Sorry about that, hun. You'll have to forgive my oversight."

"It's all right. I was just on the way to the bathroom to wash it off."

Carter's lips graze my head before I pull away in search of a bathroom.

—CARTER—

Crank's gaze momentarily follows Alex's ass and my grip tightens on the cup in my hand. Keeping my cool is necessary as Crank is a star fighter for Knock Out Champions and technically, my teammate. I can't hit him, but I still have my limits.

"Look too hard and I might have to challenge your title," I quip, raising my beer.

Crank's lips twist into a smirk and he pries his eyes away. Tipping his beer back, he relaxes against the wall next to me.

"You shouldn't bring your girl to parties like this. You can get more ass here than a toilet seat."

"Her ass is the only one I want."

"For now, you do." Crank's gaze searches through the plethora of women mingling in the hotel suite. Landing on

215

one, he rubs the back of his fingers against his scruff and makes a beeline for a tall blonde.

"Enjoy the party," his words trail off.

Before I'm caught alone, I wander to the vacant balcony. Each step reminds me of the toll tonight's fight took on my body. Purple and blue blotches and busted skin are the superficial marks left over from Reggie's ferocity, but it's my muscles that scream for me to give them the relief of a cushy hotel bed. All I want is to relax with my girl in my arms and feel the touch of her hands all over my body as I drift into oblivion.

With the chaos of fight night and the after party, we've had no time alone to talk. It's important to me to know how she felt about tonight's fight and if she's willing to come to the next one. I hope she will. Having her support and companionship during this trip has provided me with an added sense of calm. She settles the beast within.

Slender, soft fingers graze across my skin, intertwining with my fingers. Turning my head, my chest constricts, and I withdraw my hand from the dark-haired brunette staring up at me.

"Carter, right?"

"Yeah." My gaze drifts over her excessive cleavage and I intentionally look away toward the speckled horizon.

"You were amazing tonight. That was a hell of a fight. I imagine those muscles would appreciate a rub down."

One bold movement brings her hand caressing along my bicep. Uncomfortable with her advance, my muscle twitches, and I brush her hand off.

"You're a pretty girl, and I mean no disrespect—"

216

"But he's taken."

Alex's challenging tone surprises me. Stepping through the threshold of the balcony doors, she moves to my side and tucks herself inside my open arm, eyes still locked on the brunette's.

"Whatever." Her dark chocolate eyes roll before she leaves.

Adjusting my footing, I open both arms for Alex to fill them. Darkened by the night, her bold green eyes stare up at me with affection.

"I need you to know it doesn't matter how many women make advances, I will always want it to be you I wake up with each morning."

Her smile couldn't possibly get any wider. Stretching on her toes, she meets my lips, and I lure her into the desirous storm brewing beneath.

"All I want is for us to go back to our hotel room, get naked, and take advantage of that large Jacuzzi tub."

"Done." With wide, eager eyes she takes my hand and pulls me toward the exit of the suite.

Warm water flows from the silver faucet as my eyes linger over her bare body. Pink, pert nipples taunt me as the golden glow of the candlelight flickers across her skin. She dips a toe into the water, and my gaze falls to the small, dark patch revealing fleshy pink lips I'm eager to caress.

Taking her hand, I guide her into the water and help her straddle my lap. Thoughts evaporate as her warm mouth elicits aroused moans between the passion of my kiss and the strokes of my fingers between her legs.

Writing over my fingers, her moans grow louder, an arousing chorus to my ears. Switching from her tiny nub, I thrust two fingers against her tender g-spot. Grip tight against my shoulders, she begs for release. My mouth covers her dampened lips and smothers her satisfied cry.

"I need you on my cock. I need to be inside you."

Teasing the tip with the anticipation of her warmth, she lowers herself, burying me deep inside her. Leaning back against the wall of the tub, I thrust my hips up, stretching her, claiming her in the most intimate way possible.

Joined as one, I lower her mouth to mine, my hand holds her ass tight as I get my rhythm, thrusting deep and slow, giving our bodies the intimacy they crave from one another.

The decadent sound of her whimpers vibrates across my lips and I savor the sensation as we reach our orgasms.

My hooded eyes stare at the green-eyed thief before me. She's stolen more than my heart, she's broken in and seized my soul.

Tilting her head, she moves into my touch.

"The fight tonight was one of the best experiences of my life, but it doesn't compare to what I feel when I'm with you."

"Carter." The sound of my name is an emotional breath whispered from her lips.

"I mean it, Alex. When I look at you, I see my future."

This is getting deep and I know it. Maybe I'm riding an emotional high, but I feel it's more than that. I've felt drawn to Alex and wanted to be the man in her life since I met her. What's between us is the kind of stuff I imagine to be in romance books or the princess fairytales told to girls. Our relationship is progressing quickly, I'm fully aware of it, but I'm not shying away from it. I'm all in. I'm all hers.

My fingertip catches and swipes away the tear falling beneath her eye.

"What are you thinking? Talk to me."

"I never knew love could be like this."

Hugging her close, I kiss her sweet lips.

"It's only the beginning for us."

CHAPTER THIRTY-TWO

—

ALEX

"I'm so sorry we weren't able to make Carter's first fight." Jane's lengthy leg bounces over the other as her lips form a pout. "Kyle was so upset he got called into work."

Dropping my empty container into the trash next to my desk, I give her a reassuring smile. "Don't worry about it. He has another one coming up and you guys can make it up to him then."

"We will, for sure. Kyle said Carter was ecstatic talking about the fight."

"He was amazing! I thought I was going to have a heart attack after the first round, but he came into round two and owned it."

"Ugh, I'm so bummed we missed it. You nervous about the next fight?"

"I am, but not as much as the first fight. The first fight jitters are over. I kind of know what to expect at the next one."

"So, how's it feel having a soon-to-be-famous MMA fighter boyfriend?"

My mouth quirks. "I'm probably going to have to invest in a taser just to keep the women off him."

"That bad, huh?" Jane laughs, crinkling the corner of her eyes.

"Yeah, I saw how they reacted to Knock Out Champions' star fighter and Carter's a lot better looking than he is. I interrupted one chick trying to offer him a rub down."

"Oh my God, what a hussy. How did Carter react?" Leaning forward, she drops her container into the trash.

"He shot her down instantly. Didn't even consider the offer."

"He's such a good man."

"He is. He's incredible. Jane…" Her pupils narrow, intently focused on my next words. "I love him." Jane's squeal surprises me and I immediately shush her. "Mr. Kline will hear you."

"I knew it, babe. I've been getting the vibes off you for a while. Did you tell him?"

"I've told him I've fallen in love with him but haven't said I love you yet."

"Are you planning something special to tell him or going to let it flow out while you're together?" The twitching I see in her hands tells me how much she's restraining her excitement.

"I'd like to—"

My words break off at the sound of my cell phone ringing. Glancing down, I see it's Todd's number. Immediately, my chest constricts, and I hit decline.

"Who was that?"

"Todd," I snarl.

"Are you serious? Why would he be calling? Doesn't he know when to let go?"

The blinking light indicates a voicemail. "He left a message. Let's see what he wants." Raising the phone, I click the voicemail icon. His normally smooth voice is cracked and emotional.

"Alex... I need you. My father... died Friday night. Please call me." The strain in his voice is real and so was the fighting of tears he choked back.

"Shit!"

"What's wrong?" Jane is standing next to my desk, her expression full of concern.

"Mr. Livingston passed away." Pain prickles my belly. The man was going to be my father-in-law. He was kind to me, actually cared about me. Even more, Todd thought the world of him. Saw him as a role model and tried to live up to Carl's reputation. There's no doubt Todd is a broken man right now.

"I should call him."

"What? No!"

"Jane, his father just died. He's heartbroken. He deserves a phone call back."

"Ugh. I'm not going to be witness to this. I need to go back to work. I'll call you later."

The smacking of her heels on the tile floor has an exaggerated stomp in each step. She'll get over it, or I'll have to ask for forgiveness in the form of her favorite sweet treat.

Quickly, I click Todd's missed call indicator and press the call button.

"Alex."

"I got your message."

"It hurts, Alex. He's gone. He's really gone."

"What happened?"

There's an agonizing pause. "...Heart attack. He died...in his sleep. The funeral is Sunday. Will you attend it with me? I need you, Alex...so much right now."

Hearing his voice crack and the emotional struggle on the other end of my receiver pulls at my heartstrings.

"I would like to pay my respects to your father...I'll go." I'm sure he hears the reluctance in my voice, but he doesn't acknowledge it.

"This means more to me than I can express. Thank you."

His voice cracks again and I know he's fighting the overwhelming emotions. I've been where he is, except I knew it was coming. I watched my mother wither and fade before me in hospice. I truly don't know what's worse, knowing there's nothing you can do to stop your parent's death or never being able to say goodbye.

As we disconnect, the memories rush through my mind, forcing the tears down my cheeks. It's a terrible thing for anyone to lose a parent too soon.

Our last workout session together is bittersweet. Carter has morphed my body and my heart. I'm a stronger woman emotionally and physically than when I first walked into the gym over eight weeks ago, and it's because of him. But he knows the heavy weight I'm carrying this evening is not because it's our last workout from Jane's certificate. Patiently, he's been watching, analyzing, waiting for me to share what's bothering me, what has fueled each punch, kick, and block in today's defense class.

Sitting on the bench, I swish water in my mouth before swallowing, avoiding his penetrating gaze. He looks off into space, his eyes revealing his concern, but also his patience. I don't want this awkward silence to continue into tonight's dinner. It's time to rip the band-aid off.

"Will you walk me to my car?"

Carter's muscles tense. "Yeah, of course."

The heavy silence grows more daunting as we near my vehicle.

"What's going on? You seem tense, afraid." Wrinkles form across his brow as he leans against my hood. "Come here." Opening his arms to me, I move between them, enveloped in his warmth. "Talk to me, beautiful. You're freaking me out."

"I have something to tell you you're not going to like."

"Okay." I can hear the concern, practically see the wheels turning as he quickly thinks of the possibilities.

"I got a call from Todd yesterday."

"Uh huh." I can already hear the contempt in his tone.

"His father passed away. He's asked me to attend the funeral."

"With him?"

"I plan to meet him there."

"I don't want you to go." His authoritative tone startles me.

"Carter, it's not about Todd. Carl Livingston was almost my father-in-law. I'd like to pay my respects."

"Going sends Todd a message."

"What message?"

"That there's hope, that there's a possibility for him to push his way back into your life."

"You and I both know what it's like to lose a parent too soon. This isn't about Todd and me. It's about Carl's passing."

"For you it is, but not for Todd."

"It sounds like you don't trust me."

"Don't twist my words. I don't want you to go because I don't want Todd anywhere near you. I don't want him to look at you, touch you, hold your hand, or cry on your shoulder."

"Carter, I'm going. It's the right thing to do."

"When will you stop letting Todd have a hold over you?"

"He doesn't have a hold over me." Pushing out of his arms, my eyes narrow on him. "Why would you say that?"

"If he doesn't have a hold over you, then don't go."

"You're not being reasonable. You're letting your jealousy get the best of you."

"Jealousy," Carter snickers. "That's what you think I'm feeling? It's not jealousy, it's having a sense of how a man like that works. Todd will make it through his father's passing with or without you, but having you there, it's a way for him to play to your heart."

"His father just died. I don't think mending things between us is on his mind right now."

"Don't be naïve. That's exactly what's on his mind."

Heat warms my cheeks as my palms clench to fists. "I think we should postpone dinner tonight. I've had enough of your insults."

"I don't think we should postpone dinner. I think we should talk this through."

"You mean, you talk, and I listen until you've convinced me not to go?"

"Truthfully, yes."

"I'd rather not have dinner with you until you apologize."

"Apologize for what? Wanting to protect my girl? Being honest with you?"

"No. For treating me like I'm the kind of woman who's easily fooled or disloyal to the man she loves. Just because Todd asked me to the funeral doesn't mean I'm going to go running back to his arms."

Placing my fingers on the handle, I open the door and give one last glance toward Carter before slamming the door shut. Stepping away from the hood, he lowers his head, shaking it before those damaged blues agonizingly watch me drive away.

Without Carter, dinner is lonely. I miss him, but I'm still pissed at him. I knew he wouldn't want me to go to the funeral which is why approaching the subject with him was difficult. I expected him to be uncomfortable, to not want me to go, but I didn't expect him to insult my loyalty or self-respect.

The sound of the TV is background noise. I'm too mentally distracted to absorb what's in front of me. The dinging of my phone has my attention though. It's the third text from Carter. Reaching down, I finally give in to my curiosity and guilt. Swiping the screen, his texts pop up.

I'm sorry. I hate that you're upset with me.

I understand this was about you paying your respects to his father and I made it about you and Todd.

I didn't mean to insinuate you would be disloyal. I hope you can understand it's difficult for me to be at home while you're with him, even if it's for a funeral.

My head falls back as I fight tears. I hate being upset with him. I don't want anything to create conflict between us.

Raising my head, I type back.

Will you come over?

227

It's only seconds before his response comes back.

On my way.

Quickly, I order delivery and freshen up my face. It's not long before his knuckles rap at the door.

Opening it, his sullen handsome face is on the other side. No words pass between us. He steps in and wraps his arms around me. Pulling back, he cups my face in his hands, kissing me.

"Does inviting me over mean you've forgiven me?"

"Yes."

The sound of his boot tapping the door reaches my ears just before the door shuts behind him.

"Can we turn this evening around where it ends with me making love to you?"

My fingers intertwine with his. "Yes, as long as we're on the same page."

Tilting his head up, he looks off, nibbles at his lip, then returns his gaze to me. "I think I have to accept you're going to the funeral no matter what I say, and you'll have to accept I'm not comfortable with you going."

"I agree. There's no ending to this where we both get what we want."

Pulling me back into his arms, he kisses my head as I lay it against his t-shirt covered chest.

"When is the funeral?"

"This Sunday."

Large, solid hands rub up and down along my back. "I wouldn't put it past him to try to open things up between you two again. The thought of him trying anything makes me nuts. Promise me you'll be on top of your game around him. He's more conniving than you realize."

Pulling back, I stare at him confused. "What do you mean?"

"I wanted to tell you before, but I knew if I said something you'd think I was trying to sabotage your and Todd's relationship."

"Tell me what?"

"I met Todd before. He and Kyle used to come to the gym together for a while. There was a blonde woman that caught my attention. I thought about asking her out to dinner or something. It's the only reason I noticed what happened next. When Todd saw her, he noticed her too, then the next day he came to work out at the gym alone. He spent the entire time flirting with her, then left with her. It was around the time you split up. Kyle confirmed the timeline."

Turning away from him, I pinch the bridge of my nose in a weak attempt to control my tears and to absorb the information he just dumped on me.

"You're telling me Todd cheated on me?"

"Kyle said it was close to the time you broke up. I can't say without a doubt he did."

"Kyle knew about the woman?"

Carter lets out a breath as he wipes his hand across his face. Regret etches itself into his expression.

"Yes, Kyle knew Todd had a fling with the woman. He said she was a rebound, someone to get his kicks with."

Wet, warm tears stream down my face. "If your goal was to ensure I don't go back to him, then you succeeded, even though you didn't need to. What hurts nearly as much as Todd's behavior is you all knew and didn't tell me. You all let me form a new relationship with him knowing he might have cheated on me or had a sexual fling while I was a broken woman, desperately trying to recover from the horrific trauma I suffered."

Carter steps closer and I back away. "I'm angry. So angry, Carter. I don't think tonight is going to end any other way than at the bottom of a wine bottle."

"This is why I don't want you anywhere near him. Every time he steps into your life, he causes you pain."

"Right now, the pain I feel is the betrayal of my closest friends, including you."

His eyes go wide. "Would you have believed me if I'd told you sooner?"

"I don't know. I wasn't given the chance to decide that."

"I liked you, Alex. I liked you from the first day we met, but you were set on giving your and Todd's relationship a second chance. Who was I to destroy that? I thought maybe the son-of-a-bitch had got his shit together and truly wanted to make it work. I saw that you were happy and I couldn't bring myself to be the one to ruin that. So I waited. I let things take their natural course and didn't intervene. Do you think that was easy? I hated seeing you with him. The day he walked into my gym to pick you up, the asshole threatened me. He told me if I said anything about the blonde he'd make sure you believed I was trying to sabotage your relationship and threatened to have me fired. Not that he could, but the audacity of that prick alone had me ready to wipe the floor with his arrogant smirk."

My tear-soaked eyes catch the bright light of the lamp as I turn to face Carter. "He threatened you?"

"Yes, this is why I'm coming clean about all of it. I want you to know what kind of man Todd really is. You shouldn't go to the funeral. You shouldn't go anywhere near him."

My doorbell rings and Carter's attention whips to the door. "Who is it?"

"It's dinner. I ordered delivery for us."

Opening the door, Carter takes the pizza, then pays the delivery guy.

"Have as much as you want. I'm not hungry." Dropping down on the couch, I place a pillow protectively on my lap.

Setting the box on my counter, Carter joins me on the couch. Putting his elbows on his knees, he rests his chin in his folded hands.

"I've hurt you twice tonight and I'm sorry. Hurting you is something I never want to do. I want to fix everything. I want to make you feel better. Tell me how." Leaning back against the couch he stares into my eyes, studying me, reading me as best he can.

"What's done is done." I sniffle, wiping my tears off my cheeks. "I just need time to work through it. I understand why you didn't leap to tell me. You didn't know if I'd believe you over Todd and you're right. I don't know what I would've believed. I was so caught up in trying to get back what I once had, it took me a while to realize he wasn't what I wanted anymore. I wouldn't have let him woo me away from you because…I love you."

Sliding his hand into mine, he rubs his thumb over it. A small gesture, but ample enough to pull at my heart.

"This isn't how I imagined telling you, but you need to know. I love you and it hurt me today when you insinuated I could easily be won back by Todd. I realized this evening you needed to know that won't happen because of how much I love you."

His free hand extends along the back of the couch and gently grazes my cheek before brushing my hair behind my ear.

"I love you too. That's why I handled your news so poorly today. You're my girl and I'll do anything to protect you and what we have. I saw you going to the funeral with Todd as a threat and reacted like an idiot. I can't say sorry enough, not until I know you're not hurting anymore."

"You don't have to worry about the funeral. I'm not going. Not after what you told me Todd did with that woman. Broken up or not, it disgusts me. I wish I hadn't wasted my time trying to reconcile things with him. I'm an idiot. I had an amazing guy right in front of me the whole time."

A smile lifts the corner of his mouth before fading. "You did, but you were worth the wait."

Leaning forward, I remove the pillow and ease into his open arms. Holding me close, he soothingly rubs my back and kisses my head.

"Can I hear you say it again?"

"What?"

"Those three words."

"I love you."

He squeezes me a little tighter. "Yeah, those words."

CHAPTER THIRTY-THREE

—

ALEX

Cool water ripples around the lounge pool float I'm resting on. The midday sun bathes my skin in comforting warmth. Next to me, Jane's voice drags me back from the nap I was close to.

"I'm glad you came to my house today instead of the funeral."

"I feel bad missing it to be honest, but I have no desire to be near Todd."

"I'm relieved Carter told you the truth. I have no doubt it was painful to hear, but you needed to know."

My gaze shifts from the puffy white clouds against the baby blue sky to Jane's pained expression. "I was angry with all of you, but after thinking it through this week, I realized why you didn't say anything. None of you wanted me to think you were trying to sabotage the relationship because I did know none of you wanted me to be with him."

"It's true. We didn't, but we wanted you to make the decision on your own and not be influenced by our feelings toward him. Well, Kyle and Carter felt that way. I never hid how I felt about it." Her sheepish grin brings a smile to my face.

"That's why you're my best friend. You never shy away from telling me how it really is."

"Always," she giggles atop the rim of her cup before sipping her drink. "Even though you didn't get to tell Carter how you felt the way you wanted to, are you glad you told him you love him?"

"I am. Our argument brought us closer. We've been having deeper conversations about the future and what we both want."

"Like marriage and kids?" Jane grins.

"Yes, like marriage and kids."

"I'll make a hell of a maid of honor."

"Let's not get carried away. We aren't talking anytime soon."

"Sure, sure. Whatever you say, babe."

With the flick of my wrist I splash water in her direction. The carefree laughter rolling from our bellies makes me forget all about Todd and the funeral.

My feet swing through the air as I land on my couch. With my phone in hand, I read Carter's text that he'll be over later after he's done changing the oil on his mom's car. With a text back, I let him know I'll have dinner waiting for him. It's a while before I need to start cooking, so I set the phone down and swap it for my glass of wine and the TV remote.

The warm sun, drinks, and time with Jane did me good today. I feel refreshed, relaxed, and eager to see Carter. A sudden pounding on my door startles me, shifting my glass in my hand and spilling wine on my couch. "Shit!" Thankfully I chose white wine this evening.

"Just a minute!"

Carrying the glass to the kitchen counter, I set it down and amble to the door, irritated with the interruption to my relaxing evening.

With a look through the peephole I see Todd on the other side. He appears disheveled, still in a funeral suit, the tie crooked, his hair every which way as if he'd been running his hands through it. Turning my back against the door, I bite my lip. I can't pretend I'm not home. I already announced my presence. Idiot!

"Todd, now's not a good time." I wince, hoping he'll accept that and go away.

"Please, Alex, let me in." His voice is strained, broken.

"I know you're hurting. I can't fix it for you."

"Alex, please, I need you. I'm begging you."

A thud hits my door. I look through the peephole to see Todd's head collapsed against his folded arm and my door. I can hear the tears from my side. The memories of my lonely, tear-filled nights creep into my mind. Guilt picks at my stomach, nagging me.

Slowly my hand turns the bolt and opens the door. His tear streaked face meets mine.

"Thank you."

Wobbling over my threshold, the stench of alcohol is heavy.

"Did you drive here?"

"Took a cab from the bar."

With a hand to his arm to stabilize him, I usher him toward my couch. "You should sit down. You don't look well."

"I'm not," he stammers.

Letting me assist him to the couch, he forcefully pulls me down next to him.

"Why didn't you come today?" He sounds angry, distraught, not himself.

"I don't think it's the right time to explain it."

"I want to know why."

Frustrated, I confess. "Because I learned about the blonde woman from the gym—Lana."

His hand brushes through his hair, tugging at it. "Fuck Lana, she didn't mean anything to me. It was always you. You were meant to be my wife. But my fiancé couldn't stand to have me touch her. For a little while I just needed a woman to want me. I closed my eyes and imagined she was you when I fucked her."

Standing, my chest constricts, and I fight back the feeling of nausea. "I think you should go."

"I don't want to go. I want us back. I want to be inside my girl and forget all this pain."

Bold hands touch my hair, fisting it as his other arm wraps around my waist, holding me tight against him. Turning, I back out of his grasp, placing a hand at his chest.

"You've had a lot to drink tonight. You're upset and not yourself. You should go home and sleep it off."

"You're all I've thought about. Night after night. It didn't matter who I dated or slept with, you'd come back into my mind when I'd close my eyes to sleep. I missed the smell of your body next to me. The feel of your soft skin…" My back hits the counter as Todd's fingers swipe across my lips. "The way you'd react when I kissed you."

The taste of liquor fills my mouth as his tongue forces between my lips. Shoving him back a step, he stares at me bewildered.

"You need to go. I'm in a relationship with Carter. You and I…we aren't good for each other…there's too much baggage. We've hurt each other too many times."

Taking my hand, he steps closer. "I never wanted to hurt you. I tried to wait, but you shut me out. My touch revolted you. Do you know how that made me feel?"

"I didn't realize how much until it was too late."

Touching my cheek, his thumb brushes over my jaw. "It's not too late for us. I'm willing to do what it takes to have you. Let me have you. Let me love you."

Leaning in for another kiss, I press my hand to his chest, stopping him. "You're not in a good place right now. You've lost your father, you're emotional, you've been drinking. I'm going to call you a cab to take you home."

Moving to the coffee table, I pick up my phone. Todd seizes it from my grasp.

"I'm not going home. We have more to talk about."

"Give me the phone. Carter is coming over soon and you need to be gone before he gets here."

"What the hell do you see in him?"

My hand swipes across my moist forehead.

"Todd, don't do this."

"Have you slept with him?"

Glossy hazel-green eyes narrow in on me. For the first time, the look in Todd's eyes frightens me. Shifting, I try to move past him and he blocks me.

"That's none of your business."

"You did, didn't you? You spread your legs for a man you barely know, but you cry when I put my dick on you?"

"That's enough! You need to leave!"

"Why do I repulse you? I'm not the man who raped you!"

The slap echoes and stings my hand before I realize what I've done.

"I'm sorry. You need to go. We can't fight like this."

Touching his reddening cheek, his eyes transition. My phone whips through the air, crashing into the wall behind me.

"Nothing in my life is right! We would've been married by now! You'd be having my child! Your rapist didn't destroy only your life, Alex. He took away mine too!"

"I know you're hurting, but being here, fighting with me, it isn't helping."

With tears in his eyes, Todd rushes forward and forces me into his arms, burying his head in my hair.

"I'm sorry I walked out on you. I never should've let you go." One hand cups my head as the other rubs along my back. "My father told me to always go after what I want. To not give up until I have it in my hands. That's you, Alex. You're what I want. I realize that now more than ever." Easing his grip, he wipes at the tear falling down my cheek.

"Call Carter, tell him not to come. Give us tonight."

Another tear falls as I struggle with the emotions this fight is bringing out of us.

Running my hand down his arm, I shake my head.

"I can't. I don't want us anymore. I want to be with Carter."

The sudden force of Todd's muscled arm shoving me onto the couch shocks me.

"No, you don't. You think you do because it's easy with him. Love isn't easy. When you love someone, you fight for them."

"This isn't like you. I've never seen you act this way."

Dropping to his knees in front of me, he caresses along my legs. "Because I'm here, pouring my heart out to you and you're trying to shove me out the door."

Both our heads snap to the sound of my phone ringing.

"That's him, isn't it?"

When I attempt to stand, Todd pushes me back down. "Let it go to voicemail."

"Why don't we put this conversation on hold and finish it when you're feeling more yourself."

"I know you, you'll do everything you can to shut me out. Avoid my calls, texts, visits. I have you here now. Let's talk now."

"I don't feel there's anything else to discuss. We want different things."

"What changed?" Todd's grip on my knees tighten, and he drags me forward, closer to him. "You wanted us to get back together. Why don't you want that now?"

"We're different people than we were two or three years ago. I'm...a different woman. What we had is gone. We can't get back to where we were."

"But you still love me, don't you? I saw it in your eyes the day at the beach. I saw how hard it was for you to walk away from me."

My head lowers. "You're right, it was. You do hold a special place in my heart. We share a strong history together."

"If Carter wasn't in the picture, would you want to be with me?"

"It's not that simple. It's not only how I feel about Carter. It's how I feel about you. I'm...not in love with you."

His grip on my legs tighten as an uncontrollable growl escapes his chest. "Fuck, Alex. Kick a man while he's down, why don't you?"

"I don't want to hurt you. I'm being honest with you."

"Then tell me, have you slept with him?"

"Todd." I place my hands over his and try to slide them off my knees. He doesn't budge, and my nerves kick up a notch.

241

"Tell me." He reads my eyes and my silence, getting the answer he doesn't want. "That's what I thought. You let him fuck you."

Dropping down onto the floor, he lays on his back. "Jesus, Alex. How do you think this makes me feel? I wasn't sure we were done, but you've made it pretty clear we are by letting another man fuck you."

"You've had too much to drink. You were at your father's funeral earlier today. I know how much it hurts to lose a parent. I want to be there for you, but we can't keep on like this. You need to go home and get some rest."

Leaning over, I take his hand and try to raise him off the floor.

Jerking his arm, he pulls me down on top of him. Clutching me in his grasp, he keeps me from getting up. One arm raises, and he grazes his hand over my face as he stares at me.

"You've hurt me. Really hurt me."

Wiggling, I try to free myself.

His expression morphs as he recognizes my desire to break free.

"That's right. I remember how much you hate my touch."

With my hair tight in his grip, he shoves me off him. Pain ripples across my shoulder and cheek as I'm slammed into the coffee table. Buckling over, my hand goes to my face as I struggle to stand.

"Shit, Alex. I didn't mean to—"

"Leave!"

"Let me help you." Reaching his hand out for me, I swat it away.

"Get out!"

Todd stares at me, different thoughts crossing over his eyes. With a pissed off click of his tongue, he storms toward the door.

With his hand on the knob, he stops and turns back to me. "I really do love you. I never wanted it to be like this between us."

"You're an asshole. That's why I chose Carter. He'd never walk out on me, give up on me, or push me before I'm ready. He'd never treat me like you did tonight."

Jaw twitching, he looks straight ahead and breathes in deep. I watch his profile, seeing the effect my words have on him just before he turns his back to me and walks out.

The materials of my first aid kit are scattered across my bathroom sink. Rushing to tear the gauze package open, I glance in the mirror at the bruised and broken skin on my face. My time is short before Carter arrives and I'm scared of how he'll react when he sees me. I'm afraid to lie to him, but even more afraid if I tell him the truth he'll go after Todd. Any fights outside the ring can get him suspended or lose his contract with Knock Out Champions.

I reach for my phone. I can cancel tonight. Avoid him until my face is healed. My shaky fingers fumble over the touch keys as tears stream down my cheeks. I never should've opened the door. *Why did I open the door?*

My heart stops when I hear the familiar knock. Quickly, I toss everything into the first aid kit and put it back under my sink. Rushing to the front door, I look through the peephole at Carter.

"I was just going to call you. I'm not feeling well. I think I got the stomach flu. I don't want to give it to you. Let's reschedule for another night."

"I'm not worried about getting sick," Carter chuckles. "I've been anxious to see you all day. Let me in. I'll take care of you, hold your hair back."

More tears uncontrollably escape my eyes. My back goes to the door and I slide down until I'm a ball on the floor. I want him to hold me, confess to him everything that happened, but I know what will come of it, and I can't do that to him.

"I'm so sorry, I'm really not feeling well. I promise to make it up to you."

"You're really not going to let me in?"

"It's best I don't."

"All right. I'll head home. Call me if you change your mind. I don't care what time it is. Love you."

"Love you too. Thank you for understanding."

I wait as he reluctantly walks away from my door. When I know he's gone, the events of the evening playback through my mind, tormenting me, reminding me how foolish I'd been. Pushing myself to my feet, I amble to the kitchen, pour myself a glass of wine, chug it down, wipe away my tears and head to my bathroom to clean my face and shower.

CHAPTER THIRTY-FOUR

—

ALEX

"Alex, what happened to your face?" Carter's panicked tone startles me awake.

My heart jumps to my throat. Shielding my face, I look at Carter, standing over my bed, concern etched into his brows.

"How'd you get in?"

"I stopped by Kyle and Jane's for the spare key. I wanted to be here when you woke up so I could take care of you today. I didn't think you'd be going into work. Now tell me, please, what happened to your face?"

My bed sinks in from the weight of his body. I stare back at his baby blues, pleading with me to explain.

"You're not sick, are you?"

A slight whimper escapes me. "No."

"Come here."

He opens his arms and I fall into them. Tears pool in my eyes as he runs his hands over my hair and back.

"Can you talk about it? Is it why you wouldn't let me in last night?"

"No and yes."

"Did someone hurt you?"

"I'm fine. It was an accident."

I wince when his hand grazes my shoulder. Attention going to my shoulder, he examines it, then my face.

"Tell me, please, did someone hurt you?"

"Todd—"

His tone swiftly changes. "He was here last night?"

"He had too much to drink. We got into an argument. It was an accident. He didn't mean to—"

"To what? Hit you?"

"He shoved me off him and I fell into the coffee table."

"Why was he shoving *you* off him?"

"He had pinned me to him and I was trying to break free. He got angry and shoved me away."

Scooting farther back on my bed, Carter takes me with him, cradling me in his protective arms.

"Tell me everything from the moment he showed up at your door."

As I explain the events of the evening, he keeps his calm demeanor, rubbing over my body, wiping each tear that dribbles down my cheek. As I get to the end, I feel his muscles tightening, see his jaw flexing. A haze covers his usually sparkling blue eyes.

"He walked out after hurting you like that?"

"I made him. I didn't want his help. He wasn't himself last night. I've never seen him act that way."

"Alcohol and desperation can do dangerous things to a man."

"You were right." Laying my head against his shoulder, I nestle further into his arms. "The funeral would have been an opening for him to pursue something between us. That was made clear last night."

With a kiss to my head, he sighs. "I didn't want to be right. I wanted you to be safe and that didn't happen. I'd like you to stay with me for a while. I don't want you here alone if Todd comes back."

Leaning back, I study his handsome face and lose myself in the deep pool of blue staring back at me, awaiting my response. After last night's fight with Todd, the thought of being in the safety of Carter's home, going to bed and waking up in his arms gives me comfort. I don't want another visit from Todd like last night.

"You wouldn't mind having me around all the time?"

Calloused fingers send a soothing sensation over my skin as he caresses my cheek and jaw, just below the broken, bruised skin.

"I'm debating whether or not it should be a permanent move."

"Yeah?"

Leaning forward, he kisses my tender skin. "It kills me I wasn't able to protect you last night. Had I been here, Todd's face would be the one bruised, not yours."

Placing my hand on his shoulder, I rub along his arm, enjoying the feel of his soft cotton shirt and warm skin beneath my fingers.

"You're here now giving me the comfort I need. That means so much to me."

Gentle lips press to my forehead. Curling at the nape of my neck, his strong fingers caress my hair and neck as I raise my chin and kiss him.

"Will you help me pack my things?"

"Of course. Bring as much as you want. I want you to feel comfortable at my place."

Grudgingly, I move out of his arms and head to my closet to gather my luggage bags. Just inside, I lean back to look at Carter. He's sitting on the edge of my bed, his knees resting on his elbows, his chin dropped in his hands, deep in thought.

"Carter."

The hardened muscles of his back shift as he turns my direction.

"Yeah, beautiful?"

"You okay?"

"Yeah, tell me what you need me to do."

CHAPTER THIRTY-FIVE

—

CARTER

Standing in the doorway of my bedroom, I watch Alex unpack her last bag. Her fight with Todd is visibly worn on her body by her fatigued movements, the puffy, red broken skin on her cheek, and her bruised and scraped shoulder. Exhaustion, mental and emotional, has dulled her bright green eyes. Sliding the luggage bag under my bed, she crawls atop the mattress and I come to her side as she covers herself with my blanket.

"You mind if I take a nap? I feel so tired."

Brushing her chocolate hair away from her face, I caress her cheek before leaning down to kiss her. "Not at all. I have some things I need to take care of. I'll get 'em done while you sleep." Tugging at my arm, she pulls me down onto the bed with her.

"Don't go. Lay with me." Turning to her side, she tucks her back to my front as I wrap my arm around her.

"I'm not going to say no to that."

Lying next to her, listening to her breathing, I do what I've done all day, hide the rage that's been festering in my gut since I saw her damaged face this morning. Fear, true fear seized me when I saw her. In that moment, many possibilities went through my mind of what caused it. None of them were good and that fear was an excruciating ache that took hold of my entire body. I haven't tasted fear like that since I received the news my father had died in a motorcycle accident. Feeling that fear for Alex is something I never want to feel again.

When I realized her injured face was the reason she didn't let me in the night before I had a suspicion it had something to do with Todd. Quickly, she confirmed that suspicion. Staying with me keeps her safe to a certain point, but I can't be with her at all times, at work, when she's with Jane. No, there's one problem that still remains—Todd.

Carefully, I ease my arm from under her and roll to the opposite side of my bed. With one last glance over my shoulder, I check to ensure she's still resting peacefully.

Honking cars and the scent of exhaust fumes reach my nostrils as I remove my helmet and set it on my bike. With it being Monday, the city is abuzz with life—pedestrians walking with their cell phones in hand, taxis looking for work, cars driving too quickly. Glancing at my watch, I see it's nearly time for the suits to be leaving their desk jobs. Leaning against my bike, I wait for Todd to leave his office building which was easy to find with a simple Google search.

With each sparkling suit that walks out, my muscles tense, expecting it to be Todd. Finally, the fifth suit is him.

"Livingston!"

Turning his head my direction, he sees me and stops abruptly, unsure of how to react. I can see the fight-or-flight response washing over his face. Surprisingly, the bastard sticks around even walks over to me. Being a lawyer, I'm sure he's convinced the witnesses will be at his advantage. Stopping a couple feet in front of me, conveniently out of reach, he nods.

"I know why you're here."

"You left her pretty banged up."

"I tried to help her, but she didn't want it."

"And that's your justification for walking out after hurting her?"

"I didn't mean to hurt her."

"That's what happens when a man can't control his aggression after too many drinks; he accidentally hurts people."

"Yeah, all right. I was out of line. I plan on apologizing to her."

"No, man." My thumb brushes across my puckered brow. Apparently, I need to spell it out for him. "You're not going to apologize to her. You're going to stay the fuck away from her…for good."

"Is that a threat?" Todd's eyes narrow on me. The attorney in him is taking over.

"Yeah, damn straight it is. Stay the fuck away. Don't show up at her house or her work. Don't call, don't text, don't even email. Don't send her gifts either. You see her in public, walk away. Because I'm telling you now, you come near her, and I'll put you in the hospital."

His jaw flexes. He's not ready to back down.

"Don't you dare threaten me. What happened between Alex and me is exactly that, between her and me. If I want to see her, I will. Don't think coming to my workplace and making idle threats is going to scare me. Alex might think you're what's good for her right now, but we both know your foolish dream of becoming somebody someday will only drag her down with you. If it wasn't for you getting in my way, we'd still be together."

Stepping closer, I narrow the space between us. "You're more arrogant than I thought if you think I'm the reason you're not together. You're the reason you're not together anymore. She finally saw you for who you really are—a sleazy, arrogant, spoiled rich boy who can't handle it when he doesn't get what he wants."

Hazel-green eyes narrow to slits as his nostrils flare. "I can take it all away from you, you know that? I have the means and the money. I can bury you, make you wish you'd never gotten in my way."

"Who's giving idle threats now? But go ahead, try to take it all from me, try to ruin my career, she'll still love me, and knowing that eats at you. She doesn't love you. She doesn't want to have anything to do with you."

253

Grabbing his jacket, I force his face to mine. Bringing my voice low, I make sure my words are clear.

"And my threats aren't idle. I'll tear you limb from fucking limb. *Stay away from her*."

Flinging his arm up, he breaks my contact with his jacket and shoves at me. "Keep your hands off me."

His tone drips with arrogance. Nothing I've said to him got through. I didn't want it to come to this. I didn't want to have to hit him, but it's obvious putting fear in him is the only way to get through.

My arm swings, one smooth solid punch and he goes down like a limp sack. If there were witnesses, they didn't seem to care. The pedestrians keep walking as if they didn't even notice. Looking down at Todd, I finally see the hint of fear that's needed.

"Stay. Away. From. Her."

With nothing else to be said, I turn to leave. My muscles tighten at the tension of a man's hand on my shoulder. Spinning, I'm prepared to land another punch. Todd's fist clocks my jaw. A cheap shot, my back barely turned. Stumbling backward, my foot catches on the sidewalk, and the view of a royal blue hood blurs my vision.

CHAPTER THIRTY-SIX

—

ALEX

Dry lips abrasively graze my ear as he whispers to me, "It's unfortunate our time together has to end."

Cold steel touches my belly and scrapes along my skin. Around me, the pillow is saturated with my tears, but I've gone numb to all sensation. Fear has consumed me, body and soul, but it's my will that fights for life, unwilling to give up, to give in.

Sweat drenched sheets peel away from my skin as I snap awake. I grasp for Carter, but he's gone.

"Carter," I call out, my voice shaky.

Silence.

Entering the living room, I find my phone and look at the missed calls and texts as I wipe away a lone tear. There are several missed calls from an unknown number that's left a voicemail. Immediately, I listen to it. On the other end, Sandy's distraught voice asks me to call her as soon as possible. Worry seizes my chest as my hands fumble to call her back.

"Alex?"

"Yes, where's Carter? What's wrong?"

"Oh, sweetheart." Her voice breaks between tears. "You need to come to Advance Medical immediately."

My knees weaken and I reach out for the counter to stabilize myself.

"Please, Sandy, tell me he's ok."

"Just get here as soon as you can."

My body trembles with fear as I pass through the hospital's sliding doors. Sandy and Kevin clasp onto me as I reach them.

"Where is he? What's happened?" I plead.

"He's in surgery. He was hit by a car," Kevin explains quickly.

His massive arms hold me steady as my knees weaken.

"How bad is it?" I stammer.

"It's bad. Head and back injury. We won't know anything more until he's out of surgery."

"I…can't…lose him," I cry out.

Kevin's arms enfold me as I sob into his shirt. My very core ruptures in agonizing pain. Sandy's hand rubs up and down my back barely registering amidst the fear consuming me.

"My baby, he's so strong, he'll fight through this. He needs our prayers, sweetheart. That's what he needs right now."

Three agonizing hours pass before medical staff comes to find us. In the waiting room, we huddle around the weary surgeon. Lost in my emotions, all I can do to keep my composure is stare at the silver wedding band on his finger.

"He's made it through the surgery. He's resting now in an induced coma. We'll ease him out of it in forty-eight hours. He's suffered injuries to his head, lower vertebrae, and spinal cord. It's too soon to judge the permanent effects, but at this time, he's lost mobility in his right leg."

Tears pool in my eyes. Kevin's arm reaches around me, holding me steady.

"Can we see him?" Sandy asks.

Empathetic brown eyes glance at each of us. "One person, briefly, his body needs the rest."

Sandy looks to us and Kevin and I nod at her to go. She follows the doctor out, her head hanging low as she wipes at her face with a tissue.

My sobs break the silence. Kevin eases me back into the stiff hospital chair.

"Little bird, he's alive. Carter is a fighter. If they say he'll never walk again, he'll prove them otherwise. He's always been that way. Nothing stops him."

Looking into Kevin's dark blue eyes, I want to believe that. I want to have hope, but I know the cruel ways of life all too well.

"If he can't walk, he won't be able to fight. He's going to lose everything he's worked for. He didn't deserve this. He's an incredible man. He deserves so much better than this."

A firm hand rubs along my upper back.

"We don't know that yet. We have to wait. It's going to be a long, hard road ahead, but the most important thing is he's alive."

"It's excruciating not being able to go in there and talk to him, hold him, or kiss him."

"You love him a lot, don't you?"

My eyes pinch closed, fighting tears as I nod.

"He loves you too. You're the first woman to be put in the same conversation as the word marriage. Just don't tell him I told you that." He winks.

A smile tilts the corner of my mouth. "Thank you."

With a tap to my knee, he stands. His massive frame blocks out the doorway behind him.

"I know you don't want to leave, but you should go home and rest. We won't be able to talk to him until he's out of the induced coma. He wouldn't want you waiting uncomfortably in these shitty chairs for the next forty-eight hours."

"I moved into his house today. If I go back there, I won't be able to stop crying."

"What about at your place?"

A sullen feeling drops to the pit of my stomach. "I don't want to go back there either."

"That got anything to do with the cut on your face?"

I'd completely forgotten about it until now.

"Yeah," I admit, embarrassed.

Studying my face, he tries to read me. "Is there somewhere else you'll be comfortable?"

"I'll call my friend, Jane. I'll stay with her."

With a nod, he seems satisfied. At the sound of Sandy's return, Kevin and I look to her, observing her emotional state.

"He's sleeping, but I still talked to him. I told him how much we all love him and that we'll be praying for him and be here when he wakes up."

Fresh tears sting my eyes at the sight of Sandy's struggle to stay composed. Kevin moves in and hugs her, giving her the comfort she needs.

"Uh, uh," a man clears his throat behind us.

Two men stand side by side, one in a hospital uniform and the other in a police uniform.

"Mrs. Maxwell, this officer is here to speak with you all."

Our attention turns to the officer as he steps farther into the room. He's tall in stature, a little round in the belly, and exudes authority.

"Mrs. Maxwell, I'm officer Carnes. I'm here to inform you there's been an investigation opened in response to your son's accident."

"What do you mean?" Sandy asks, confused.

"The driver of the vehicle who hit your son reported that a man pushed your son into oncoming traffic and that's why he was hit."

"Someone pushed him? Why would they do that?" Her tone sounds as horrified as I know we're all feeling.

"The accident happened on Morris Avenue. Do you know anyone who works or lives around there?"

My hand goes to my mouth as I gasp. The light in the room suddenly seems blinding, the air thick. I lose sense of direction and barely feel Kevin's hand touch my arm.

"She's about to faint. Get a nurse." I hear someone say.

The cool glass of water in my hands does nothing to soothe my dry throat. Across the table, Officer Carnes awaits my answer. We're alone in a borrowed room of the hospital. He insisted on speaking with me as soon as the nurse checked my stats and gave me the clear.

"And it was Mr. Livingston who shoved you into the coffee table, causing the injury to your face and shoulder?"

"Yes."

"Would you be willing to let me take pictures of your injuries for evidence?"

The memories of the last time an officer asked me that sends chills down my spine.

"Yes."

"And you believe Mr. Maxwell went to Morris Avenue to confront Mr. Livingston about your altercation?"

"Yes. As I stated before, that's where Todd works. His office building is there. Carter must have gone to talk to him."

Officer Carnes' face contorts into an expression of sympathy as he watches me wipe stray tears off my face.

"It's all my fault this happened. If I hadn't opened the door and let Todd in, he wouldn't have hurt me, and Carter never would've gone to confront him."

Officer Carnes closes his notebook and leans back in the chair, meeting my gaze.

"Miss DeMarco, I've been doing this job for over ten years. I've seen many horrible things and more times than I can count, I've seen women blame themselves for things that happened that were completely out of their control. You can't see the future, nor can you control what another human will do. Don't blame yourself. It's a guilt too strong for any one person to carry." His smile, even though it's brief, is comforting.

"Please wait here. I'm going to call a crime tech to come to the hospital and take photos of your injuries and Mr. Maxwell's."

CHAPTER THIRTY-SEVEN

—

ALEX

It's two days later and I fearfully walk into the hospital. After breaking down and telling Sandy and Kevin everything that happened, I expected them to be furious, to blame me and tell me to stay away from Carter, but they didn't. They comforted me through my tears, listened to everything and insisted I come back today.

As I pass through the sterile halls, I'm more aware of the sounds and smells of the hospital than before. I notice the multitude of staff and how busy they are rushing from one place to the next. Reaching the elevator, I press the button to Carter's floor. I'm incredibly eager to see him, talk to him, show him how grateful I am that he's alive.

The elevator dings and I step off onto his floor. Making my way to his room, I stop just outside of it when I hear the doctor and Sandy talking.

"How long do you think this will last?" I hear Sandy ask.

"It's hard to say. It can be a temporary effect from the head trauma or it could be permanent. It's something we'll have to monitor. For now, bring him photos and things that are a part of his life, talk about memories, but most importantly, be patient with him, explain who you are to him, and try not to get upset when he can't remember. It will cause further stress and confusion to his brain."

A lump forms in my throat. Turning into his room, my eyes go directly to him and the heart monitor next to his bed. Asleep, he looks peaceful, but my stomach churns at the bandage on his head and the bruised and broken skin on his face and arm.

Approaching the bed slowly, I fight back the distressing tears. Sliding my hand beneath his, I stare at him, unable to fully absorb all that has happened. All that I've just heard.

"He's lost his memory?" The words are barely more than a whisper.

"I'm sorry to say, he has. We don't know yet if it's permanent."

"When he wakes up, he'll have no idea who I am?"

"Unfortunately, no. He'll remember what things are, what they're used for, but the part of his brain that processes the emotional connection to memories and retrieves them has suffered trauma."

My eyes pinch close as I bring his hand to my lips. Kissing it, I long for this to all be a bad dream. The tears I've cried endlessly for two days pour down my cheeks. It's an agony as painful as my assault. The man I love has no memory of what I mean to him.

Sandy comes to my side, rubbing my back. "I know, sweetheart, I know how much it hurts. He didn't know who I was when I came in his room this morning. He was frightened. The doctor gave him something to relax him."

"I encourage you all to continue to visit, but we need to ease him into it. It's best he's not overwhelmed. To him, you're all strangers. He doesn't understand the emotional connection you each have with him. I'll arrange for a therapist to meet with him. She's very good, she's a friend of mine who works here at the hospital. She'll be able to help him transition and cope with the unfamiliarity of his environment."

"Thank you, Doctor Keller."

"I'll do everything I can to help your son recover. He'll wake up soon. Be prepared to introduce yourselves."

Doctor Keller quietly slips out to attend to his other patients. His tall frame leaves my peripheral, but I never take my eyes off Carter. Caressing his cheek, I lean in and kiss him, fully aware this is the only time I'll be able to steal a moment of the Carter I know and the man who loves me.

Carter stirs, and I ease my hand out of his and quickly wipe my tears from my cheeks. Sandy does the same and we both take several steps back from his bed.

Grimacing, his eyes open. He reaches for the water next to his bed and I move to get it for him. His eyes lock on mine. Studying me, he reads my face, the same way he always has.

"I'm Alex," I say, handing the cup to him.

Tipping the glass to his lips, he lowers it and stares at me and Sandy.

"I know both of you, don't I?"

"Yes, I'm your mother, Sandy, and Alex is your girlfriend."

Gaze steady on me, his expression is unreadable, but his blue eyes spark as he looks at me.

"I imagine this is awkward for you, being told complete strangers are your family and friends. I have a few pictures on my phone if you'd like to see them. For entertainment purposes, at least."

The corner of his mouth lifts. "I wouldn't mind seeing them."

Pulling my phone from my back pocket, I swipe the screen and find the pictures. Stepping closer to the bed, I hold the phone out for him to see.

Taking my phone from my hand, his fingers graze mine, and I force myself to shove my leaping emotions back down.

Swiping right, he looks through my pictures. He studies them with the same look of concentration as he did me.

"We look really happy together. Are we?"

"Very," Sandy replies. "Happiest I've seen you with a woman."

My head lowers and I try so hard not to cry.

Raising his hand, he offers the phone back. "I can see you're hurting. I'm sorry I can't remember you. I wish I did."

"It's okay, don't feel guilty. Please. I don't want you to feel bad when you see me. If you don't mind, I'd like to come visit you often, let you get to know me…again."

His baby blues roam over my face, studying me again, seeming to take in every detail about me. "I'd like that."

Relief fills me from head to toe. Behind us, the sound of Kevin's heavy footsteps enters the room.

"Bro, you're awake. About time."

Carter's face tenses. He looks at Kevin, startled—in his mind, he's seeing him for the first time. Kevin observes Carter's uncomfortable expression and goes silent.

"Kevin, step out with me. I need to talk with you."

"Sure, Ma."

The door closes behind them and Carter's gaze switches from the door to me. "That's my brother, huh?"

"Yeah, you two are…were super close. He's a year older than you and weighs probably twice as much as you."

The corners of Carter's eyes crease when he chuckles. "He is a big dude." Attention returned to me, his mouth twists. "Alex?" He pauses, as if afraid he doesn't have the right name.

"Yeah?" His expression relaxes when I respond.

"How long have we been together?"

"A couple months, but I think we both feel like it's been longer."

"My family seems to really like you."

"I adore them. Your family is wonderful. They accepted me with open arms and have treated me with nothing but kindness."

"What about your family? They like me?"

266

"My family consists of my best friend, Jane and her husband, Kyle. My mother passed away six years ago. My father remarried and moved to the UK. I have a sister, but we haven't spoken to each other in years."

"Why is that? If you don't mind me asking."

"We dealt with my mother's death in very different ways. I stayed by my mother's side and my sister came to see her in hospice twice. She's a lot like my father. They run from their emotions."

"You miss her?"

Talking with Carter is easy. I step closer to his bed and lean on the edge. His body language indicates he doesn't mind.

"I do sometimes. There are times I wonder how she's doing. If she's gotten married, had kids."

"Do you have any…kids?"

I shake my head. "Never married, no kids."

"If you don't mind me asking, how old are you?"

I chuckle. "Maybe you should guess first."

"You're stunning. I'm guessing you're older than you actually look. You're in shape, clearly take care of your body. Mmm, twenty-six?"

"Close, I'm twenty-eight."

Carter laughs to himself. "I have no idea when my birthday is. How old am I?"

"You're thirty. Your birthday is March eleventh."

"What's the date today?"

"June fourteenth."

"When's your birthday?"

"May eleventh."

"Our birthdays are on the same day?"

I laugh at the astonished look on his face. "They are. Different months, same days."

"What do you do for a living?"

"I work for a company called Kevlar and Kline. They make the bulletproof vests for law enforcement. I'm their operations specialist. I handle their contracts with clients."

"That's a great job."

"Thank you."

"What do I do?"

"A few things. You work at a gym as an instructor and personal trainer. You teach kickboxing, self-defense classes, and more. You also have a contract as an MMA fighter."

"Wow, MMA, huh?" Carter looks down, examining his body. "I don't think the MMA contract is going to work out. The doctor told me I've lost mobility in my right leg and have nerve damage from the car accident. Is that how you got the cut on your face? Were you injured in the accident too?"

My head drops, and I struggle to find the right words.

"Alex, don't answer that. I can see that topic hurts you to talk about."

"I'm so sorry, Carter."

The tears unleash, and my fear forces me to run, rushing out of the room, afraid of causing him any added stress.

CHAPTER THIRTY-EIGHT

—

CARTER

When the woman, Sandy, my mother told me Alex was my girlfriend it was a strange feeling, but I didn't dislike the news. One look at her and I was smitten, memory or not. She's gorgeous and sweet and I could tell she has a sense of humor beneath the sorrow. When she ran out, I didn't like seeing her go, but I understand this is hard for her in an entirely different way than it is for me. I don't know her, but she knows me better than I know myself.

Kevin, my brother, told me she's been through a lot and that she's taking my accident the hardest out of everyone. I asked why, but he kept it vague, not diving into detail. It seems no one wants to say much about my accident except the doctor. Maybe it's still too hard for them to talk about.

I haven't seen Alex in two days, but I've thought about her. I can't help wondering when she'll come back or if she'll ever come back.

After meeting with a therapist, I got a better understanding of how to cope with the overwhelming emotions of my family and friends. She encouraged me to ask questions, start a journal, and note anything I feel is important. She suggested I view everything new as an opportunity to discover things about myself. We started with something simple, coffee and tea. I drank both and discovered I'm a fan of tea as long as it's got honey in it.

My family has brought photographs in and a few memorabilia items like my bike helmet. Kevin says I love that bike more than a man should. He's a jokester, I like that about him. Talking to him is effortless. He knows a lot about my past and answers my endless barrage of questions without complaint.

Another man, Kyle, stopped in. Says he's my best friend, besides Kevin. He's got a pretty wife who kept looking at me like I was a fascinating science project. She didn't stay long which left time for Kyle and me to get reacquainted. He knows Alex well. Had a lot of nice things to say about her. I asked him where she was, and he said she was struggling to cope with some things and needed some time. She's been staying at his and Jane's place. I learned she was moving in with me just before the accident. Kyle said she stayed at my house last night.

After he left, I laid in bed wondering what my house looks like, how Alex felt being there alone. It's an odd sensation having guilt for another person's pain you barely know, but I saw it in her eyes when she looked at me that first day. There was a longing there that pulled at me, drew me in, and left its imprint behind.

A rustle at my door opens my eyes and draws my attention. Alex stands in the threshold, with an iPod in hand. Her chocolate hair is down and wavy, her makeup fresh. The mark on her face is barely visible. She looks beautiful in her green top and dark fitted jeans.

"Can I come in?"

Sitting up, I smile at the light I see in her emerald eyes. She's in a better mood and I'm happy to see that.

"I brought you your iPod. You use it when you're working out. I added some more music I know you like. I thought you might like to have it."

Taking the iPod from her hand, I smile appreciatively. "Thank you. I would."

The faded red chair by the window scrapes across the floor as she drags it closer to the bed.

"You doing ok?" I ask, genuinely concerned.

"Better than the last time you saw me," she replies, wringing her hands together. "I took some time to get a handle on my emotions. I'm sorry I ran out on you."

"Don't apologize. I understand this is difficult for you."

"Not as difficult as it is for you. Everything is new, unfamiliar, and strange."

"It is hard, but you've all been patient and let me ask questions and get to know everyone without making me feel bad for not remembering. The therapist has been helpful too. I met with her yesterday."

"I'm really happy to hear that talking with her helped. I want to do anything I can to make things easier on you. I cleaned your house, thoroughly, yesterday. I wanted it to be nice for when you're released from the hospital."

She doesn't know it's going to be awhile before I'm released, and the question springs to mind whether I'll want

271

to honor my previous arrangement of having her live with me. As much as I'm attracted to her, I'd like time to get acquainted with my life and who I am without the added stress of trying to be the man she remembers.

Her gaze drops to her lap. The awkward tension passes between us. If I remembered her, would she be closer, affectionately touching me, kissing me?

"How comfortable are we in our relationship?"

With a minute change in her expression, her thoughts appear to scatter.

"As in…like…sex?"

I can't help smiling at the flush to her cheeks. "Yeah."

Pinching her lip between her teeth, she thinks of how to respond. Putting her on the spot like this is entertaining me a little too much.

"We're intimate with one another."

Tension rushes to my groin. I can't help wondering if sex with her is as amazing as I imagine it to be.

"Would you mind doing something for me?"

"Yes, of course."

"Being in this bed, I'm pretty stiff all over. Would you mind rubbing my shoulders a bit? I'd ask a nurse, but honestly, I'd be more comfortable if you did it."

That last part brightens her eyes and gives me a glimpse of that gorgeous smile of hers.

"Is it ok for you to sit up like that?"

"Yeah, the doctor said he did an interlaminar implant between my lower vertebrae. It's some kind of u-shaped device he put in to put space between the vertebrae. They were smashed together in the accident. It's good for me to

272

move, but it's painful. I'll be starting physical therapy in a week or so to help strengthen the muscles in my lower back and work on getting better movement."

She sits on the edge of my bed, her expression filled with concern.

"What about your leg?"

"Doctor thinks the trauma to my spinal cord has caused the loss of muscle control and sensation. He's not so sure I'll get function back in my leg, but I'm not taking that as an answer."

Her troubled eyes glisten with the sheen of oncoming tears, but her lips crease ever so slightly.

"That's just like you not to accept defeat."

"So I hear."

Instinctively, I raise my hand and gently swipe at the stray tear that escapes her pretty green eyes.

"About that back rub." She giggles and scoots even closer.

"I might be more excited about this than you are."

The start of my laugh is abruptly cut off by the moan that escapes my mouth. With each stroke of her firm touch, my muscles ease, and I relax. Closing my eyes, I focus only on her touch and nothing else. Not of the man I once was or the man I am now, not what anyone expects of me, or my confusion of what to expect from myself. All thoughts and feelings are obliterated by the feel of her soft, warm hands massaging me.

My hand goes to hers and she stops. Striking green eyes blink twice. In the unusual lines and curves of her irises, I see the longing. With her hand in mine, I feel it. The strange pull to her I can't explain. My mind may not remember her, but I'm pretty sure my heart does.

"Would you mind rubbing underneath this itchy gown?"

A crease forms at the corner of her mouth as she shyly nods.

Carefully, I lean forward, and she tugs at the gown, creating an opening for her to slip her hands beneath it.

Rubbing along my shoulders, she moves to my chest. My eyes open slightly and admire the satisfied expression on her face. Her massage is giving my body the relief it needs, but I can see it's also giving her the connection she craves.

"I don't know if you've seen it yet. You have an intricate tattoo that goes across your abdomen, chest, shoulder, and arm. Part of it is in memory of your father."

"I was able to look at some of it in bed. I like it. From what I can see, it looks pretty badass."

The flush to her cheeks has me curious of the cause.

"The first time I met you, I got a glimpse of it as you were putting a fresh shirt on. I found it very attractive. I found you very attractive."

Hearing that brings me a surprising amount of joy. I assumed she found me attractive since we were a couple but hearing her admit it to me now provides me with a sensation of satisfaction.

"How did we meet?"

"My best friend, Jane bought me a certificate for eight weeks of personal training with you. It was for kickboxing and self-defense classes."

"Did I do a good job?"

With her thumb in my shoulder, she focuses on a knot and works at it.

"You're an amazing instructor. You helped me more than I can express in words. And I don't mean just as my instructor, you became an incredible friend and someone I could lean on." Lowering her hand, she grazes her fingers across my abs and her eyes dance with a desirous spark that my cock notices too well.

The last thing I need right now is a full-on erection I can't do shit about. Using my good arm, I adjust the blankets, and her eyes, of course, go right to where my hand is. Fuck me, she needs to stop looking. I'm about to grow a semi thinking about her stroking it.

Touching her hand draws her attention to my face. "I appreciate the massage."

Her fingers lace between mine and her full lips split into a smile. "Anytime."

Rubbing my thumb along her hand, I enjoy the touch of her soft skin. The scent of vanilla drifts my direction, giving me a reprieve from the sterile scents of the hospital.

"I'm glad you came to visit me. I hope you keep coming."

Her rosy cheeks swell with her smile. "I will."

275

CHAPTER THIRTY-NINE

—

CARTER

I'm thankful I start physical therapy today. I've had as much as I can take of the one window room, the scents of plastic, sterilizing solution, and my own body odor. The nurse had a fit when she found me taking a piss on my own today, but the hell with her scolding attitude. My body is fit, it's not like I can't use my arms and one good leg to get around. The best part was telling her I'd be taking a shower and dressing on my own. Yeah, that went over well, but damn if I didn't win that argument. It's time I start learning how to get around the way I am. It's been over a week I've been stuck in a hospital bed. I can't take much more. Cabin fever is setting in.

Apparently, word got out about my stubborn attitude because they sent a male nurse to my room to take me to physical therapy. His green scrubs contrast against his chocolate skin. He's a big guy with kind, dark brown eyes. They were smart to send him. All the sweet little nurses struggle to help move me.

Waving my hand, I turn down his outstretched arm.

"Nah, Seth, I can get into the wheelchair just fine on my own."

"I'm sure you can, but it's best not to push it. If you lose balance and fall, you can injure your back further."

"Well, that's what you're here for. To catch me if I fall," I quip.

Seth's mouth curves and he takes a step back, arms outstretched and ready to catch me if needed.

Wobbling on one leg, I brace my hands on the bed, turn, and drop down into the chair. My attention is drawn to the door not only because it's my first time getting to leave, but there's a gorgeous brunette beauty standing in the doorway with her eyes fixated on me.

"Aren't you a sight for sore eyes."

"I'm happy to see you too."

"Visiting will have to wait. He's headed to physical therapy."

There's a mixture of emotions that cross her face. I find myself wanting to know what each of them are and the reason.

Alex has been visiting me every other day and I look forward to her visits. They're the highlight of my boring days. She always visits for at least a couple hours and every time she brings me something new to try. My favorite being the food. Hospital food is made for sustenance, certainly not taste.

"Can she come?"

Seth shrugs. "I don't see why not."

Her smile brightens and seeing it tugs at the corner of my mouth. Setting her bag in the room, she settles into a casual stride alongside us.

Down a few floors, I'm rolled into the physical therapy room which is large, full of equipment and many injured people and their physical therapists. Several windows along the right wall give a nice ground view of the trees and landscaping outside. The left corner has a desk with two associates working at it.

Stepping out from behind the desk is another guy in black scrubs, gelled blond hair, and unusually hairy arms. With a clipboard in hand, he heads right toward me.

"Carter Maxwell?"

"Yeah."

"Pleasure to meet you. I'm your physical therapist. My name is Jeff Myers."

"Nice to meet you."

"So today we're going to start off light with focusing on stretching and dynamic stabilization exercises, then gradually we'll add in core strengthening exercises and muscle strengthening. I hear you're a personal trainer, so this should all be familiar to you."

Familiar, that isn't something I've felt since I woke up in a hospital unable to remember anything about myself. I chuckle, and Jeff looks at me confused.

"I lost my memory, bud. I'm not sure how familiar any of it will be."

"Sorry to hear that. Although the good news is some things we do could still be familiar to you. Your mind might remember what it's supposed to do in response to the workouts."

There's a spark of hope that flourishes in my chest. I'd love to remember something, anything, about the man I was.

"And you are?" Jeff's attention switches to Alex. I can see the attraction in his eyes when he studies her, and I twitch at the pang of jealousy it causes.

"Oh, sorry. I'm Alex, a friend of Carter's."

"Girlfriend. She's my girlfriend."

Did I really just bark that at him? Am I really trying to stake my claim on her? Alex's gaze whips to me and the look on her face sparks something in my chest I can't quite put my finger on. Fuck it, yes, I am. Maybe I don't want another guy to take her from me.

Jeff's expression contorts. His disappointment is obvious and it pleases me.

"It'll be good for Carter to have your support. Let's get started."

Alex takes a seat in a nearby chair while Jeff insists on helping me onto a bench. The stretching exercises consist of Jeff manipulating my body into several positions for the next thirty minutes while I grimace through each of them.

When that's through, he has me lay on a mat on the floor and attempt several stretches on my own. He does it first, then I copy.

The last twenty minutes I spend working on what he calls stabilizing exercises. Unfortunately, nothing we do throughout the hour-long session is familiar to me, and when he asks if any of it was, it only irritates me more.

279

Seth helps me into the wheelchair and we all quietly walk back to my jail cell...I mean hospital room.

Alex touches Seth's arm and indicates for him to follow. They walk out of the room and I wheel myself over to the window. Looking out it, a sudden sensation of sorrow consumes me. What if I never remember my past or the man I was? What if I never walk again? This might be my new life, and even though this week I put on a positive attitude I'm okay with it, I'm really not.

Alex steps back into the room, and although her smile usually lightens my mood, it doesn't do the trick this time.

"We're leaving."

"What?"

"I'm taking you out of the hospital. Seth gave me permission to wheel you outside. There's a path that winds around the backside of the hospital. We're going there."

And with that, my mood lightens. "Let's go."

Pushing the wheels forward, I follow her out. She gets the elevator and before long we're passing through halls on the way out. As soon as the fresh air hits me, I stop and breathe it in deep. The evening sun is falling, leaving behind a pink and orange glow across the horizon. The air is the perfect temperature of warm with a light breeze. Alex continues forward and I join her side.

She walks, and I wheel in silence for several minutes. Stopping at a bench, she sits down, and I park in front of her.

"Thank you for asking to take me out. I needed it."

"I know you did."

Vivid green eyes linger over my face which has a bit of scruff that needs to be shaved, but thankfully, my head is free of its bandage. Staring back at her, I sense that longing I can usually feel emanating from her. Bracing my hands on the wheelchair, I struggle to raise myself to a standing position. Immediately, she jumps to her feet. Placing my hand in front of me, I stop her from reaching out.

"I want to sit next to you."

Creases on her forehead reveal her concern, but her eyes spark with life.

"Okay." She scoots down the bench making room for me. I use the bench as leverage to pivot and sit down next to her.

"You called me your girlfriend."

The corner of my mouth raises. "Technically you are. We haven't broken up, have we?"

Her eyes glisten with moisture. "No, we haven't."

"I like you. I don't want you to stop coming to see me."

"I don't want to stop seeing you either."

Glancing down, I notice her hand close to my leg. Sliding my hand beneath it, I intertwine my fingers with hers. Her hand is warm and the contact comforting. Her gaze lingers over me, then our hands. She nibbles her lip and I wonder what she's thinking.

"Do you miss him…I mean me, the man I was?"

A single tear rolls down her cheek. "Yes," she admits.

"Did I tell you I loved you?"

Her gaze looks off, she's fighting more tears. "Yes."

"Did you feel the same?"

She wipes at her cheek. Seeing her pain is a struggle for me.

"Yes."

She's confirming what I already assumed. I'll never be able to explain how foreign it feels to be a stranger inside your own body and mind. This beautiful woman had a relationship with me. One I believe was a strong one, and now, that's been taken from her.

"Are you still staying at my house?"

"Sometimes. I…uh, should probably stop. I'm beginning to feel like I'm invading your privacy and space."

I remain silent. As much as I want to keep seeing her, I'm not comfortable returning to my home with her there. There's too much for me to cope with without her there, let alone with her there.

"The doctor said I'll be released in a week if my physical therapist signs off on it. I'll have to keep coming back for my appointments of course. There's a lot for me to figure out. Sandy has spoken with my employer, and they're giving me a temporary leave of absence, but if I can't walk, I can't instruct. I might have to look into some desk jobs. Hell, I don't even know what I can do. And tomorrow I meet with a man named John. Sandy says he's my MMA manager. I was supposed to have another fight in six weeks. It's been canceled. The hospital has been a bit of a security blanket. I haven't really had to deal with what my life is going to be outside of it. I admit I'm not sure where my life is headed next."

Reaching up, I wipe away another one of her tears.

282

"But I know I'd like to keep seeing you, I just, need to figure a lot out for myself."

"I understand. I moved everything back into my place already. I stayed the night a couple times because I..." Pulling her hand out of mine, she covers her face as she fights back the outpouring of tears. "Wanted to be close to you."

Her pain is palpable, the tension unbearable.

"I should probably get going. I'll walk back with you."

"Alex."

Struggling to compose herself, she turns her head, the sorrow in her eyes cuts right through my heart like a knife slashing delicate fabric.

"I'm sorry."

"You have nothing to be sorry for. I'm the one who owes you an apology. You wouldn't be in this position if it wasn't for me."

"What do you mean? What happened? I feel like there's more to my accident than anyone wants to tell me."

"It's my fault." Her breathing is raspy between controlled sobs. "The mark on my face was because of my ex. You went to confront him. During the confrontation something happened, I don't know what, then you were hit by the car. If it wasn't for me, you wouldn't have been there, you wouldn't have confronted him. You wouldn't have the memory loss or injuries. You wouldn't have to worry about losing your MMA career. All of this is my fault."

Her eyes are full of desperation and agony awaiting my response. My chest constricts. Hearing the truth about my accident doesn't give me the relief I expected. But regardless of what happened, she's wrong, this isn't her fault, and she shouldn't carry that kind of pain with her for the rest of her life.

"My accident wasn't your fault."

"How can you say that?"

"Did you ask me to confront your ex?"

She shakes her head.

"Does your ex have a history of violence?"

Again, she shakes her head.

"Did you know I went to confront him?"

"No."

"Then how is my accident your fault?

When she can't answer, I know my words have sunk in.

"Alex."

The moment my hand touches her back, she collapses into my chest. At first, it surprises me, but then I find myself wanting to comfort her. Placing my arms around her, I rub up and down her back. Beneath my fingers, her hair is soft, and her vanilla scent appealing. It's a scent I'm beginning to savor each time she's near.

"Do you forgive me?"

"There's nothing to forgive." Leaning back, I place my hand beneath her chin and raise her face to meet mine.

"I want you to promise me something." Around her pretty green eyes are splotches of pink, but even with her sorrow I still find her beautiful. "I want you to promise that you won't let my accident destroy you."

With a sniffle, she nods. "Only if you promise me something too."

"What?"

"That you won't let it destroy you either. That you'll fight like you have for everything in your life."

Her request hits me deep, snuffing out the pity and anguish I've been wrestling with. It gives me a new reason, a new purpose.

"I promise."

CHAPTER FORTY

—

CARTER

Jeff grins with his silly ass approval as I step with my good leg up to the walking rail.

"You're making good improvement and I'm about to sign off on releasing you. You sure you want to chance it?"

"C'mon Jeff, no pain, no gain. If I'm going to be able to walk, we have to push it. I have to learn to balance and put weight on it."

"You sound like you know what you're talking about."

"Yeah, I know. I think you were right about my mind remembering the training I used to give. Sometimes I know exactly what you want before you ask and how I need to do it."

"I've noticed." Setting the clipboard on the stand, he puts an arm out, ready to help me if needed.

With my left hand on the rails, I use my right arm to adjust my right leg, aligning it with my left. With both hands on the rails, I slowly put weight on my right leg so I can step with my left. Keeping my hands on the rails stabilizes my balance and lets me use my muscles to lessen the weight on my leg if needed.

One step and my grip tightens on the rails. Breathe in, breathe out. Another step. Pain ripples up my hip and to my lower back. I grimace, but don't stop. Another breath in, another breath out. Step again.

"Fuck."

"It's time to stop," Jeff insists.

"No," I bark.

Another breath in, another breath out. Step.

When I reach the end of the nine-foot walking rail, Jeff has my chair ready for me to collapse into. Sweat beads off my forehead and along my upper back. My hands are shaking. I grip the wheelchair arms to hide it.

"You did better than I expected, but that was too much for your first time. I can see it on your face."

"Every day, Jeff. If I do it every day, soon it'll get easier."

"That's usually how it works, but if you're going to insist on doing this at home, have someone there to keep an eye on you. Last thing you want to do is fall and cause further injury."

"Got it, Boss."

Jeff pats me on the shoulder before handing me his clipboard. "Sign here. This is your release form. From now on, your sessions will be by appointment…from outside the hospital."

Taking the clipboard gives me a sensation of relief and apprehension. I'm ready to leave the hospital but unsure of where to begin outside of it. The one good thing is the insurance agency of the driver of the vehicle that hit me was quick to pay my medical bills, and on top of that, the hospital received an anonymous donation toward my account. I'm leaving the hospital with having to pay barely anything. It's one major concern I can now mark off my list.

Back in my hospital room, I gather the few items that are mine and toss them in a duffle bag. Thanks to Kevin, I have a new phone. After a police officer stopped in my room to speak with me, I learned there's an investigation into my accident and my clothing and cell phone were collected for evidence. Don't imagine I'll ever see that phone again which is unfortunate. It holds many pieces to the man I was.

There's a knock at my door and I turn my wheelchair to face the visitor. When thinking about who I wanted to take me to my house, Alex was my first thought, but after thinking about it more, I called Kevin. Walking back into my home is going to be rough. If I have a breakdown, I'd rather she didn't see it.

Kevin nods. "Ready, bro?"

"Very." I toss my duffle bag at him and he catches it with ease. "Thanks for the ride."

"Anytime. Honestly, don't hesitate to call and ask me for anything even if it's getting off the toilet after taking a shit."

Laughter rolls out of my chest. "No wonder we were close. You're all right, man."

He pats me on the shoulder. "I'm serious though, anything at all."

"Thanks."

For not knowing him long since waking up with the memory loss, I already feel a brotherly connection to him. I have no doubt we were close before. I hope we can be that way again.

The drive to my home isn't long. On the way, we stop for burgers and I roll down the window and enjoy the rest of the ride with the breeze cooling the tension off my body.

Pulling up to my house reveals a tan siding, ranch style home with brown trim on the windows and front door. Kevin says it's a two bedrooms, two bathrooms, and he and I redid the flooring and remodeled the kitchen a couple years ago.

"It's yours now," he says, looking from the house to me. "You didn't have much left to pay on it. I paid the remaining balance for you."

I'm completely shocked. "Wow, Kev, that's—"

"Don't mention it. Us Maxwells stick together. I wasn't going to have you worrying about losing your home while you're trying to recover. With the money we received after our father died and the added money you saved, you had the balance nearly paid. There wasn't much left to pay, so don't feel guilty about it, all right?"

Leaning over, I pull Kevin in for a hug. "Shit, bro. Thank you. This means a hell of a lot to me."

Kevin pats my back, then leans back. Staring at the house, he sighs. "I wasn't there to protect you. This is my way of making up for it."

"Don't let it haunt you. The things I did the day of my accident were my choices. No one else's."

"Your girl, Alex. You were fighting for her that day and I don't blame you. You were doing what you thought was right to protect her. I would've done the same. I would've wanted to beat the shit out of her ex too. He hurt her more than once."

"What do you mean?" My muscles tighten hearing those words. "Did he abuse her when they were together?"

"No, not that I know of. You told me he walked out on her after she was raped."

"Alex was raped?" My hand wipes over my face, rubbing uncomfortably at my stubble.

"Yeah, by a serial rapist. Over a year and a half ago. She was his last victim before the police caught him and shot him. It took her a long time to recover. You told me you're the first man she's been with since her attack. The first guy she's let in. I actually Googled that shit after you told me. There's articles about it. It was in the news."

"That's fucking horrible." My fist tightens into a ball. Hearing this causes a twinge in my chest, an ache in my gut.

"I know. You should've seen the look on your face when you told me about it. If her rapist wasn't already dead, I think you would've hunted him down yourself and taken him out. There's something about Alex that brings out a different side of you. It's the same as I am about my wife, Carrie."

"I like her, Kev, but—"

"You don't know her."

"I'm trying to get to know her to see if there can be something between us. It's hard. When she looks at me, I feel like she wishes I was a different man, and I don't know who that man is."

"I get it, bro. You mind if I give you a piece of advice from your older, more experienced, married brother?"

I chuckle at the older as I know he's only a year and a couple months older. "Of course."

"Don't try to be the man she remembers. Don't try to fill those shoes. Just be you. Start the relationship fresh. Discover what it is that made you fall in love with her in the first place."

Going silent, I absorb his words. If I'm honest with myself, I want Alex to look at me and see me, the man I am now, not the man she remembers.

"That's damn good advice."

Kevin's hand goes to the door handle, a grin smeared across his face. "Let's head in. You have a new home and new shit to get acquainted with."

Leaning against the car door, I wait for him to pull the wheelchair out of the trunk.

"I have more good news for you, C."

"Yeah, what's that?"

"You're going to be an uncle."

CHAPTER FORTY-ONE

—

ALEX

As I pull my blouse over my head, I glance at Carter's t-shirt I took from his house. Maybe it's creepy, maybe it's pathetic, but I don't care. I needed to have something of him close. It smells like him and is the last shirt I saw him wear before the day of the accident. Reaching out, my hand grazes the fabric. The soft blue cotton slides between my fingers and I swallow down the lump swelling in my throat. I will not cry. I cannot cry.

Jane is on her way over, insistent on taking me out today. She's concerned with my emotional state, worried I'll withdraw into myself like I did before. My heart has been shattered once more, but I made a promise to Carter I plan to keep. I don't want him to only see the sad and emotional Alex. There's more to me than that and he deserves to get to know the strong and fun woman I can be. I owe him that, and more importantly, I want him to see the woman he fell in love with.

At the sound of knocking, I release Carter's shirt from my hand. On the other side of my front door is Jane. She swoops in and hugs me, squeezing me tight against her.

"Hey, babe." Soft lips pucker against my cheek.

"Good to see you too. You ready?"

A dimple forms as she beams with a smile. "We're changing our plans."

Brows creased in confusion, I wonder what she's up to. "How come?"

"We're going to my house instead because Carter is coming over to hang out with Kyle."

"He is?" Instantly, my stomach does a loop-the-loop in excited anticipation. "It's not going to be weird you left to come hang out with me, then we show up, is it?"

"I got it covered. When Kyle told me he was going to Carter's house to pick him up, I told him not to tell Carter I left to go hang out with you, that way we can show up like it wasn't planned."

"I love you."

"I know you do. Now let's go pick up some food, then you can seduce your boyfriend."

Laughter rolls out of my chest as I close the door behind me.

Pushing through the front door, Jane carries the bag of wings while I carry the pizza. Walking through the entryway, I can't see Carter yet, but my nerves have already started tingling across my chest and shoulders. Jane sets the bag on the counter, and as soon as I move next to her, I see Carter's back. Turning, he looks right at me and I'm grateful a smile spreads over his face.

"Hey, honey. Hey Carter. It's nice to see you. It was a good night to come over. Alex and I got pizza and wings."

Kyle stands from the couch and winks at Jane. "Did you girls have fun?"

"Yep," Jane replies innocently before walking around the counter and kissing him. "But now we're ready to veg out. Can we join you?"

She looks to Carter and he sets the Xbox controller down on the coffee table. "Yeah, of course."

Looking at me, I see his eyes brighten. "Hey, Alex." He pats the couch cushion next to him. "Come have a seat."

Jane opens the cabinet and pulls out several plates. Grabbing one, I lift the pizza box. "How many slices you want?" I ask him.

"Two would be great. I'll have some wings too."

After filling both our plates, I carry them into the living room and hand one to Carter before sitting down next to him. Jane brings in drinks for us, and we take them with a 'thanks.' She and Kyle take the chairs by the couch and ignore us, focused on their meals.

"How you been?" Carter asks. "I haven't seen you since I left the hospital." He sounds a bit disappointed and I'm pleasantly surprised.

"I figured you needed some time to get settled."

"I did. Thank you. I'm happy to see you though. I missed you."

It's been a week since I've seen him, and he has no idea how much I've missed him. Hearing him tell me he missed me is amazing to hear and it's sweet. I can tell he's flirting and I like it.

"Yeah? Maybe we could get together sometime soon."

"Speaking of that." Our gazes switch to Jane. She sets her slice of pizza back on her plate. "Before the accident, Kyle and I had planned on inviting you both to his father's beach house in Key West for a long weekend. We still wanted to ask because we thought you both would like the getaway and I mean, who doesn't want a free stay in Key West?"

Carter and I both go silent. It's obvious we're both unsure of how to respond or how the other one feels. I'm still practically a stranger to Carter, I can understand if he isn't interested or ready for a trip like this.

"I'm game."

My gaze whips to Carter in surprise. His shoulders shrug, and he glances at me briefly before looking at Jane and Kyle.

"I think it'd be good for me to go somewhere fun with my friends. As long as y'all don't mind my limited mobility."

"Not at all," Kyle quickly replies. "I'm happy to help you any way I can."

"We all are," I reply, placing my hand on his knee.

Glancing down at my hand, a smile forms his lips as he places his hand over mine and rubs it. "Thank you. Does that mean you're in for the trip too?"

Feeling his hand caress over mine causes butterflies to do a slow swirl in my stomach. Looking at his hopeful blue eyes, my heart skips a beat. "I am."

"How fun!" Jane squeals. "Alex, do you think you can get Friday off work?"

"Yeah, I haven't had a vacation day yet. I know Mr. Kline won't mind."

"Ok, great, because the Marco Island Key West Express leaves on Thursday and comes back on Sunday. Does that work for you Carter?"

"Yeah, that'll work. I'll do physical therapy that morning and if you don't mind picking me up after."

"I can pick you up," I tell him.

Carter gives my hand a squeeze, then reaches for his pizza. "That's perfect."

With our bellies full and a few drinks in, we move to the dining room table for a card game. As I stand, Carter reaches for my hand.

"Wait a moment, I'll walk with you."

Still holding my hand, he places his other on the couch arm, using both to help him stand. On his feet, he positions his hands on my shoulders.

"Good?"

"Yeah."

Slowly and carefully, I lead us into the dining room. Behind me, I hear him wince a couple times and feel his grip tighten on my shoulders. It's obviously painful for him to walk, but he doesn't complain or ask me to stop. We make it to the square table, and he reaches out for the red leather chair and sidesteps, dropping into it.

I slide into the chair next to him and he brushes my hair off my shoulder. His hand lingers, rubbing my back. The sensation creates goosebumps along my neck and shoulder. Longing for more of his touch, I remain still, indulging in the affection.

"Thank you for the extra hand."

"You're welcome."

With the alcohol in my system, I stare a little too long at him, and he grins, his cheeks slightly pink.

Removing his hand from my back, he caresses his thumb across my cheek, and I lean into it. With a wink, he removes his hand, attention switching to the game being set up in front of us.

Thankfully I know the rules because my attention is entirely on Carter. I feel like a lovesick schoolgirl, desperate for my crush's attention. Taking a breath, I rein in my emotions.

The cards are dealt and we each look at the answers written on our cards. Each of us laughs at something we've read.

"Ok, let's begin," Jane insists.

She reads her card and we each search through our hands for an answer we feel is the funniest. We each slap the card of our choice face down and slide it to Jane. Picking them up, she looks at the first one.

"Ok. It ain't no sunshine when she's... getting humped by a vicious Chihuahua... sticking a chili pepper where no chili pepper should ever be stuck… when Aunt Flo comes to town."

We all burst out laughing and wait for Jane to pick the one she thinks is the funniest.

"I'm going with getting humped by a vicious Chihuahua. Who's was it?"

"Mine," I cheer.

"One point for you. Your turn to read."

Over an hour later and a couple more drinks in, my cheeks are hurting from how much I've laughed and smiled. Jane tallies the score and points to Carter. "You're the winner," she beams.

"What do I win?" he jokes.

"A kiss from Alex, of course." Her sneaky grin widens as she gathers the cards to put back in the box.

"I'd take that." Glancing at me, he winks.

Helping Jane, I gather cards and drop them in the box. "Let me know when you're ready to cash it in." I give a sideways glance and wink back.

His smile is playful and his gaze seductive as he watches me, carefully standing to his feet. "I'm holding you to that."

"Please do." I nod, grinning.

Carter's smile widens before he looks at Kyle and pulls his cell phone from his jean pocket. "Unfortunately, it's getting late. I'll call a cab to pick me up."

"You're welcome to stay here. I can drive you home tomorrow morning if you want," Kyle tells him. "We have a guest room."

"You should stay too," Jane adds, putting the game box back in the cabinet.

"Sure, I can take the couch."

"No, I'll take the couch," Carter insists, putting his cell back in his pocket. "You can have the guest room."

"It's fine. I promise. I don't mind."

"I do. I want you to have the guest room."

Opening the fridge, Jane pulls another beer out. "Why don't you both use it?"

My gaze shifts to her, eyes narrowing.

"Or not," she giggles. "Let's go to bed," she tells Kyle, running her hand over his shoulders.

Following quickly behind, Kyle smacks her ass, and she rushes into their room. Kyle closes the door after him, leaving Carter and me awkwardly at the table.

"We won't see them again until morning." I laugh. "But we'll hear them."

"How long they been married?"

"Four years, together for five. They met through a mutual friend and hit it off instantly. She told me shortly after meeting him he was the man she was going to marry."

"They're great. You all are. I'm lucky to have such good friends."

"You're pretty awesome yourself."

Putting his weight against the table, he adjusts his footing, I notice the grimace he makes, and it pains me to see it.

"You're doing really well getting around, but it hurts, doesn't it?"

"It does, but it's also because I'm pushing my body."

"Do you have anything to take that can help?"

"Yeah, but I don't want to take pain pills. I have to work through it and manage it." His face twists, another grimace of pain.

"Let's get you into a comfortable bed. You look tired," I state, walking toward him at the end of the polished black table.

Without arguing, he places his hands on my shoulders, and I lead us to the guest room. Reaching along the wall, I flick on the switch, then help him ease down onto the bed.

"You need anything?"

Raising his shirt over his head, he sets it on top of the comforter. Using his arms, he scoots his body back to the headboard. With each push of his arms, his muscles flex, and my gaze is drawn to the contours of his chest and abs. My hands twitch with the need to touch him.

"I'm good. Thanks."

"How about a massage?"

With a tilt of his head, the corner of his mouth raises. "Not going to say no to that."

The bed dips beneath my weight as I crawl across the mattress to him. Staring back at me, his eyes have lost the look of pain and have filled with something new—desire.

"Lay down."

The soft fabric of his jeans fills my hands as I tug at him, helping him to lay on his back. Raising one knee, I straddle his thighs. His gaze doesn't stray, remaining fixed on me.

"I'll start on this side."

Firm hands hold tight, just below my ass. With the alcohol coursing through me, I'm feeling confident. Taking his hands in mine, I move them up. Cupping my ass, he continues to watch me, awaiting my next move. My hair falls to the side, brushing across his chest as I lean down, putting my lips within a whispered reach of his.

"How about that kiss?"

Lifting his head, his lips touch mine and a fire ignites, blazing through my body, burning straight to my core. The kiss doesn't end quickly. One hand tangles in my hair as the other squeezes my ass. Pushing my hips forward, I press into his growing erection. A moan escapes us both.

With a grip tight on my neck, I feel his arm wrap around me. I'm flipped to my side, his mouth ravaging mine. A calloused hand slips beneath my shirt, caressing up my side, resting just below my bra.

Under my hand, I feel his erection and work to unbutton and unzip his jeans. With the material aside, I slide my hand into his boxer briefs and stroke him. His moan fills my mouth.

"Alex—"

"Ssh." Placing my finger to his lips, I stop his words. Pulling out his erection, I lower myself, taking him into my mouth. Turning onto his back, his fingers wind through my hair.

"You sure about this?" he asks, his tone so caring it turns me on more.

I answer by putting him to the back of my throat.

"Fuuck, you feel so good."

He practically purrs through my passionate sucking. Hand in my hair, he fists it tight, moving his hand and arm with my head. Blue eyes watch me take him in and out of my mouth, filling with a carnal desire, making me wet with need. Fingers wrapped around his base, I lick and suck, taking him deep. Warm cum fills my mouth as he moans through his orgasm. As my tongue licks the tip of him clean, he lets out a breath of satisfaction.

Pulling me to him, he looks me in the eyes, a mixture of emotions cross over his face. Caressing my waist, he plays with the top of my jeans.

"Can I make you feel as good as you just made me?"

"Yes, always yes," I whisper.

Taking his hand, I place it into my jeans. His mouth tilts into a satisfied smile, finding me completely wet for him. Sliding his hand out, he unbuttons my jeans, then tugs them off my hips.

"Sit on my lap," he instructs.

His expression is wicked as he watches me remove my jeans and underwear and slide onto his lap. With my back to his chest, he kisses along my neck and shoulder, sending an arousing sensation throughout my body. Lost in his kisses, I don't notice his hand wrap around me until his touch centers between my legs.

My breath catches as he slides two fingers into me. With his other hand, he winds my hair around his fist and tugs my head back. Warm lips burn a trail across my neck and shoulder as his fingers work me into a moaning, aching, and pleading woman eager for release. When my orgasm sweeps over my body his warm lips feather my ear.

"You're beautiful when you come." Turning to face him, he kisses me deep, still caressing between my legs. "I don't want to stop touching you. You feel perfect in my hands."

"I don't want you to stop either. I love the way you make me feel."

"Is this how it's always been between us?"

"Yes." Strong fingers caress my head, tugging my hair, sending a ripple of pleasure through me.

"I want more. So much more of you." His lips feather mine, teasing me.

My hands caress him everywhere, running through his hair, down his neck, touching his muscled shoulders and chest.

"I want to be with you. I want to feel you inside me."

"Fuck, Alex, I've thought of being inside you. I feel like a bastard for saying so, but it's true. I've imagined you riding me, coming all over my cock."

"I've thought about it too." Taking him in my hand, I stroke him with a fierce need.

His head drops, a groan escaping him as he shakes his head. "How is it you've stolen so much of my thoughts when I barely know you?"

My head falls back as his thumb moves over my clit. "I don't know. Maybe there's a part of you that remembers."

"Maybe." Holding me close to him, his kiss is rough and dominant. My body responds willingly to his demand for control. "I feel like I should be gentle with you, but you make me wild. I want to spend the night exploring you, touching you, tasting you, but it's not the right time or

303

place for it." Tilting his head back, his eyes pinch closed. "You're making it so hard not to."

My stroking eases. "I'll stop…for tonight."

Beautiful blue eyes penetrate me deeply, giving me a hint of the Carter I know. Brushing my hair behind my ear, he caresses my cheek. Between my legs, he stills, resting his hand on my inner thigh.

"I want to do it right. I want to make new memories with you, earn your love and trust. I want to make love to you knowing it's me, the man I am now that you want. I don't want to take advantage of you because you already love me."

My forehead rests against his. "You're already making it happen. Tonight, the way you've made me feel, the things you've said. I want the same things. I want to feel your love again."

CHAPTER FORTY-TWO

—

ALEX

My eyelids flutter open at the caress of fingers tracing the shape of my curves. Giving sensuous kisses, his lips leave a sheen of moisture along my neck and shoulder. Fully waking from sleep, I move my body, wiggling closer, putting my back to his chest. Lacing his fingers with mine, he places our arms together around me. A firm erection presses into my backside, rousing me completely out of my sleep as my body tingles with want.

"Good morning, beautiful."

Hearing those familiar words affects me more than I want to show. Moisture fills my eyes, and I bite into my lip, fighting the emotions sweeping over me.

"Good morning, handsome."

Turning in his arms, I face him, staring into the swirls of his blue irises. He stares back, admiring me, studying my face like I am his. Leaning forward, he kisses me, and we both pull back smiling.

"Does last night mean I'm officially your new girlfriend?"

Playing with the end of my shirt, he raises it, brushing his fingers affectionately across my skin.

"Yes, I want you to be my girlfriend. I don't want you to date any other men. I want you all to myself. I want to give us a chance."

"I don't want any other men. I only want you."

"This ex of yours that I fought with, is that over?"

Hearing the concern in his voice tugs at my heart.

"It's been over for a long time. I didn't realize that right away and I regret it. I told him I chose you. That's what made him flip out and shove me into my coffee table."

"I can imagine how upset I would've been. Hearing it now upsets me."

"You hid it well that day. I didn't know the extent of your anger."

"I shouldn't have hid it from you."

"It's okay." Touching his hair, I run my fingers down his neck and shoulder, caressing him lovingly. "Don't feel bad about things you don't remember. I'm sure you had your reasons."

Tugging at my hip, he pulls me closer, kissing me.

At the end of our kiss, I rest my head against his chest and arm. The distinct scent of his cologne mingles with his natural masculinity. With each breath, my body relaxes, feeling at home in his arms. My mind clears as his fingers brush through my hair, tugging at the ends, sending a pleasured sensation throughout my body.

"Are you free on Tuesday night?"

"I am."

"Good. Sandy is having a family dinner. They have them every month. I'd like to take you."

A smile forces its way to my lips. "I'd love to go."

"Have you been with me before?"

"I have."

His chest vibrates beneath my cheek as he chuckles. "It's humorous that my girlfriend will be more comfortable and familiar with my family than I will be."

"For now. It won't be long and everything that is new about us will become familiar to you."

"I do like discovering new things about you." Placing his free arm around me, he holds me against him.

"What have you learned so far?" I kiss his chest and the pressure of his hand rubs along my back in response.

"You're kind, caring, affectionate, passionate, beautiful, loyal. The list is growing, and I haven't discovered anything that concerns me, which concerns me," he laughs. "Each time we've spent together, you've left me wanting more of you. To be honest, not seeing you this week was rough. I got used to seeing you every other day. I thought you wanted space, maybe were going to stop coming around. That bothered me. I didn't call you because I was working through my own feelings and what to do next, and truthfully, I didn't know what to say. The last time I saw you, we left with things uncomfortable between us."

Wrapping a leg around his thigh, we lay above the black and white comforter, joined together, tightly holding one another.

"I wanted to give you space to take care of the things you needed to. I was worried I was overwhelming you, maybe even coming on too strong."

Our heads turn toward the sound of the bedroom door opening. Jane takes one glance at us, grins happily, then immediately closes the door. I giggle, and Carter kisses my forehead.

"I think she liked what she saw."

"She did. She's always wanted us together. She even played matchmaker, setting you up as my trainer, then arranged a party here so we could get to know each other better. We played a blindfolded coin search game. We were teammates. We had our first kiss at that party."

"History is repeating itself. We had our first kiss here again."

"Yes, we did," I laugh. "Our second first kiss was even better."

Tracing the curve of my ass, he squeezes it and I giggle.

"Maybe other second firsts will be even better."

Leaning my head back, I see the lasciviousness in his eyes and it excites me.

"I have no doubt it will be."

He thumbs my bottom lip, his gaze sensual as he leans in to kiss me.

"I have something else to tell you," he shares, caressing along my side. "I haven't told anyone else yet."

Rubbing my hand along the top of his boxer briefs, I curiously await his news.

"What is it?"

"I've gained feeling in my right leg. Just a little, in my butt and thigh. It's why walking is so painful. Before leaving the hospital, I couldn't feel anything in my leg. Now I feel pain and some sensations."

Raising on my elbow, I stare at him with I'm sure is an astonished expression. "Carter, this is amazing news."

"I have an appointment with Doctor Keller on Wednesday to get checked out. He was happy to hear the news."

"I am too, so happy." With excitement coursing through me, I pull him in for a passionate kiss. He leans over me, laying me beneath him.

"It's good we're here at Jane and Kyle's because if we weren't, I don't think I'd be able to keep from ravaging you."

"*Keep from ravaging* are words I never want to hear," I tease. "I want to be ravaged. Over and over."

"In time beautiful, in time. This is hard for me too. I can't help feeling like I'm taking advantage."

"At some point, you'll have to stop feeling that way." My fingers tug at the band of his briefs.

"Until then, I'll take my time exploring you."

Lowering his head, he nibbles between my legs, pulling my panties between his teeth. The graze of his warm mouth sends a titillating sensation over my thighs and up my abdomen.

Please, yes. Explore.

CHAPTER FORTY-THREE

—

CARTER

Sweat droplets form on my brow as I lift the weights over my chest for the last rep. I've discovered I like to work out, and thankfully, my spare room is a mini gym. I've been home for over a week, and every morning, I start my day with a workout, strengthening my upper body, and keeping up with Jeff's at home stretches. Since being home, I've gone through all my things, hoping something would spark a memory. Nothing yet.

I can't complain too much though. I'm adjusting to my home, family, and friends. Even though I felt like I was moving into another man's house, I've found myself growing more comfortable here. I like my home, the style of furniture, and my clothes. Even more, I like Alex. Seeing her Saturday left me departing Sunday with a lightness in my chest. She's a beautiful woman, clearly adores me, and so far, there isn't anything about her I don't like. I'm looking forward to the trip to Key West and spending the entire weekend with her, getting to know her better, and doing more exploring of her gorgeous body.

I need to give myself a pat on the back. She says I'm responsible for how toned she is. Thank you to my prior self, I appreciate your handy work. And it's not just her body. Those stunning green eyes of hers—each time she looks at me with longing makes me want to rip off her pretty, lacy underwear and claim her as mine long into the night. I don't get how this woman has made me this infatuated this quickly. It's as strange to me as my memory loss. There has to be something about her my mind is remembering, or maybe, just maybe, our connection was that strong.

Either way, I'm glad I get to see her again today. She's picking me up to go to my family's dinner. I'm looking forward to that too. I'd like to get to know all of them better, especially Kevin. He's a fun guy to be around.

Easing the weights down, I sit with my hands braced on the weight bench. Pushing against them, I raise myself into a standing position. The usual pain shoots up my hip and lower back. Grimacing, I reach for the cane Sandy got me and slowly walk to the shower. Each step is difficult because I can't feel my foot, so I have to watch each step and tell my mind it's there, I'm stable on it, and able to push off it to step again. I'm getting used to this way of walking, but I hope with all my heart that I can continue to improve.

I want Alex, I want to be the man in her life, but I don't want her to see me as weak and unable to care for her. That's something I won't be able to handle. If I grow to

311

love her, I'll want to protect her, and how can I if I'm barely able to walk, let alone run, lift her in my arms, or knock a guy out who thinks he can steal my girl away? In my condition, he could. Another guy could flirt with her, dance with her, kiss her, pick her up in his arms, and walk off with her, and there's nothing I could do about it. Just thinking of it locks my jaw. It's an excruciating feeling of helplessness.

Turning the knob of the shower, I brace my weight against the bathroom wall and set the cane in the corner. Sitting on the toilet seat, I undress, and with careful movements, I get myself into the shower. Beneath the warm water, my back twitches and my muscles relax. Thoughts of Alex and our night together fill my mind. Chocolate hair brushes over my skin, and I remember the sensual gaze of her green eyes as she took me into her mouth.

Hand fisted, I urge the swell of my cock with each stroke. I want this woman in my bed. I want to feel what it's like to be inside her, thrusting deep, feeling her legs tight around me as I come inside her. Mine. I want her to be all mine.

An image flashes quickly. Then another. My thoughts jumble and I struggle to focus, to make sense of the images.

Staring up at me, her desire is evident as she places her hand around my cock. Warm, her hands so warm, her tongue wet. Her pink lips soft as they surround me. My hand strokes her hair, her face.

The water takes my orgasm with it and the image fades. Inhaling a deep breath, I lean against the wall of my shower. The realization hits me hard and I focus on my breathing. A memory, a real fucking memory. Wiping my hand over my face, the emotion cuts me deep, overwhelming me. Tears moisten my eyes.

Alex.

—ALEX—

Entering my silver Audi, I close the door and start it up. On the drive to Carter's house, I can't help thinking about all that's happened. I spent a week worrying Carter needed space, worrying I needed to back off. Maybe it was a good move because his response to seeing me Saturday was better than I expected. Spending the night with him was incredible, but it was also strange for me. I felt like I was cheating on the old Carter with the new Carter.

When I told Jane this, she laughed at me and said I needed to stop thinking so much. She's right. I've spent so much time thinking lately, I'm causing myself headaches. A reason for one of the headaches was created by a phone call to the investigator on Carter's case. He said Todd was charged with attempted battery but bonded out of jail within twenty-four hours. Todd told the officer Carter punched him first, and he retaliated with his own punch but didn't intend for Carter to trip and fall in front of the car.

313

The investigation is an open case while they wait to see if Carter gets his memory back as there are no other witnesses besides the driver to confirm or deny the altercation. Going on the driver's statement alone, attempted battery is the appropriate charge. I'm not surprised Todd bailed out immediately. I also struggle with what to believe. Todd isn't a violent man. The way he acted at my house wasn't like him. I find it hard to believe he would've intentionally pushed Carter in front of the car, but I wasn't there, and things might've got very heated between them.

Each day that passes I wonder if I'll hear from Todd or if this was the final action to make him move on. I hope he has moved on.

Pulling into Carter's drive, all my thoughts scatter as my body warms with excited jitters. With the light on inside, I can see his silhouette through the front window, slowly moving through the living room, toward the front door. Stepping up to the door, I knock, and he opens it right away.

"Alex." With jeans, a dark grey t-shirt, a brown leather bracelet, brown belt, and his hair styled, he looks like the rugged rocker I remember. Above a wide smile, his blue eyes are alight with joy. "Come in."

As the door opens farther, I see the brown, wooden cane in his hand. My chest tightens, but I don't let my gaze linger. "Thank you."

Closing the door, he faces me, opening his left arm. "Come here."

Instantly, without hesitation, I fill the space and rest my head against his shoulder.

Atop my head, his kiss sends a warm sensation over me.

"I'm glad you're here."

"I am too."

Pulling back, my gaze lingers over his face. Emotion fills his eyes as he looks at me just before he touches my chin and brings me in for a kiss. A kiss that's passionate and full of need. With a stroke of his hand, his fingers follow the length of my hair.

"You look gorgeous."

Having decided on a knee length dress with sleeves and a loose curl to my hair, I appreciate he's noticed my effort and likes what he sees.

"Thank you."

Carter opens the door for us. "You ready?"

"If you are."

"Yeah."

He remains still, waiting for me to walk through the door first. Stepping over the threshold, I glance back at him, unable to withhold my smile. If the night is going to be anything like the start, it's going to be an amazing time.

Carter's steps are slow, methodical, but he closes and locks the door behind him, and with careful steps, he walks to the car, the cane assisting him. I keep pace alongside him, and he slips his free hand into mine.

"Oh, Alex, you look beautiful." Sandy's arms wrap around me as soon as I step through her front door. "It's so good to see you."

With a loving embrace, I squeeze her back. Tears moisten my eyes as she holds me close. I believe we share an understanding of the similar pain we hold down deep. Easing out of the hug, Sandy turns to Carter, her body language indicating she's unsure of how to greet him.

Carter reaches an arm out, and her face brightens, filling with a smile only an appreciative mother can have. It doesn't matter that Carter doesn't remember all of us. He's still the incredible man we all know. That hasn't changed.

Thunderous steps enter the kitchen and I know it's Kevin. His black t-shirt is stretched over his solid muscles and slightly tucked into his black jeans. His height towers over everyone else, making me wonder if their father was just as tall.

"Hey C!"

Kevin moves in for a brotherly half-hug and a pat on Carter's back. Carter's tight muscles instantly relax and his expression transitions to one of relief.

"Hey, bro."

"There's a fight on. You want to join us?"

Carter's gaze switches to me, I immediately nod. "Go. Please. I'll help your mom in the kitchen while you guys enjoy watching the fight."

Taking my hand in his, he brushes his thumb over it. "You sure?"

"Yeah." Leaning in, I kiss him on the cheek.

Sandy's already made herself busy and Kevin turns back toward the living room. Carter takes the moment of privacy and pulls me to him. "I appreciate it and I appreciate you." With a kiss, he steals my breath.

Nibbling my lip, the butterflies flap in my belly as I watch him make his way into the living room.

Sandy comes to my side, bumping me with her hip. "Even with his memory loss, he still adores you."

"I think there's something he's not sharing. He seems emotional, more affectionate than normal…than what *was* normal," I correct.

"Give him time. He'll share it with you or with Kevin. I know that for sure. Even though he's lost his memory, he's still the same man, still the son I know."

"He is. I'm falling in love with him all over again."

"I'm very pleased to hear that," Sandy grins, handing me a wine glass.

"We're taking a trip with Jane and Kyle this weekend to Key West." Standing in front of the counter, I busy myself helping her.

Over her shoulder, she gives an approving smile. "That'll be good for him and your relationship."

"He did say on Sunday, I'm officially his girlfriend."

317

I can't contain my giggle as Sandy's eyes brighten and her smile widens. A knock at the door interrupts our girl talk. Annalise and Phillip walk in and I greet Annalise with a hug.

"Hi, Alex. Where's Carter?"

I nod toward the living room and Phillip wastes no time rushing in there. Following behind him, I watch Carter observe him and work through his recent memory of what Phillip's name is.

"Carter!"

Phillip's body language indicates he wants to hug his cousin. Carter notices and struggles to stand, slowly stabilizes himself, and hugs Phillip.

"I got in! I got into Florida State," Phillip beams at Carter.

"Congrats," he replies, carefully sitting back down.

"It was because of you. You helped me fill out the application. You pushed me to work hard at baseball, and now, I've got a scholarship."

Carter's expression indicates his emotional struggle.

"Is it true? You really don't remember any of us?" Phillip's sudden change in tone pulls at my heart.

"I'm sorry. I wish I did."

"You don't remember me," Phillip's head drops and the disappointment is evident, "do you?"

Everyone's attention has become drawn to their conversation.

"I'm sorry, Peter, I don't, but—"

Carter's voice trails off as Phillip walks out of the living room and out the back door. The door slams behind him and Carter swallows, the emotion on his face is heartbreaking.

His hand runs over his hair. "Shit, I said something wrong."

Kevin pats him on the back as he rises from the couch. "Don't worry, I'll talk to him."

"Alex," Carter calls. Sitting down next to him, I rub his back as his head rests in his hand. "That's not his name, is it?"

"It's all right. Kevin will help him understand. Carter..." Placing my fingers on his chin, I turn his face to mine. "You have nothing to be sorry for. It was an honest mistake. Phillip is upset because you were very close. You're a father figure to him."

Annalise steps in and explains, "After the divorce, Phillip started looking up to you. You came to his games, encouraged him, and kept him out of trouble. This is hard for him because he feels like he's losing a father all over again. I told him about your accident, but he didn't want to believe it was true that you'd lost your memory. He cried a bit at the thought of you not remembering him."

Carter's silence and locked jaw give away how upset he is. I look to Annalise and Sandy. "Can you give us a moment alone?"

Sandy places her hand at Annalise's elbow, and the two walk out the back door.

"This is hard for you, I know."

Turning abruptly, he pulls me into his arms and lays his head against mine. Beneath his chest, I hear the heavy heartbeat and sense his sorrow.

"I had a memory of you today. It was brief, so brief, I stood there clinging to it, wishing it would come back. I want them all back. I want to remember you, all of you."

A warm droplet touches my head and I know he's shed a tear. Pulling out of his arms, I place my hands on his face. "I understand this is hard, there are days like this that make you feel like a foreigner with your own family, but it won't be this way forever, I promise. New memories will be made, and in time, you'll feel better and more comfortable around all of us."

Taking my hand in his, he moves it to his lips and kisses it. "I already feel comfortable with you."

My smile is followed by a kiss. Carter's hand lays at my thigh as his lips move against mine in an affectionate dance, each of us needing, wanting, but restraining. The opposite hand brushes through my loose curls.

"I'm glad you're here with me tonight."

"I am too. Are you ready for me to invite them back in?"

"Yeah, I owe Phillip an apology."

I caress Carter's shoulder. "I know Phillip will be happy to watch the fight with you. Ask him questions. He's talkative, enjoys talking about sports and MMA with you."

"Alex," he stops me, taking my hand in his as I stand. "Thank you."

With my kiss, I reply, "I'm here for you, always."

CHAPTER FORTY-FOUR

—

ALEX

Walking through Carter's door, I'm filled with relief the dinner at Sandy's took a turn for the better. Carter, Kevin, and Phillip bonded all evening, chatting about everything and anything. As we left Sandy's, it was obvious how happy he was and that he'd had a genuinely good time.

Taking my hand in his, he twirls me in front of him. "Stay the night with me."

Giggling from the spin, I rest my palms against his chest. "I'd love to."

Placing his fingers on my jaw, he raises my chin, his blue eyes filled with sensuous desire. "I wish I could carry you to my room."

"I don't care how I get to your bed as long as you're in it." Winking, I scoot off to his kitchen to gather a couple drinks.

Carter watches me, a smile raising the corner of his mouth as he gradually makes his way to his room.

As I enter with two beers, I stand in the doorway mesmerized by his naked torso. The intricate ink across his skin and the indentations of his muscles create a work of art in the light. Approaching him, I place both beers on the nightstand. His heated gaze follows my movements as I slowly trace my fingers over his skin, following the trail of ink.

"There's a Native American healing quote I found in my things. It says *The tragedy of life is not death, but what we let die inside of us while we live.* It stuck with me. Do you know why?"

Sensually tracing my finger, I shake my head.

"Because I don't want the man who I was to die and be forgotten, but I want the man I am now to live."

My hand is wrapped in his fingers as his mouth claims mine, taking me with a need so strong, so fierce, I moan beneath his kiss, hungry for his touch, his love.

His weight shifts, and I feel him adjust his footing, putting his weight on one leg. Strong hands lift me briefly, placing me on his bed. He falls above me, arms on each side of me, blue eyes piercing. The fabric of my dress is raised as his hand caresses up the outside of my thigh. My breathing increases as I'm already wet with desire.

"I want to be inside you. I want to feel you fall apart beneath me, wanting me as much as I want you."

Taking his hand, I guide him between my legs. "I want you, you, the man in front of me."

My head falls back as his fingers slide into me, caressing me. Warm lips kiss my neck, my chest, my cheek as his fingers pleasure me, making my body tingle with satisfaction.

Reaching down, I unbutton his jeans, releasing his erection. Taking him in my hand, I smile against his lips as he moans with relief.

"I need to see you, all of you," he whispers.

Removing his fingers leaves me aching with want. Sitting up, I gather my hair over my shoulder and turn, my back to him. With a gentle movement, he lowers my zipper. Fabric collecting at my arms, I stand to face him, lowering my arms and letting the dress fall to the floor.

Seductive blue eyes look me up and down, admiring what he sees. "You're gorgeous."

Taking my time, I thumb each side of my underwear and lower them off my hips.

Carter sucks in a breath, his gaze falling to my trimmed, dark patch. Reaching out, he takes hold of my hips and pulls me to him. Leaning forward, his mouth closes over my nipple, licking and sucking, then switching to the other, bringing my body to a state of desperate need. My ass fills his hands as I climb above him, straddling him. Pushing me forward and back, he moves me over his erection.

"Do I need a condom?"

As I shake my head no, Carter's eyes light up.

Fisting his erection, I slide onto him. Wet, slick heat is combined with the incredible sensation of him filling me. Head falling back, his grip tightens on my hips as I move up then back down.

Raising his hips, he lowers his briefs and jeans farther down his ass and thighs giving me more room to ride him. Gazes locked, I place my hands on his chest, riding his cock. The slick sound of us coming together fills my ears as I increase my pace. His grip on my hips helps rock me and pushes his head just where I want him. With each thrust of my hips, my body hums with pleasure, and my breathy moans fill the room as I near my orgasm.

My release courses through me, and my sigh is smothered with a sensuous, dominating kiss. Arms enfold me, rubbing my back and hair, keeping me close to him as he thrusts one last time, reaching his own orgasm.

I'm pulled down to his chest, and we give into obsessive, fervent kisses. Minutes pass before we pull apart, breaths slowing as we stare at one another.

"I already want more of you."

"We can make love all night until we pass out with exhaustion. I love the feel of you inside me."

"So much for me doing the right thing." A hint of regret etches into the creases of his brow.

"I wanted this as much as you did, don't feel guilty." My eyes close, indulging in the touch of his hand stroking my face and hair.

"I'm a lucky man to have you as my girlfriend."

"I'm just as lucky to have you."

His kiss comes sweet and loving. "Let's take a shower together. I'll help you get clean."

Carter's small chair in the shower came in handy for me to sit atop his lap while he washed my hair. Stepping out of the shower, I wrap myself in one of his velvety green towels. Giving him a hand, he uses my shoulder to carefully step out of the shower to his sink. He winks at me when he catches me admiring his uncovered package.

Moving into his room, I give him privacy in the bathroom. With my underwear pulled over my hips, I look through his closet and pull out a shirt to wear. When he enters his room, a towel wrapped around his waist, his cane in hand, he stops and admires me sitting at the edge of his bed, drinking one of the beers. His smile is wide, his eyes light with contentment.

"You look good in my shirt." He nods toward his jeans on the floor. "Toss me my phone."

I do as instructed, and he fusses with his phone for a moment then aims it toward me and snaps a photo. Laughing, I set down the beer. "I probably look terrible."

"Not possible. Lay on the bed, I'll take another."

"Take one of us." I pat the mattress and the corner of his eyes crease as he smiles.

Dropping the cane as he reaches the bed, he sits next to me. Pulling me closer to him, he reaches out and snaps a photo of us. A giggle escapes me as he kisses my cheek and snaps another. The phone is tossed aside, and I laugh as Carter flings me to my back. My giggles continue as his

325

lips and tongue tickle across my stomach. Opening his shirt wider, he reveals my chest.

My laughter settles as kisses are placed on each breast, my nipples pulled between his teeth. Each nipple tightens to a pointed peak, and Carter touches each one, massaging them between his fingers before nibbling on them again. My breathing turns to excited moans as he touches between my legs.

"Do you want me?"

"Yes," I breathe.

Tugging at the towel, he reveals his erection. Raising my hips, I pull down my underwear. The touch of his tongue to my clit ignites a fire at my core. I tug at his hair as I moan out in pleasure.

Laying on his chest, his caresses up and down my back nearly lulling me to sleep.

"This has been an amazing night."

A kiss to my head brings a smile to my lips.

"It has. I don't want tomorrow to come. You'll have to leave, and I don't want you to."

"I'll come over after work. Cook you dinner if you like."

"I'd like that."

"Any special requests?"

"Italian. It seems to be my favorite."

Inside I'm beaming. "I have the perfect dish."

Carter's caressing stops, his hand stills on my back. His breathing becomes rhythmic, and I lay against his chest, thankful to be falling asleep in his arms.

The tip of the blade scrapes across the skin of my inner thigh. With all my strength I withhold my cry of fear. It only fuels his sadistic torture further.

"I can end this. Slice this blade across your artery, you'd bleed out, and this would all be over. You want that? For this to be over?"

Inside I'm screaming, begging, pleading for my life, but to him I say nothing. There are no words that will satisfy him.

Warm sweat beads across my forehead, chest, and back as I'm awakened to my own screaming and thrashing. Protective arms instantly wrap around me and rock me against his chest.

"I'm here, Alex. No one is going to hurt you. I'm right here. I got you."

My tears stream down my cheeks and drip onto his chest, but he doesn't care. He holds me tight until my own body stops trembling. Hands, loving and careful, stroke my hair and back.

"Do these nightmares happen often?"

"I have them more often if I've been stressed out."

"You've been coping with my memory loss and injury on your own, haven't you?"

327

Against his chest, I nod. "I talk to Jane some, but I don't want her to worry I'm going to withdraw and get depressed again."

"You're not still carrying guilt, are you?"

"A little, it's hard not to, but I've kept to our promise. The week not seeing or talking to each other was hard for me though. I was afraid it might be the beginning of a breakup, but hoped you only needed space to take care of things and get settled in."

"I'm sorry I didn't call you." I can hear the guilt in his tone.

"Please don't feel guilty. Everything has worked out. I'm just being honest about how I felt, why I was stressed." Easing me out of his arms, he wipes the tears from my cheeks. The moonlight streaming in his window illuminates his handsome face.

"I don't want you to be stressed or worried. I've realized we have something special. I admit, I've had a pull toward you since the first day I saw you in my hospital room. It was strange to me at first, but I had to adjust to so many things, it was overwhelming. My therapist had me start a journal. I wrote about you every time you came to see me and sometimes in between. Little things stayed with me like your vanilla perfume, your soft hair, your stunning green eyes. I'd close my own eyes and see yours. You had me infatuated and I barely knew you. I didn't know how to handle it and when I came here, I had to adjust to a new environment again. I wanted a clear head to focus on what I needed to do next. When you're around, I'm too distracted to have a clear head. When you're around, you're all I think about."

My hand goes to Carter's cheek, pulling him to me. Kissing him long and ardently, I move with him as he lays us back. A single tear falls down my cheek and Carter wipes it away as he stares into my eyes.

"I don't know what I'm going to do for a job yet if I can't walk fully, but I know one thing for sure, I want to stay close to you."

"*This* is why I fell in love with you because of the man you are. It's why I'm falling in love with you all over again."

With his hand over mine, the slow tenderness of his kiss fills me with an overpowering sensation, a feeling of complete and utter love.

CHAPTER FORTY-FIVE

—

ALEX

Carter holds me in his arms, rubbing along my back like we did before falling asleep. In the warmth of his arms, I feel safe and wish I didn't have to return home at all. Staring at the clock, I watch the minutes pass. Unable to sleep, he stays awake, caressing me.

"These nightmares you have. They're from what happened to you?"

"Yes," I admit uncomfortably.

"Kevin told me. What happened to you is horrible. It upsets me you were hurt like that."

"It was terrifying and yes, horrible." My fingers squeeze around his. "He hurt me more than just physically. He broke me."

"Why you?" Carter's grip tightens around me protectively.

"I lived alone and fit his preferences and pattern— shorter brown hair, mid to late twenties, one hundred and

330

twenty to one hundred and forty pounds, no pets, no roommates."

"How'd he find you?"

"I don't know. I'll never know. The investigator said he probably saw me somewhere like a coffee shop, at a grocery store, something like that." A shiver runs over my spine and he goes back to stroking me.

"We don't have to talk about this."

"It's okay. I've never talked to anyone about it other than a therapist."

"You don't have to share anything with me if it makes you uncomfortable."

"Talking about it will always make me uncomfortable, but I don't want him to have that hold over me. I shouldn't have to feel ashamed."

His kiss to my head is affectionately placed. "Never feel ashamed."

Hugging him, I keep my head resting against his chest as I begin, "I was naïve. Didn't think about how easily someone can attack you. I remember that day as if it was yesterday. The doorbell of my apartment rang, and I opened it wide to see a man standing there with a package. The uniform was the right color even had a name tag. He handed me the package, and I turned and bent down to set it on the floor. He'd walked farther into my apartment and closed the door partially. He smiled and handed me a clipboard. Looking down at it, I was confused. It was a blank sheet of paper. My attention returned to him, and the last thing I remember was dropping the clipboard as I attempted to fight him off and keep him from putting the cloth to my mouth.

"I woke up, handcuffed to my bed, ropes tied to my ankles, keeping my legs spread apart. At the bottom of the bed was the very package he delivered. It had all his *tools* he needed. The very package I accepted, held in my hands, was his box of torture." Shivering, Carter squeezes me and continues his caressing, silently listening to all that I have to share.

"He had a knife and was running it across my stomach. Pushing the blade into my skin, he told me if I screamed for help, he'd cut me open, side to side. He blindfolded me so I couldn't see what he was doing, but I still knew. I still heard and smelled everything. He put a condom on, then lubricant. He tore off my underwear, gripped my legs, and shoved into me. I cried out from the pain and shock of it. He slapped me so hard, it knocked the sound of my scream out of me. Then he shoved into me even harder."

Tears moisten my eyes, and my chest constricts, but I continue struggling through the words.

"He... raped me more than once. He'd take a break, toy with me, touch me, then when he was ready, he'd rape me again, each time more violent than the last. The more I cried and begged for him to stop, the more it fueled him and his violence.

"What saved me was something so small. One single mistake he made. He'd parked in the wrong spot at my apartment building, an area where cars often got towed. A police officer stopped by with the tow truck. He ran the plates of the truck, and it put up a red flag. He'd been on

332

their radar. He was their lead suspect in similar rape cases. The police and FBI came to my apartment. He pulled a gun, put it to my temple, and told me to stay quiet.

"As soon as he walked away from the bed, I screamed. I screamed so loud my throat was raw. I didn't care if he shot me. I wasn't going to go through any more of what he'd done to me. They burst through the door and I heard gunshots. I was terrified. When a man's hands touched me, I cried. The officer told me it was okay. That it was over. They covered me with a blanket, took the blindfold, cuffs, and ropes off."

My wrists tingle from the memory. I jerk my hand toward myself instinctively and Carter takes my hand and brings it to his lips and kisses it tenderly before holding it on his chest.

"I was taken to the hospital. They did a rape kit and treated my wounds. Gave me pain medicine. After the reports, I was free to go home." I laugh, "*Home*. There was no home after that. It was a prison. A constant reminder of what had been done to me."

The memories of my old apartment and bed flash through my mind. I grimace at the thought of them.

"Todd came over the next day and I couldn't look at him. I couldn't bear to be touched. He wanted to console me, but I couldn't stand the contact. I slid into a deep depression. Lost my job, but I didn't care. I was broken, ashamed, disgusted. I wanted to die. I was so far gone, I took a bath and laid there staring at the bottle of pain pills. All I had to do was take them all and go to sleep, and it would be over, but I couldn't do it. I couldn't let him win.

I'd fought to survive his torture, I had to fight to survive for myself.

"Shortly after that, Todd left me. He couldn't take my constant state of misery. It broke me, but I didn't blame him. I was a walking corpse. My first step forward was moving out of the apartment. I moved in with Jane and Kyle while I sought therapy and a new job. Once I was hired at Kevlar and Kline, I got a new apartment. Gradually, I rebuilt my life, learned to live as the scarred woman I am now."

Pulling out of Carter's arms, I sit up, a frown etched into my expression.

"Do you feel differently about me knowing what happened?"

Sitting up, he takes my face in his hands. "Yes, you're even stronger and more beautiful than before. Your body isn't tainted if that's what you think. Your body is stunning, and when I look at you, I only see you, an amazing woman I care for deeply."

My fingers wrap around his wrists and rub affectionately as he pulls me in for a kiss. As we lay back down, I turn, and Carter wraps an arm around me, tucking my back to his front. Gentle kisses are placed on my cheek and behind my ear. The pleasurable tingling sensation sweeps over my neck and shoulder.

"I love that."

"Good to know your soft spot."

Nuzzling closer to him, I pull the blanket up over us and link my fingers with his.

"Thank you for listening and not making me feel like something is wrong with me."

"That took a lot of courage to share your story with me. I understand it was difficult, but I want you to know, you never have to feel ashamed or embarrassed with me."

I love you, Carter. So much.

"Thank you."

"I'm here for you, always," he whispers.

CHAPTER FORTY-SIX

—

CARTER

Dr. Keller's white coat shifts as he takes a seat in the black chair across from the one I'm occupying. Setting a folder on the sterile, silver counter in front of him, he opens it, then switches his attention to me.

"I'll have the results of your CT myelography in twenty-four hours. Until then, let's go over what we know. You've gained sensation in your right hip and upper leg and you've had two memories come back to you."

Rubbing my thumb over the top of my cane, I nod. "Correct, I had another memory come to me this morning. It was a memory of me training for a fight."

"This is good news. Your body is healing. I had hopes after the interlaminar implant, the pressure would be taken off your spinal cord and nerves. When I discovered your loss of leg mobility, I hoped it was temporary. As for these two memories, this means your memory loss is likely not permanent."

"I'll get all my memories back?" My enthusiasm is difficult to suppress.

"I can't guarantee it, but usually with retrograde amnesia, as patients heal from their injury, long-term memories tend to return. They return in bits and pieces and in random order. Because of the head trauma and swelling, your brain suffered a chemical imbalance. As brain chemistry normalizes and brain systems begin working normally again, the memories start to return. I don't know how quickly this will happen or if you'll remember the same things you did before the accident, but these two memories are a start."

Dr. Keller smiles at my expression. No doubt I look happy with the news. I'm thrilled with the possibility that all my memories might come back to me. I feel lost, without a purpose, or a place I belong, and those memories can fill the deep void.

"How are the sessions going with Dr. May?"

My thoughts disperse, and I return my gaze to him. "Good. During the sessions, we work on memory exercises, and she's helping me cope with my disability and memory loss."

"That's good to hear." Head lowered, his pen moves along the paperwork in his file. "Are you feeling depressed at all or struggling to remember new things?"

"Sometimes names, where I left something. There are brief moments where I feel overwhelmed, lost, but when I'm around my girlfriend, I don't."

"And she was your first memory?" Intelligent brown eyes study me.

337

"Yes."

"What was the memory of? Were you with her when this memory occurred?"

"The memory was of us being intimate. No, she wasn't with me when I remembered it."

Pen moving swiftly, he adds to my file. "Are you having any difficulty gaining an erection during arousal?"

I chuckle, and Dr. Keller smiles, clearly humored by my laugh. "I know it's an invasive question, but it lets me know you don't have any nerve damage correlating with sexual function."

"I'm not having any trouble getting an erection."

"And ejaculation is normal?"

"Yes."

"Good." He scribbles some more, then places the pen in his coat pocket.

"I want you to continue your rehabilitation program— physical therapy twice a week and sessions with Dr. May once a week. In your file, Jeff reported you are working on walking on your own." He points to the cane resting across my knee. "By the looks of it, you're walking, but with assistance."

"Yes, I practice walking every day. I force my mind to accept my leg is there and is able to receive my weight. I work on lightweight resistance to keep the muscles strong, that way my leg can hold my weight, but because of the numbness, it's easy for me to lose my balance. I feel with practice, strengthening my muscles, and working on balance, I have the potential to walk without a cane."

Thumbs touched together in his lap, his brows furrow, his expression hard pressed as he speaks, "We have to wait and see how you continue to heal. I wish I could say the partial paralysis will heal and muscle mobility and sensation will fully return, but I can't guarantee it, unfortunately."

"I understand."

"On a good note, it appears your experience as a personal trainer is being retrieved from your memory which is surely assisting in your recovery."

"I think you're right. This question might be unusual, but I'm curious. If my mind is remembering my personal training experience, do you think a part of my memory remembers my girlfriend? I'm asking because I can't remember anything we've done together or how we met, but she feels familiar to me and so does my brother, Kevin. When I'm with her, I feel… infatuated and I barely know her."

Closing my file, he sits back in his chair. "Your brain is a complex system—consider it like a library full of storage files. Events go in one file, scents in another, colors in another. When you see your girlfriend, your brain is walking through the library in search of memories and things that are familiar, the storage files for events have been misplaced, but your mind finds the scents and color files. It retrieves those for you and says this woman is familiar, but I can't provide you with why. As you spend more time with her, I believe she'll trigger more of your memories."

My thumb rubs over the head of the cane, the fine wood smooth beneath my skin. "There's something that's bothering me."

"Yes?"

"I'm struggling with the fact I used to be a strong man capable of taking down another man fairly easily, yet now I can't protect her."

Dr. Keller's eyes narrow in curiosity. "What do think she needs protecting from?"

My gaze absently passes over several objects before returning to his. "I'm not sure."

CHAPTER FORTY-SEVEN

—

ALEX

My hands tremble as I peel back the envelope. Seeing Todd's name on it sends a chill over my neck and shoulders. Clammy hands withdraw the letter from inside. Sitting on my couch, I open it and read the contents.

I knew you wouldn't want to hear from me and would avoid all attempts to reach you, so my only option was to write a letter. I owe you a deep and regretted apology. I've hurt you in a way I never thought myself capable of, and because of it, I'll live with this regret the rest of my life. I never stopped loving you but managed to push you away, time and again, because of my own ego and my own selfish needs. I realize now how many mistakes I've made and more than anything I hope you can someday forgive me.

I admit, Carter and I had an altercation. He swung first, and I reacted by doing the same thing and punched him. What I didn't expect was for him to trip and fall, putting him dangerously in front of a moving vehicle.

Whether you believe me or not, this is the truth. I know I've made mistakes, but if you know me at all, you know I would never intentionally try to harm someone like that.

Since our argument and the altercation between Carter and me, I've seen a therapist who helped me cope with my father's passing, my guilt of hurting you, and my guilt about Carter's injury. In my efforts to make peace with my actions, I have anonymously donated a large sum toward Carter's medical bills. I feel responsible for his suffering and owe him the opportunity to heal from his injury without struggling with overwhelming medical fees.

I miss you, Alexandria, and if we never speak again, I hope you find happiness. All I ever wanted for us was to be happy together. There was a time when the sight of me brought a light to your eyes I'll never forget. A time when my touch drew the very breath from your lips. A time when I possessed the love from a woman who more than anything wanted to be my wife. I'll forever miss her.

Folding the letter closed, a single tear cascades down my cheek, his words leaving my gut in a tight knot. Looking back, it pains me to think about how far Todd and I fell from loving one another. So much chaos and heartbreak surround us. It's pity I feel when thinking about how happy we once were versus where we are now.

My phone dings, and I jump, my thoughts scattering. Swiping the screen, I read the text.

Dinner last night was great. I'm looking forward to seeing you today. :)

Me too. On my way shortly. ♥

342

Just the thought of Carter washes away all the negative feelings surrounding Todd. Placing the letter back in the envelope, I put it inside a drawer in the kitchen and gather my bag.

My gaze sweeps the horizon and watches Marco Island become smaller in the distance. With my hands wrapped around the white bars of the boat railing, I raise my chin, enjoying the touch of the sun on my skin and the cool, salty breeze sweeping over my face. The familiar touch of Carter's hands overlaps my fingers as he molds his chest to my back. With a tender kiss, he sends a warming sensation rushing over my skin. His head rests against mine, holding me closely as we both look out at the landscape ahead of us.

"What are you thinking?" he asks, the graze of his lips tickling my ear.

"How glad I am that we've taken this weekend to spend together."

"I am too. It'll be a struggle to come back." In his words, I hear a troubled tone.

"Are you okay?"

"Yeah, a few things on my mind is all."

Muscles tense, he goes silent. Looking over my shoulder at him, he seems lost in thought. A moment passes, and his escalated breathing worries me.

"Carter?"

At the sound of my voice, he snaps out of his trance. "A fight," he blurts out, seemingly disoriented.

"Did you have a memory?"

"Yeah, I think it was my first MMA fight."

Turning in his arms, the boat railing is hard on my back, but I don't care.

"That's wonderful! This is your third memory this week."

A frown tugs at his lips. "If only they'd come faster."

Touching his cheek, I rub my thumb across it. "I know."

Adjusting his footing, he puts more weight on his stable left leg. Placing his hand over mine, he brings it to his lips and kisses it.

"I want to remember more of us."

His forehead touches mine, and I fight back the pressure of tears.

I want you to, too.

The three-hour boat ride to Key West gave us too much time to get buzzed off multiple alcoholic beverages. I can't stop giggling and Carter can't stop pawing my ass. As people line up to exit the vessel, Carter grips the ledge behind me, leans his weight against me, putting me up against the wall of the first-floor sitting area. Dipping his thumb into my jean shorts, he pulls my hips flush against him. The flavor of whiskey and beer tease me as his tongue darts in and out.

"C'mon, you two lovebirds," Jane calls, interrupting our delicious moment. Pulling back from our kiss, his eyes glisten with arousal. He winks, and my delicate little lady parts yearn to have his touch. With a quick kiss to my lips, he squeezes my ass before grabbing his cane.

Carefully, he walks down the ramp holding my hand in his free hand. He draws attention from folks looking in our direction. I imagine it's odd to see such a handsome, tatted, fit man with a cane, but Carter pays no attention to the onlookers. With a quick cab ride, we're exiting the vehicle outside our tropically decorated, one-story home for the weekend. Palm trees align both sides of the walkway, leading up to a large, brown door framed with two white pillars.

Inside, the home is just as glamorous with shiny tile floors, white walls, and beautiful beach and wildlife paintings on the walls. The entryway opens into a living room with a kitchen and dining room to the left and two bedrooms to the right. Behind the living room are two sliding glass doors that open onto a stone deck surrounding a large swimming pool, and to the right of that, a hot tub partially tucked away behind palm trees and pretty landscaping.

After exploring the beach house and picking our rooms, Jane and I find a store nearby to stock up on drinks and food for the weekend. Coming through the front door, I get distracted carrying bags in when I see Carter doing the best he can to complete laps across the pool. He's not as fluid and powerful as the last time I saw him swim, but he still manages to force himself across.

"Alex."

Jane's voice snaps me back.

"Yes, I was totally gawking."

"You two seem like you're doing really good." With a turn of her head, she returns her attention back to the kitchen. Hoisting the bags onto the counter, I open and empty the first one.

"We are, but it's still hard. There are moments I want to tell him how much I love him, and moments I miss how much he loved me." My eyes moisten with the tightening of my chest.

"It's just as hard watching him struggle to walk. I'm worried he's going to lose his personal trainer job and MMA contract."

"He's got a few more weeks leave with his job and twelve weeks until he has to commit to another fight. Things might work out. He's doing really well."

"Even if he does heal, I'm worried about him fighting again and getting re-injured."

"Has he said anything about wanting to fight again?" She shuts the refrigerator door, emptying the last of her bags.

Removing the wine bottle from the brown bag, I dig through drawers for a bottle opener.

"He hasn't. He seems worried about what he's going to do next for a job. I think he's hoping to go back to being a personal trainer but preparing for if he can't."

Jane gets two beers out of the fridge for her and Kyle.

"Hand me one of those."

Taking it from her, I set it next to my wine to take out to Carter. Jane finds the bottle opener and hands it to me.

"I can imagine how stressful that is for him."

"He said he wants a job close to me and to his family, I'm sure." Pouring the wine glass full, I take a few swallows. "I hope this weekend he can have a break from having to worry about any of it."

Bathing suits on, drinks in hand, we move out to the pool. The midday sun is warm, and from where we are, we can view the horizon and above it, the bright blue sky and puffy white clouds as far as the eye can see. Beyond the pool, the ocean waves can be heard crashing onto the shore.

Kyle kisses Jane as she hands a beer to him. Carter is sitting on one of the chairs, facing the ocean, lost in thought. Hand over his shoulder, I hand him a beer, interrupting whatever thoughts he had. He smiles up at me, taking the bottle.

"I saw you swimming. You did well."

"It was harder than I expected."

Pulling a chair close to him, I admire his smooth, shaved face and strong jaw. He catches me looking and places a hand on my thigh, caressing it.

"Would you like to take a dip in the hot tub?" Running his thumb farther up my thigh, it makes my skin tingle.

"Yes," he replies, his lascivious gaze meeting mine.

"We're going to take a walk on the beach. We'll see you guys later," Jane shares from behind us.

Thank you, Jane.

"See you later." I wink as she passes by our chairs, observing her cheeky grin.

With a little assistance walking to the hot tub, Carter sits on the edge and swivels, dropping onto the seat. With his hand extended, he helps me in. Pulling me forward, I straddle his lap, and he rubs along my back. Resting his head against the hot tub, he admires me, his thoughts clearly still troubling him.

"Will it bother you if I'm like this permanently? If I can never walk down the beach with you, run with you, or remember how we met, what you meant to me?"

"No, it won't, and it doesn't because I lo…"

The touch of his warm hand caresses along my cheek, his eyes softening as they look at me.

"Say it. I see it in the way you look at me. I want to know how you feel."

"I love you." Like a bird fleeing its cage, my words give my emotions freedom. "I love you so much. You're the same man you were before the accident, the only difference is you don't remember everything I do. You haven't changed. You're still the same man I fell in love with and your limited mobility isn't going to ruin how I feel about you."

With gentle pressure, he brings me forward, kissing me.

"Did I ever tell you before how beautiful you are inside and out?"

"You did," I grin.

"I'm a smart man."

As the warm bubbling water pools around us, he snuggles me as close as he can while looking up at me.

"You still wanted to date me after being told by strangers I was your girlfriend. You had no idea who I was, and you gave me a chance, anyway. You're more than smart. You're incredible, and I love you." Giggling, my cheeks become warm. "I'm sorry, I've wanted to say that to you for a while now and it feels so good to be able to."

"I know you have. I wasn't ready before, but now...I want to hear it because I'm all in. I'm falling for you, but I'm afraid of losing you."

"You won't lose me because I'm all in too." Pressing my head to his, I caress along his muscled shoulders and arms. "My heart is completely yours if you want it."

"I want it, beautiful. I want this to last. You're the only constant in my life. The only time I feel needed and useful."

"Give it time. Focus on healing. I know it's hard for you, you probably feel stagnant and unsure of what's next, but whatever you end up doing, you're going to be great at it. That's who you are. You never give less than a hundred percent in anything you do."

The corner of his mouth lifts briefly, then his smile is gone, stolen by his thoughts.

"How do you feel about being back in your apartment? You feel safe there?"

Nerves tickle my belly as I answer honestly, "I do worry about Todd showing up unexpectedly."

"He hasn't tried to contact you, has he?"

"He sent me a letter because he knew I wouldn't take his calls or messages."

"I can hear it in your tone. Talking about him upsets you."

"He hurt you. I'll never forgive him for that."

"He lost it when you told him it was me you wanted?"

"Yes. He'd lost his father and had been drinking. He wasn't in the right mind to accept that I love you and wanted to be with you."

"And you were ready to move in with me?"

"I was. I love sleeping in your arms and waking up to you each morning." I chuckle at a memory. "That's something you said to me once."

Fluid strokes of his hands caress along my back as he kisses me, his kiss reaching deep within, touching my heart, branding my soul.

Sexy blue eyes playfully wink at me as his hand tugs at the string on my bikini top. "I love having you in my arms...and on my lap."

Rubbing over the fabric of his shorts, I stroke his growing erection. His kisses feather my lips as my bikini top is dropped into his hands and tossed onto the ledge of the hot tub.

"I want to be on more than your lap."

Palms massaging my breasts, his thumbs swipe over each nipple, pinching them between his fingers.

"I won't keep my girl waiting then."

Lifting his hips, he slides his shorts down. My palms take hold of the ledge as his fingers slide my bikini bottoms to the side and his others tease his head to my opening.

"Just the thought of being inside you makes me stiff."

Sliding onto him, his head falls back.

"Hearing you talk like that makes me want you even more."

Dominating lips claim mine as he pulls my hips toward him, pushing deeper in. With his kiss stealing my senses, I lose myself to the motion of my hips gliding through the water and the sensation of us coming together, our need for one another deeply seated with more than just desire.

CHAPTER FORTY-EIGHT

—

CARTER

All day, I haven't been able to keep my hands off my girl. Whether she was sunbathing, swimming, shopping, it didn't matter. I wanted to be close to her, touching her, knowing the smile on her face is because of me. It's tough not being able to lift her and swing her around or carry her to the bed, yet she still manages to make me feel like a man with the way she treats me. There's never a moment where she's disappointed in my limited mobility. Instead, she behaves like it's a part of who I am, and she's okay with it.

To have a woman so openly accept me the way she has makes me realize how amazing she is, and that I need to do everything I can to make her happy. In my world of chaos and uncertainty, she's the only thing that makes sense. I understand why I fought for her like I did. Why I confronted her ex. She's worth protecting.

The sound of Jane's voice snaps me out of my lovesick haze.

"Where do you guys want to go tonight? Did you see that restaurant and bar with live music we passed on the way back?" Jane asks, falling into Kyle's lap with a beer in hand. Twirling his hand through her hair, Kyle smiles at Jane, his expression of a man content with his wife.

"That sounds good to me, babe."

"How about you guys?"

Jane looks at us, sitting together on the patio chair. I rub along Alex's back as her sun-kissed face turns to me.

"You up for some drinks and music?"

"I'm all for sitting back with a beer and watching you dance."

Cozying up to me, she kisses me before sliding off my lap.

"Let's figure out what we're wearing," she says to Jane as they dash off to our room.

I sit back and relax, knowing Kyle and I have a while before we need to get ready.

"You good going out again? You seemed tired today from last night's outing."

"Nah, I'm good. It's the most physical activity I've had which is why I'm tired, but I can handle it."

"You sure? I don't mind telling Jane it's a night-in kind of night."

Letting the empty bottle slip from my fingers, I set it on the stone patio next to my chair.

"Whether I sit here or at the restaurant doesn't matter. Thanks for the concern though. I appreciate it."

"Of course. Honestly, it's good to see you recovering so fast. I didn't expect you to be up and moving like you are this quickly."

"I'm determined to walk fully on my own again."

"Don't push too hard though. I don't wanna see you injure yourself."

"I need to push my body. I can't keep a woman like that with only one good leg."

"Are you kidding me? Alex isn't going anywhere. You're it for her whether you're on one or two legs. Before your accident, I was sure you two were heading toward marriage."

With the setting sun, the air has shifted. Along my skin, the hair raises against the cool ocean breeze. With my hands braced on the chair, I carefully raise to my feet.

"Then I had to go and fuck it up, along with my career."

Kyle instantly stands, ready to help me if needed. I wave his outstretched hand away and hobble forward, attempting to walk without the cane. With the next step, and no feeling in my foot, my knee buckles forward. Stable arms hook under my pits and catch me.

"Easy now. That last beer probably did you in."

Kyle moves to my side, ensuring I'm stable.

"You're tore up, man. I get it, but you don't need to be so hard on yourself. It was an accident. No one could've predicted what happened."

The tension in my chest tightens, frustration building. "I don't want to lose the way she looks at me. She looks at me like I'm some damn hero, but I feel far from it."

Kyle shakes his head. "If only you knew how broken she was before meeting you. You helped her heal and trust again. You are her damn hero, so stop feeling sorry for yourself and get ready to have a good time with her tonight." With a pat on my back, his words diminish my brooding mood.

"You're right. I need to get out of my head, but it's hard sometimes. I don't know where my life is headed next. If I'm not walking by the time my leave of absence is over, I won't have a job. I'd like to return to the job I once had. In my gut, I know I'd like it, probably love it. But the reality is, I have to accept I might have to do something else. I applied for several jobs last week. One called me yesterday and left a message they want to do an interview. It's got my head messed up. I'm not sure what I'm going to do."

Movement in the house draws our attention. The girls are giggling inside, almost ready. Seeing Alex's chocolate wavy hair brush over her shoulder as she smiles loosens the knot in my chest.

"I need to figure it out though." My gaze remains fixed, watching her beneath the interior lights. "I need to focus on the future and stop worrying about what was in the past."

The band is on a raised platform in the restaurant bar, belting out familiar sing-along songs. The waitresses in their barely-there outfits are busy dishing out large plates of food and giant beer mugs to customers in the booths and high-top tables beyond the dance floor. It's Friday night and the place is packed. We had to wait thirty minutes for our own booth, but the food made the wait worth it.

Having shared a seafood sampler and fish tacos, I sit back in the booth, bringing the beer to my lips as Alex rubs my leg under the table, her pretty smile turned my way.

"That was some of the best seafood I've had."

"I'm full and happy." With a hand to her belly, she leans back into my open arm. Her head lulls to the side as I rub along her upper back. "That feels so good. Keep it up and I'm going to fall asleep."

Chuckling, I kiss her hair.

"No," Jane squeals. "We need to dance."

"C'mon." Reaching across the table, she captures Alex's wrist in her hand.

Pulled from my arms, I watch the two of them stroll onto the full dance floor. Kyle and I look over the table of empty plates and liquor glasses.

"I don't know how they have the energy. I'm exhausted."

"They're running on alcohol. We'll be carrying them to bed." A frown tugs at the corner of my mouth, but I shove the emotions down.

Seeing Alex get into the music is a wanted distraction. Toned and tan, her long hair sways as she rocks her hips back and forth. She and Jane are lost to the music, laughing and dancing. Both beautiful women enjoying the moment.

"What was she like before me?"

Pulling his gaze from his wife, Kyle brings his attention to me, his brows furrowing.

"Terrified of being touched. Afraid she was going to be alone for the rest of her life. You wouldn't know that now, would you? Not with the woman you see in front of us."

"No, all I've seen is how strong and caring she is. Did I pursue her?"

"Yeah, you met her when she was still struggling. You looked past her wounds just like she does yours."

"You really care about her, huh?"

"Like a sister, yeah. She's a sweetheart. I was thrilled to see you two get together."

Eyes narrowing, my muscles tense when I see a tall guy with messy wavy hair moving in to dance with Alex. Hand wrapping around her hip, he goes for her ass, and she backs away, her body language indicating she doesn't want the contact. Sliding to the end of the booth, Kyle catches me on the other side.

"I can handle this."

"No."

Adrenaline pumping, I take a step with my good leg first, then the numb one. My leg tries to give. Clenching my fists together, I take a breath and push more weight onto my foot, knowing it's there. I focus on the sensation I have going into my thigh. Another breath and I clench my teeth, forcing my movements, pushing through the numb and awkward sensations. Concentrating on the feeling in my thigh with each step, it gets easier until I'm within reach of Alex and the fucker pawing her ass. My grip slams down on his forearm, instantly drawing his attention.

"Take your hands off her."

Blue-green eyes pierce mine, fear filling them. An unfamiliar face blends with the face in front of me.

"I can take it all away from you, you know that? I have the means and the money. I can bury you, make you wish you'd never gotten in my way. If it wasn't for you getting in my way, we'd still be together."

"You're the reason you're not together anymore. She finally saw you for who you really are—a sleazy, arrogant, spoiled rich boy who can't handle it when he doesn't get what he wants. I'll tear you limb from fucking limb. Stay away from her."

Flinging his arm up, he breaks my contact and shoves at me.

The man in front of me has broken from my hold, his hands up in the air.

"Sorry, man. I don't want any trouble."

Kyle is at my back, letting me know he's there to help. I nod to the guy, and he slips through the crowd, disappearing.

Taking each side, Kyle and Alex catch me before my leg gives out.

"You okay, bro? You don't look good."

Head foggy, I shake it and try to focus on the here and now.

"Let's go back to the house," Alex insists. "He needs to rest."

"Yeah," is all I can mutter amid the confusion.

Outside, the cool night air is refreshing against the stickiness of my damp shirt and skin. Arm around Alex, she's staring at me, concern filling her beautiful green eyes.

"What's wrong? You look like you don't feel well. Did you hurt yourself walking?"

"No."

Adrenaline plummeting, the physical exertion and the harsh memory of my fight with Todd has me rattled, my body tensing. Kissing her cheek, I give a forced smile.

"I'm okay."

"You're not okay, I can tell."

"I'll be okay, I promise. I just need some sleep."

Ahead of us, Jane is calling a taxi. With Alex's assistance, I take careful steps toward the bench along the street. An ear-piercing squeal of tires draws our attention to the road. Bumper to bumper, a blue car and a white car crash into each other. The clash of metal is a strident echo into the night. The sounds shake me to my core.

Looking down at Todd, I see the hint of fear.

"Stay. Away. From. Her."

I turn to leave. My muscles tighten at the tension of a man's hand on my shoulder. Spinning, Todd's fist clocks my jaw.

"Fuck," I blurt, collapsing onto the bench.

Turning the corner, I see a gorgeous woman standing by the entrance of the gym. Bold green eyes are filled with lust as she watches me lower my shirt.

"Hey, you must be my nine o'clock. I'm Carter."

"Carter? Are you ok?"

359

Alex's voice is distant, my head aching, the memories coming too fast.

"Kyle, can you get him some water, please? He looks like he's going to be sick."

Arm resting on the weight machine, I toss my towel over my shoulder.

"I've seen you in here trying to bulk up. You mind if I give you some pointers?"

"For sure, especially if it gets me biceps like those," Kyle jokes, pointing at my arms.

"Carter? You all right?"

"Jane's planning a party at our place. You should come. Alex will be there."

"Carter, look at me."

A soft hand on my face, my eyes are met with emerald ones.

"Focus on me, take a slow, deep breath."

Pulling her against me, I hug her tight, breathing in her vanilla scent as more memories flash in and out of my mind.

Showered and in my briefs, I lay against the pillow, Alex tucked under my arm. My beautiful Alex, sleeping so peacefully. Caressing my hand along her arm, I indulge in the feel of her soft skin and the way she smells. All familiar to me.

Taking her hand in mine, I raise it to my lips and tenderly kiss her fingertips. She stirs slightly, snuggling closer to me.

"I love you, beautiful."

Awakened by my voice, she moves her body, running her hand over my chest, giving me wanted pleasure with her touch.

"Mmm, Carter…you okay?"

"Yeah, don't worry. I'm feeling better. Thank you for tonight. You helped calm me down."

With an expression full of adoration, she looks up at me, rubbing her hand along my cheek and jaw. "I'm here for you…always."

Words I once said to her and I know she means them. She's been there since the moment I woke up with endless support and patience.

Turning her on her back, I lower myself, kissing her sweet lips. She melts beneath me, her body going soft, her hands holding me close. With slow, anticipative movements, I slide her underwear off her hips, never taking my lips from hers.

Hand to my briefs, she slips beneath them, stroking me in her hand. Biting her bottom lip, I release it gradually.

"Tell me you love me again."

"I love you, Carter, more than anything."

"Nothing sounds sweeter than those words coming from your lips."

Removing the fabric between us, I slide between her open legs, completely losing myself in her love.

CHAPTER FORTY-NINE

—

CARTER

"Shit, man, you remember?"

Glancing over Kyle's shoulder, I ensure the girls are out of earshot. Toes in the sand, they're both sunbathing by the shore.

"How much do you remember?" Standing by the pool, his brown eyes are wide with enthusiasm.

"A lot. The memories have been coming since last night and after I woke up this morning. Dr. Keller was right, they're coming in pieces and in random order. Some of it's confusing, but I remember the first time we met. Playing Xbox at your house. I remember the St. Patrick's Day party where Alex and I had our first kiss. The memories started coming after I remembered my fight with Todd. The son-of-a-bitch took a cheap shot to my jaw. I don't remember what happened after that."

"Sounds like something he'd do, knowing face-to-face, you'd annihilate him. But fuck that, your memories are coming back! This is great news! When are you going to tell Alex?"

"I'm not ready to tell her yet. I want to surprise her, and the timing needs to be right for that. There are a few things I need to do first."

Kyle pulls me in for a hug, patting me on the back.

"I won't say anything until you're ready. But damn, man, it feels good to know you remember."

Coming out of his hug, I tip my head toward the girls. "They're on their way up here."

Dropping into a patio chair, I smile up at Alex in her dark green bikini and sexy beach wavy hair. Her grin is wide as she falls into my lap, kissing me on the cheek.

"I have an idea if you guys are up for joining me."

Looking at her with interest, I twirl a strand of her chocolate hair around my finger.

"What do you have in mind, beautiful?"

"I want to get a tattoo."

Mouth curving, my eyes roam over her sexy body, then return to her exquisite eyes.

"What would you like to get and where?"

"A saying that has stuck with me. I was thinking here," she points to her lower, left side.

Grazing my thumb across her bare skin, I imagine how gorgeous she'd look with ink there. Eyes full of lust, she watches me as I caress her skin. I have no doubt we're both remembering last night and how good it felt.

"It'll hurt getting it on your side, but I'll hold your hand through it."

With a quick squeal of excitement, her smile beams.

"I'm going to get one too," Jane grins. "I want something cute on my wrist."

Kyle drapes an arm over her shoulder. "Tattoos are addictive, babe. You can't get just one."

"We'll see. I only want one. Just something small and cute."

Kyle kisses her cheek and pulls back smiling. "Yeah, we'll see."

"I looked into the options before coming and there's a shop called Paradise Ink that had a lot of great reviews online."

"You want to go now?"

"Yes," she says, her enthusiasm evident.

"You won't be able to get in the ocean, pool, or hot tub for the rest of the night," I warn.

"That's okay. I'm hoping going early can get us in."

"All right. Let's get cleaned up and get going."

It doesn't take us long to find the tattoo shop. When I enter, I hear the familiar buzzing of tattoo needles, and I'm brought back to the day I got the tattoo in memory of my father. Pain, harsh and unexpected slams into my gut.

"It looks good, C. Dad would like it," Kevin tells me, looking over my fresh ink.

"I miss him."

"I do too."

A visit to see Kevin is one of the first things I'll be doing when I get home. I can imagine his reaction now. Glancing over at Alex, I see she's nervous, nibbling her lip. Putting my arm around her, I rub her back.

"It'll be fine," I assure her. "You'll love it when it's all done."

With my reassurance, she stops nibbling her lip and leans into me.

A tall man, with his hair pulled back into a ponytail and tattoos covering all his visible skin except his face looks up at us and tips his head.

"Welcome to Paradise Ink. Coming in for a tattoo or piercing?"

"Tattoo for her," I tell him.

"All right. I can get you in, in about thirty minutes. Just need your driver's license and for you to fill out this form and sign it." Handing Alex a clipboard, he points to the highlighted signature line.

"I'm going to get one too," Jane shares, stepping up to the counter.

"Are either of you getting something big or detailed?"

They both shake their heads no.

"Ok, then I can get you in too. Driver's license and sign here."

Thirty-five minutes later, Jane and Alex are sitting in tattoo chairs next to each other.

"What do you want done today?" Ponytail asks.

Raising her shirt, she points to her lower side. "I'd like, *She conquered her demons and wears her scars like wings,* written in cursive with some kind of bird or wings."

"All right. Let me put together a drawing and see what you think."

He walks off, and I wink at her. "That's gonna be a beautiful tattoo."

With a girly grin, she takes my hand into her lap, rubbing her thumb over my fingers.

"I'm nervous it's going to hurt really bad."

"It will at first, but then your endorphins will kick in, and it won't be so bad. Plus, I'm here. When it hurts squeeze my hand."

"I love you. I'm so glad you're here with me."

Brushing her hair away from her face, I caress her cheek. "I know, beautiful. It means a lot to me that I get to be here with you for your first tattoo, especially one so special."

"I love it!"

Jane's voice pulls our attention her direction. Her tattoo artist has the ink outline on her wrist. She's staring at it, grinning.

"What do you think?" she asks, raising her wrist for all of us to see.

It's an infinity symbol with a small phoenix bird outline as part of the curved side of the infinity symbol. The artist did a nice job drawing it. It looks good.

"It's adorable! I can't wait to see it when it's finished," Alex replies, excited.

"You ready to begin?" Jane's artist asks.

"Yeah," she enthuses.

While we wait for Alex's tattoo artist to return with his drawing, Jane's begins.

"Oh, my fucking God!" she screams. "That hurts!"

Kyle holds her hand, looking down at her in amusement.

"You'll be okay, babe. Suck it up."

367

If she could move, I think she'd smack him. Her flip-flopped feet try to wiggle, but Kyle gives her a stern expression, warning her to be still. Biting her lip, her cheeks get rosy as she muscles through her pain.

Alex's hand instinctively squeezes mine as she watches Jane struggle. Bringing my chair closer, I lean into her ear, using my other hand to massage her shoulder and upper back.

"Don't be nervous. You can handle anything."

Head turned my direction, she looks me in the eyes, studying me. The recognizable longing fills her irises followed by the expression I've come to love, the one that tells me she adores me and loves me with all she has to give.

Soon, beautiful. Soon I'll make everything right.

Ponytail arrives, and she takes a calm breath before looking at his drawing. Moisture fills her eyes as she stares at it.

"It's perfect."

"Turn to your side for me."

Shoulders lowered, she's composed as she raises her shirt. Placing the paper on her skin, he smooths it out, getting the guidelines set correctly. Peeling the paper off, we both look at the drawing on her skin. Emerald eyes light up as she looks at it, then at me.

I know what this emotional journey is like for her. It's more than just ink on her skin. This is her way of letting go, another step toward healing. It's her way of saying, I have scars, but I've overcome the wounds.

Taking my hand, her green eyes look up at me with a mixture of apprehension and self-assurance before she pinches them closed.

"Open your eyes. I want to know how you're feeling through this."

Sitting up, she removes her tank top then lowers herself as I move between her legs. Holding my tip, I move it against her clit, and her eyes close as I'm covered in her silky wetness.

"Open your eyes, beautiful. I want to see everything you're feeling."

Bright, green eyes meet my gaze as I slowly slide my head into her. Beneath me, her pleasured moans grow louder as I thrust deeper.

"Carter...you feel incredible."

"You do too, beautiful, so damn good."

"Please don't stop loving me like this."

The arousing memory fades, and I bring her fingers to my lips, kissing them as the needle touches her skin.

An hour and a half later, Alex gradually rises from the chair, stretching her arms and shoulders. Keeping her shirt lifted, she walks to the mirror, and her pretty eyes are alight with joy.

"It's stunning. I love it!" Finger curving around the inked and red skin, she traces the outside of the tattoo.

"Let's get it wrapped," Dillon, her artist, tells her.

Hurrying back to the chair, she sits still while he puts cream on it then covers it.

"Remove the bandage within three hours, then wash your tattoo with anti-bacterial liquid soap. Gently pat your tattoo dry with a paper towel. For the first four days, rub a small amount of ointment on your tattoo. Stay out of the ocean, pools, and hot tubs. You can get an infection because this is an open wound."

"Got it," she assures him.

Lowering her shirt, she stands and comes to me, her grin wide and her cheeks rosy as she throws her arms around my neck.

"I would not have been able to get through that without you. Thank you."

Needy for her kiss, I claim her lips, holding her head in my hand, tangling my fingers in her hair. She pulls back, blushing, and I give her ass a squeeze.

"You handled that like a boss."

She giggles, and I wink at her.

"Let's check out, beautiful. It's our last night here and I want it to be unforgettable."

Sitting on the sand, the cool ocean water whips across my feet. Arms folded on my elbows, I stare into the yellow and gray horizon. Awake before Alex, I practiced walking without a cane, determined to have my feet touch the ocean water without assistance. Keeping my mind focused on the sensation in my thigh with each step, I was able to achieve my goal. It may be a small feat, but it tells me I can do this. With practice, I can walk on my own again.

Behind me, I hear someone approaching. Quietly, Alex sits next to me. Reaching my arm out, she snuggles up to my side and leans her head against my chest.

"It's so beautiful here. I don't want to go home."

"It is. This trip has been the escape I needed."

"Me too. I loved every minute of it. Especially being with you and waking up with you."

Looking at her, I see the sadness in her eyes. For her, she feels like this is a separation, going back to two separate homes, two separate lives.

"Alex," placing my hand under her chin, I raise her gaze to mine. "I want you to move in with me."

"Are you sure?" Eyes full of surprise they moisten with emotion. "This isn't too fast for you, is it?"

Always so caring, so considerate of me. Rubbing her cheek, my mouth creases into a smile.

"No, it's not. I know what I want, and that's you…in my life, in my home, and in my bed." A single tear falls from her eye and I swipe it away. "Will you, move in with me?"

She laughs to herself as if my question is foolish.

"The better question is when can I move in?"

371

Running my hand over her face and hair, she tilts into my touch.

"This weekend."

"That's perfect." Leaning up, she holds my face to hers, giving me as much passion in her kiss as I know she feels.

CHAPTER FIFTY

—

ALEX

As I load up my car with my first run to Carter's house, a feeling of elation courses through me. I've barely seen him this week, but he's made it a priority to call and text me often and came over for dinner and to stay the night in the middle of the week. He's apologized for being busy, but I understand. He's had a job interview, physical therapy, an appointment with his therapist and Dr. Keller, and spent a lot of time this week with his family, especially Kevin. It's made me miss him though and even more thankful we'll be living together.

Climbing into the car, I become a bundle of nerves and excitement on my way to his house. My phone dings and I quickly glance at the message.

I've missed you this week. See you soon, beautiful.

Arriving at his house, I'm surprised he doesn't come out to greet me. Leaving the bags in the car, I head inside to find him. The door is cracked open and I carefully open it before stepping in. At my feet, I see a gold wrapped chocolate coin. Lifting it from the floor, I notice a note is taped to it.

The first time I met you I knew you were someone special.

Clutching it to me, I spot the next coin a few feet ahead and quickly go to it, lifting it off the floor and immediately read the note.

The first time we kissed I knew I needed more.

Rushing to the next coin sitting on the back of the couch, I pick it up and read it.

The first time we made love I knew I was yours.

The coins are leading me to his bedroom. I hurry to the next one.

The first memory I had was of the woman I love.

Glancing up, I see the next is just inside the room.

To me, she's everything I need.

Looking at the bed, I see another. Setting all the other chocolate coins aside, I pick it up.

And I want her to always be mine. Will you marry me?

"Alex."

Turning toward his voice, he's standing in the doorway of his bedroom. Tears pool in my eyes as my emotions overtake me.

"You remember."

With careful steps, he comes forward. I rush to him, removing the distance between us. Arms tangled around one another, we get lost in our kiss. Tears escape my eyes, but I can't break the connection. I need him like the air I breathe.

Putting his head to mine, he holds me close, his hands around my face, fingers laced in my hair.

"Yes, I remember. I love you, beautiful. So damn much."

"I love you too. You're everything to me."

"You're everything to me too. Since the moment I met you, I wanted to know you, to have you all to myself. When I woke up from the accident, there was something about you that I couldn't let go of, and it's because you're meant for me. You're the woman I want to spend the rest of my life with."

Tears rolling down my cheeks, he kisses me through them, his loving embrace mending every broken piece of me.

"I never thought I'd have a love like this. You've given me a second chance, Carter. A second chance at happiness. Before you, my heart was broken, I was living in a shell. You saw past my scars and had the patience to show me what real love truly is."

Pulling me to his chest, he holds me tight, kissing my hair. The familiar scent of his masculinity surrounds me, giving me as much comfort as his affection does.

"We've both been given a second chance and I realized that in Key West when my memories came back. You don't know how hard it's been this week, not being able to tell you, but I needed time to plan this and to get this."

Releasing me, he reaches into his pocket, pulling out a little black box. Opening it, he shows me the diamond and white gold ring.

"Carter, it's beautiful."

Pulling the ring from the box, he holds it out for me. Striking blue eyes gaze down at me, filled with anticipation.

"Alexandria DeMarco, will you marry me?"

"Yes, a million times yes."

Sliding my finger into the ring, I take his hand and lead him to the bed. Lifting me onto it, I lay back as he joins me. Sliding his tongue between my lips, he reaches for the button of my jean shorts. Undressing me slowly, he admires every curve, running his fingers along my body. Raising my leg, he kisses the inside of my thigh, then again closer to my aching core. When his lips touch my clit, my head falls back.

A trail of warm, loving kisses continues up along my stomach, reaching my breasts, lingering over each nipple. Taking my mouth with his, our kiss is slow, passionate, loving. Laying between my legs, he fills me, moving with care, intent on pleasing me. His tender kisses continue along my cheek and neck as he thrusts deeper.

Every nerve in my body is attentive to his touch, to his affectionate movements. Along my ear, his lips tease my lobe.

"I love you."

EPILOGUE

—

ALEX

Snuggled up next to Carter on our couch, he caresses along my arm, calming me as I nervously make this phone call to my sister. The ringtone sounds and I await the answer on the other line.

"Hello?"

"Amy, it's Alex."

"How are you?" She seems pleasantly surprised.

"Really good. I'm getting married."

"That's wonderful. I'm happy for you."

"I'm calling…because I'd like you to come…to our wedding," I announce anxiously.

"I'd…love to. When is it?"

A smile pulls my lips up as I look at Carter. Happy to see me smiling, he leans over and kisses my cheek.

"In a couple months, March third."

"I'd like to be there. I'll ask for the time off. Who is the special guy?"

Staring up at his beautiful blues, I intertwine my fingers with his.

"His name is Carter Maxwell. He's the most amazing man I've ever met."

"What does he do?"

"He's a personal trainer and an MMA fighter."

"Oh wow! I don't watch MMA, but I'd be willing to watch one of his fights."

"His next one is after our wedding in April. I'll get you the details for the wedding and his fight."

"You sound really happy, Alex. I'm glad you called."

"I am too. I've missed you."

"I've missed you too. I'm sorry I didn't reach out."

"It's okay, I don't think I would've been ready to open up, but so many things have changed. I hope we can reconnect."

"I'd really like that. I'm married, and we just had a little girl. I'd like you to meet them. I'll bring them to the wedding."

"I look forward to meeting them and for you to meet Carter."

"If he won your heart, he must be a really great guy."

"He is."

Carter squeezes my hand before raising it to his mouth. The familiar touch of his lips to my fingertips warms my body, giving me pleasure from head to toe.

"I love you," I mouth to him.

"I love you too," he whispers back.

TWO MONTHS LATER...

Looking in the mirror, I run my fingers over the smooth beading and fine lace of my wedding dress. The dress fits perfectly, and I can't stop staring at my reflection. I'm mesmerized. Our day is finally here, and in a few minutes, I'll be marrying the man I love.

Soft hands touch my bare arms and a pretty face with blond ringlets comes into view in the mirror.

"Are you ready to become Mrs. Carter Maxwell?" Jane asks, her smile beaming.

"I am, Jane, I'm so ready."

"You look stunning. He's going to be awestruck."

"Thank you." A giggle escapes me, my excitement unable to be contained.

"Your father is waiting outside."

"Can you believe he came?"

"Yes, you're his little girl, and it's your wedding day."

"Jane," Turning to her, I hold her hand close to my chest.

"Thank you for pushing me, to take that leap. If not for you, I never would've met Carter. Besides you, he's the best thing that's happened to me."

With a kiss on my cheek, she pulls back, her eyes full of moisture.

"I might have lead you to him, but it's the two of you who fell in love. You two are meant to be and I'm so happy for the both of you."

Hugging her tight, I fight the oncoming tears.

"Okay, I need to get out there before I ruin my makeup."

"Yes."

She quickly pulls back and takes my hand. Together, we walk out of the room. Outside, my father is standing in a tailored gray suit, with a pretty blue vest and tie beneath. At first sight of me, his eyes water.

"You look beautiful, Alexandria."

My head lowers, blushing. I force the tears back.

"Thank you, Dad."

"I'm honored to be able to walk you down the aisle."

"Thank you for being here. It means so much to me."

Putting his elbow out, he awaits me to take it.

"Thank you for calling me. It should've been me calling you."

Placing my hand on his arm, I smile up at him.

"I'm glad you're here now."

"Me too."

Meeting my sister at the Villa doors, her eyes light up when she sees me.

"You look gorgeous."

With an excited giggle, we all line up. Two waiting staff members open the double doors. Amy and Jane disappear through them. Jittery with excitement, I wait for our cue. Stepping forward, we turn left, and everything comes into view. Beyond the doors is a white walkway through rows of white chairs filled with guests. At the end of the walkway is an archway of blue and white flowers and beneath it, the man I long to be with.

With the rhythm of the music, we take our steps, my father escorting me down the aisle. At the end, he hands me to Carter. With my hands in his, I stand before him, ready to say the words that will promise my devotion and commitment.

Blue eyes alight with love, he stares down at me, holding my hands tenderly.

"There's nothing more beautiful than the woman in front of me. You're breathtaking, Alex, completely breathtaking."

"So are you. You're incredibly handsome in your suit."

A smile that can make me feel loved on my darkest day beams before me.

"In mere minutes I'll finally be your wife. I've longed for this day."

"I have too."

Behind us, the officiate is grinning. "You may all be seated."

The movement momentarily draws Carter and my attention from one another.

"We're all here today to celebrate the relationship of Carter and Alexandria and to be witnesses and supporters of the commitment they share with one another. You all are the most important people in their lives and they've brought you here to publicly recognize you've all played some special part in the love they share today."

Never taking our eyes from each other, we wait to say our vows.

"Carter and Alexandria, these vows are your way of openly declaring your promise to one another as well as to all of those who are here in attendance today."

With his mesmerizing blue eyes, he gazes down at me.

"Alex, my beautiful fiancée, I had no idea how much love can move an individual until I met you. Your strength and kindness know no bounds. Your love has no limits. And it's that very love that has brought us to where we are now. It's your love that gave me the strength to overcome my obstacles. It's your love I wake up and long for each day. There is nothing in this world that can stop me from loving you…today and every day we have together."

A single tear rolls down my cheek as my entire body shakes with the need to be closer to him, kissing him, holding him. With a gentle swipe of his thumb, my tear is wiped away.

"Carter, there was a time I'd lost myself, and in that journey to find myself again I also found you. You became the wind and strength I needed to be able to spread my wings. It was your patience and your love that mended my heart. Every day I wake up thankful to have you in my life, thankful to have your love. You're the most kind, caring, loving man I know and I'm so thankful you love me too. I promise to be there for you no matter what life throws at us. I promise to cherish you until the very last breath we take."

Stepping closer together, Carter holds my face in his hands as he kisses my cheek, his lips lingering. "I love you so much."

As he pulls back, my tears unleash and stream down my cheeks. "I love you too."

"Carter and Alexandria will now exchange rings to symbolize their commitment. The wearing of the rings is a visible, outward sign they have committed themselves to one another."

Taking my hand in his, Carter slides the ring onto my finger.

"I give you this ring, as a symbol of our love, for today and tomorrow, and for all days to come. Wear it as a sign of what we have promised on this day and know my love is present even when I am not."

Taking a breath, I force the tears back as I slide his band onto his finger and repeat the same vow.

"By sharing your vows and exchanging rings here today you both have decided to share the rest of your lives together. You are no longer two separate people, but one couple together.

"Alexandria, do you take Carter to be your husband, to love him, comfort him, honor and keep him, in sickness and in health, and forsaking all others, be faithful to him as long as you both shall live?"

"I do."

"Carter, do you take Alexandria to be your wife, to love her, comfort her, honor and keep her, in sickness and in health, and forsaking all others, be faithful to her as long as you both shall live?"

"I do."

"By the power vested in me, I now pronounce you husband and wife. Carter, you may kiss your bride."

Arm around my waist, hand lost in my curls, he pulls me to him, kissing me, giving my body the needed connection. Sealing our love and promises. Making me his.

LASAGNA RECIPE

Ingredients:

1 – 26 oz. jar of garlic & herb spaghetti sauce (brand of your choice)

1 – 26 oz. jar of marinara or tomato and basil spaghetti sauce (brand of your choice)

2 cups ricotta cheese (16 oz. container)

6-8 slices of provolone cheese (6 oz. package)

2 cups shredded mozzarella cheese (6 oz. package)

½ cup parmesan cheese

¾ cup diced turkey pepperoni

1 lb. of lean ground beef

1 package of lasagna noodles

Tsp. garlic salt

Tsp. black pepper

Tsp. Italian seasoning

Tbsp. Sugar

Cook 1 lb. lean ground beef in frying pan without any oils. As it browns add a teaspoon of garlic salt, black pepper, and Italian seasoning. Once ground beef is browned, set aside. Put both jars of sauce into the cooking pot. Mix with sauce - 1 lb. cooked ground beef, ¾ cup diced turkey pepperoni, 1 tablespoon of sugar. Stir ingredients in saucepan over medium heat.

Boil 1 package of lasagna noodles. (Add a tablespoon of vegetable oil to keep noodles from sticking together). Once boiled thoroughly, drain pot of noodles almost completely. Leave some water to keep noodles moist while layering the lasagna.

Layering Lasagna:

Pre-heat oven to 350 degrees.

Spread a small amount of sauce on bottom of large 9x13 baking dish instead of oils. Add first layer of noodles, covering bottom of baking dish. Add 2 cups of ricotta cheese on top of first layer of noodles. Cover ricotta cheese and noodles with the sauce/meat mix. Repeat layering with another layer of noodles, add the 6-8 slices of provolone cheese, then sauce. Repeat layering with another layer of noodles, add the 2 cups shredded mozzarella cheese, then sauce. Complete layering by sprinkling the ½ cup parmesan cheese over the top of the lasagna. Bake 45 minutes at 350 degrees. Remove the oven and let sit for 5-7 minutes before serving.

MORE BOOKS BY BETTY SHREFFLER

CASTLE OF KINGS
(A Kings MC Romance)

CLIPPED WINGS
(A Kings MC Romance, Book 2)

FIRE ON THE FARM
(A Second Chance Cowboy Romance)

MY HOT BOSS
(A Sexy and Witty Office Romance)

WHEN HUNTER MEETS SEEKER
(A Sexy and Suspenseful Paranormal Romance)

EMBRACE THE DAWNING
(Book 1, The Covenant Series)

CRUEL TEMPTATION
(Book 2, The Covenant Series)

DARK AND BEAUTIFUL NIGHTS
(Book 3, The Covenant Series)

View any of Author Betty Shreffler's books at:
amazon.com/author/bettyshreffler

Betty Shreffler is an Amazon Top 100 bestselling author of paranormal romantic suspense and contemporary romance. She writes sexy and suspenseful stories with hot alphas and kickass heroines that have twists you don't expect. She also writes beautiful and sexy romances with tough women and their journeys at finding love. Betty is a mix of country, nerdy, sassy, sweet and a whole lot of sense of humor. She's a fan of photography, reading, watching movies, hiking, traveling, drinking wine, bubble baths and all things romantic. She lives with her amazing hubs and five fur babies; two rescue pups and three cats. If she's not writing or doing book events, then you can find her behind the lens of a camera, in the woods, or sipping wine behind a deliciously steamy book. Ways to stay in touch with Betty:

AUTHORBETTYSHREFFLER

GROUPS/AUTHORBETTYSHREFFLER

BETTYSHREFFLER

@BETTY_SHREFFLER

@BETTY_SHREFFLER

BETTYSHREFFLER.COM

Made in the USA
Columbia, SC
18 October 2018